The Hole That Must Be Filled

Stories

Also by Kenneth J. Harvey:

Brud

Directions for an Opened Body

The Hole That Must Be Filled

■

Stories

■

Kenneth J. Harvey

Little, Brown and Company (Canada) Limited
Boston • Toronto • London

First published in Canada 1994 by Little, Brown and Company (Canada) Limited.
This edition published 1995 by Little, Brown and Company (Canada) Limited.

Canadian Cataloguing in Publication Data
   Harvey, Kan J. (Ken Joseph), 1962-
     The hole that must be filled

   ISBN 0-316-34983-6 (bound) ISBN 0-316-34985-2 (pbk.)

   I. Title.

   PS8565.A67H6 1994   C813'.54   C94-930307-0
   PR9199.3.H37H6 1994

Author Photo: Kenneth J. Harvey
Cover Artwork: Wet Day, Bulley Street, 1993, Alistair Drysdale
   (courtesy of the author's collection)
Cover Design: Adams + Associates
Interior design and typesetting: Pixel Graphics
Printed and bound in Canada by Best Book Manufacturers Inc.

Little, Brown and Company (Canada) Limited
148 Yorkville Avenue, Toronto, Ontario, Canada

Acknowledgments

"Birthdays" first published in *TickleAce*, Spring/Summer, 1993

"Break and Entry" first published in *Exile*, Vol. 17, No. 2, 1993

"Buffer Zones" first published in *University of Windsor Review*, Vol. 24, No. 1, 1991

"Heber Peach" first published in *TickleAce*, Fall/Winter, 1992

"The Hole That Must be Filled" first published in *Dalhousie Review*, Vol. 72, No. 4, 1994

"Into the Places of Those Lost" first published in *Grain*, Spring, 1993

"The Law" first published in *Event*, Fall, 1991

"Mime" first published in *Event*, Summer, 1992

"Muffled Drum" first published in *Event*, Summer, 1993

"Rabbit's Pa" first published in *Event*, Summer, 1990

"Three Distant Lakes on Fire" first published in *Queen's Quarterly*, Summer, 1992

"The Throat" first published in *Grain*, Winter, 1991

"Into the Places of Those Lost" was a winner in the fictional prose division of the 1993 Newfoundland Arts and Letters Awards

"The Muffled Drum" was a winner in the fictional prose division of the 1992 Newfoundland Arts and Letters Awards

"The Hole that Must be Filled" was a winner in the fictional prose division of the 1991 Newfoundland Arts and Letters Awards

The author wishes to express special thanks to the Newfoundland and Labrador Arts Council, whose unfaltering support made the completion of this book possible. Thanks must also be offered to the Canada Council for funding via a project grant. Further heartfelt appreciation must be extended to Janet Power, who gave support and validation to these stories when they first lurched forth, hobbling on shaky legs.

Contents

This book is dedicated to:

my mother, Sonia Dorothy Neary

and

my father, Josiah Boyde Harvey

Break and Entry

Someone is parked across the narrow street, blaring their car horn. It is a high-pitched, irritating sound and whoever sits in the driver's seat will not let up. I am lying in bed, unable to sleep because I am too tired. My eyes stare toward the window. My alert ears listen. I am exhausted and the sound forces me wider and wider awake and I tell myself that I can wait, control what I think, stop myself from doing what I want to do, what I know I must do, until the horn keeps on bomping and drilling outside the row house, and I am out of bed, on my feet in an instant, striding down the stairs and through the front door, across the street, kicking at the passenger door of the car with the heels of my bare feet, bouncing back and hopping and bending my knee and straightening it, kicking and kicking dents in the thin metal and shouting about how stupid the driver must be. "There's no one home there. Can't you even see, you stupid," kicking, "stupid," kicking, "idiot." I have to move along because the car begins to pull away, the driver not looking at me. I have to shout, "They should kill every last one of you stupid fuckers. That would fix the world."

The car is gone. My limbs shiver delightfully. The street is calm and still and a few of my neighbours stand in their doorways, smoking cigarettes, holding brown beer bottles in their hands, or simply watching things move around, unable to sleep as well in the all-too-quiet summer night. A thin woman further up the street staggers out onto her front step. Her dark hair is oily and her face is long and ruined. Quick fiddle music merrily spills from the small kitchen behind her. The woman laughs with an opened mouth, then claps her hands in a sloppy way and loosely nods and winks at me, calling in a scratchy voice, "Yays, buddy." She claps once more, slapping her hands together so that they almost miss each other. Then she stops and stares at the curb, stricken by a sad look, as if she has spotted something there that she remembers will do her no good. Her black dog Slash runs my way, crazily searching the asphalt with his nose. He does not bark at me as usual. Instead he wags his tail and sniffs the ground at my feet as if in tribute.

"Atta tell 'im," Jim calls down from his window, one house over. "Da...Dats what we nuh...nuh...nnnn...needs more of."

I look up and Jim is there in his white t-shirt with his grey hair sticking up, his slow glassy eyes staring down, and his big grey lips (like bloated worms) open as if to speak, but he does not say another word. His numb smile holds his expression.

I wander back to my doorstep and pass in through the open doorway, up the stairs, coming wider and wider awake, raging against exhaustion, replaying the movements of the confrontation in my mind as my heart punches against the need for sleep. In my bedroom, I move straight toward the dresser in the corner. There are photographs in my bottom drawer. I kneel against the carpet, ease open the drawer and move the clothes away from the corner in the back. Some of the photographs are in colour, others in black and white. The same woman is posed, or caught off-guard undressing, in each picture. They are not professional snap-shots. They are blurry, or the woman is blinking, the lighting off — too dark, too bright. They are the real thing. I take the glossy stack and walk on my knees toward the bed, lay out the photographs so that my chest is level with them for a tighter look. I bend my face close and analyze the images. Patsy lying on her stomach, wearing a pullover top but no pants or underwear, her naked backside seeming perfectly smooth, her face looking back at me over her shoulder, where I was standing at the foot of the bed. Slipping the photos

away from each other: Patsy in her bikini on the beach in
Foxtrap Cove, standing awkwardly with the hard grey beach-
rocks beneath her feet, her low breasts held in place by the
bikini top, her hips pleasantly wide, her thighs pressed together, giving fullness to the tight V of the bikini bottom. I
touch the smooth sheen of the third picture: Patsy in her bra,
sunbathing on the verandah in the backyard of this house, her
hard nipples plain through the white lacy material along the
top half of the bra, her eyes closed, sweating and slippery, easy
to touch, all of her skin, quickly. There were other photos as
well; Polaroids that Patsy tore to shreds days after they were
taken. Close-ups of fleshy compromised fittings into vulnerable points of entry. The images in these pictures swim
warmly in my guts. Such strong loving feelings, such despera-
tion, and only one way to blend the two, to brace release, only
one truly accommodating stroke. Pulling down my shorts, I
take hold of my cock, feel it growing instinctively thicker and
heavier in my hand as I whisper harsh words of longing against
Patsy, but I do not know if I will come or cry. It seems as if
things could go in either direction. The pictures make me hard
and soft at once, hinting at what I am truly made of, uncertainty making me the man I do not want to be, saliva rising in
my mouth, prompting an urge. My thoughts: I spit on you
Patsy because I love you so much, because I love you so
fucking much and you have left me, sliced this love down its
center, split its nucleus, allowing division into this new
wounded monster: half hate, half love. And both of them growing with the accelerated metabolism of a giant.

The corner of Slattery and Freshwater is a prime location for
the sign that I set up there. A fine selection of fairly well-off
people pass by, heading toward downtown on foot. I have my
sign on a tall stick of one by two and lean it against the brick
wall of the building that houses the Roman Catholic School
Board. People passing by glance at the sign and read: OUT OF
WORK, RATHER BEG THAN STEAL and I know what they
are thinking. They offer a few coins because they are pleased
that I am one less person who might be breaking into their
houses on the lovely streets running off Freshwater, and this
measly payment is like a tad of insurance that will make them

feel slightly better. Other people think that it is honest of me (honesty, a virtue truly worthy of reward), others believe that I am merely a product of poor economic times. They sympathize with what the government has done to me; their mismanagement of our country has wreaked such havoc upon my lifestyle. These types of thoughts bring me coins as well. The sign appeals to all sorts, even the young ones and the hippies who stroll up and read, smiling, "Right on, man," because they can relate to the ungoverned mind-set of statements such as this.

No sweat. I get my money, then I send flowers every day over to Patsy's new address, which I managed to squeeze out of her brother Nix. I send the flowers without signing the card because I have already signed a bond to stay away from Patsy, so I cannot let her know who it is (no attempt at contact permitted) or she can notify the police again to arrest me for violation of these laws put in place to keep all of us so conveniently apart.

After five thirty there is not much sense remaining at the corner. Work is out and, by this time, everyone is home for supper, so I carry my sign back to my room, and eat a tin of chili or spaghetti in the cramped downstairs kitchen, devour a few slabs of white bread with plenty of butter that tastes so good when you sop up the juice from those tins. Then I am out again, on the street (no point in staying home, alone) and I find my way over to Patsy's to catch a glimpse of her when she leaves for bingo down at the Legion. She has a car (a shiny new red number) because her wages are fairly reasonable working cash register for the government in one of their tax offices. She has a brand new car and a nice apartment in the basement of a house in a neighbourhood with lawns and driveways and trees and generous spaces between the houses. Quiet and everything in its place. Totally still and I know what the people who live here all need to wake them up. A good look at me. A good close look at my face when they wake up in the night and I am standing over their beds in their nice comfortable darkness, standing with a smug smile lit by their wonderful little nightlights shaped like their favourite fantasies. I have a thing or two to say as my hand comes down, pressing against their mouths.

"Listen to this," I whisper to the wide-open eyes. Slowly leaning down, I speak carefully, touching the places that are meant to be kept so private, hidden here, hidden behind the bland identical facades of these immaculate houses, "You have so much to learn about closeness."

When Patsy is a safe distance from her house, I stroll over, my hands in my pockets, not looking around, casual, down her driveway, and around back. The man who owns the house lives upstairs. He travels quite a bit and only finds his way home once a month or so and I appreciate the idea of that. I thank him in my mind for improving the general quality of my life.

Fitting the skeleton key into Patsy's lock, I hold the knob with my other hand. Carefully. Gently. Turn and push open the door to smell the hidden air that lingers within. It was an easy con to get the key. Weeks ago, I purchased a lock exactly like the new one on her door, taking note of the trademark printed right there. Then I carried my lock down to Safety's and explained how I had lost the keys, hinting at the idea that the lock was kind of contrary, sticking, so I required a key that was a little liberal in its give and take. The man behind the counter winked, saying, "No problem," quick to brandish his knowledge of the trade. "This one'll do the job," and he handed me the key with an easy expression. I gave him my best 'you saved my day' smile and my 'you know a hell of a lot more than me' shake of my head. And I ended up with a skeleton key that works in most of the locks like Patsy's. A valuable gift — these things that very few people have the slightest notion of. A special exciting feeling that makes me calm and brings a treasured smile to the lips when I am standing in a house that is not mine and the furniture is new and there are precious items on the tables and frames on the bedroom dressers with happy pictures of people I do not know, a few of nice-looking girls so that I am now aware of what they look like and where they live in case I decide to return, knowing they are there, knowing where they sleep, knowing... I have even removed a picture or two from a photo album, a snapshot of a woman in her bathing suit or in her underwear, laughing and putting up her hands against the flash, or a woman completely naked, posing in a way that you would never expect from her appearance. I have taken these pictures and studied them, then returned to the same location the following day, waited across the street from the woman's door to be entertained by how she has herself done up so professionally and me knowing what is underneath all of her neat clothes that try to hide her sweet body away. I see her husband and her children and I know that she is mine. Her half-undressed or naked image in my pocket. I have seen the lines and fleshy curves of her body and she is mine now. Touched. Secretly.

Patsy has left a coffee cup on the counter. I curve my fingers around its width and find that it is still warm. Shiver at the thought. Smile the smile of reassurance, the one that stimulates and charms my very own self, right to the bone. I review her cassette collection to discover what is new, what blend of notes is making her dream. Turn on the radio, then turn it off to discover the silence once again. The new lovely silence. The silence of another person's empty home. Patsy's bedroom door is open and the bed is made without a wrinkle, her work clothes on a hanger hooked over the top of the closet door. Everything is neat, a sparse arrangement of items on her dresser, the carpet uncluttered and freshly vacuumed. I move to the bathroom and open the cabinet above the sink, see the brown plastic bottles of pills, her tubes of makeup and the antibiotic cream for her occasional minor cuts and scratches. I lift out her birth control pills to see that they are being used in order. This idea pleases me in an encouraging way because I think of what I have planned for her and I realize the need to make certain nothing will come of the act, no tiny gurgling bundle of torso and limbs formed from the punitive mania of what I am now forced to do.

"I love you, Patsy," I whisper from my place in the closet. She is sleeping with her face toward me, vague light brushing her skin. The room is almost in complete darkness, only the dim glow from her nightlight shaped like a small country house and plugged into the socket in the hallway.

"I love you, Patsy," I whisper, a touch louder this time, tempting, fingering for her warm awakening.

Patsy's lips fall open and she breathes through her mouth.

Her short brown hair rests against her plump cheek and her bangs are cut straight across her forehead. A cotton nightdress lays thinly against her skin and I see that she is not wearing a bra. The shape of her bare breasts is obvious behind the material. I thrill at the way they move when she finally rolls over onto her back, tossing the blankets away in her sleep, lying there in the heat with her nightdress twisted up around her white thighs so that the center rise of her bright white panties is in plain sight. A dampness in the heat makes my fingers stir.

I use my imagination, just as I have been taught to do throughout my many years of forcing against the physical clutter that becomes each person's life. The imagination is all that rescues us. The closing of our eyes. It works well and soon my heart is racing with sexual intention, but I do not move. I simply think, admiring the goodness of this ability.

An hour later, Patsy rolls over again, onto her stomach. I remember the photographs that are mine, the ones kept in my bottom drawer. I recall a lone image: her naked backside. But now her panties press into the rising curves of her behind. The panties that would come down so easily (imagination), and I would show her how much I truly loved her (fact), with all the force that my body could let loose (biology), the steaming semen that is the spin-off from my soul gushing free of the flesh that says everything so clumsily (Imagination with a capital 'I').

"I love you, Patsy," I whisper loudly, so that my voice practically reaches normal speaking level. But Patsy does not wake and I remain right where I am, watching the slight movements of her body embraced by sleep, the quiet sounds from her lips and from the bedclothes, the slow growing of the light, before I carefully open the closet door as dawn begins to reveal itself, to bring everything to pure and vivid life. I step soundlessly along the carpet, closer to the bed where I stare down, observing the full length of her body, my eyes on her toes, skimming upward to the side of her face, knowing the stillness that I can step through if I kneel there, pressing her from sleep to see me, feel me against her in this closeness that is the body's purposefulness, its natural plea for intimacy.

I think, Why this foolish bargaining?

"I love you, Patsy," I whisper, quietly again, reaching out, but holding back, understanding that what I intend to do is not what I feel at all, but merely a bastard attempt at my body's own uneducated explanation. Sleeplessness sharpening my senses to the point of honest and plain understanding. But my body tells me other things. It would be so easy; to force the love into her, to splash her womb with my sticky markings, pretend that this is all it takes to ensure that she is mine, forget the slow delicate entries to the heart, the precision of compliment and courteous inflection. The skillful and charming penetration that is named Romance, but leads to the identical form-fitting procedure of clamping onto the cock. Either way, a woman is raped. It can be pretty or it can be brutal. Consent falls within the boundaries of that silliest of abstract arguments — Interpretation.

I stand on the corner of Slattery and Freshwater. The day is bright and sunny with a breeze that rises quickly then settles, forgetting us. I watch the women walking and driving by and I see Patsy in some of their faces and I believe I see her driving with a man in a pickup truck, but the woman's hairstyle is somewhat different, even though I would have sworn it was her.

A few coins are tossed down into my tobacco tin and I reply, "Thank you, have a good day," to the passing man who will not look at me, simply paying his insurance, tossing off a rattling bit of anxiety. A younger woman, a teenager, strolls up and stares at my sign, then regards me with a potent youthfulness in her eyes. She smiles appreciatively and nods at what she was just reading, "That's pretty good."

"Thanks," I say, troubled by a familiarity about her face, trying to place it. The girl stays close, leaning against the wall a few feet away. When she glances off into traffic, I see her profile and something clicks. An image of her in her pale blue bra and panties, a special pale blue dress laid out on her bed. A photograph taken of her, posing saucily with her hands on her hips and her head tilted to the side. Another photograph of her caught by surprise as she puts on her makeup in her bedroom mirror. The photograph is one of my favourites, back on, but including the reflection of her front in the mirror, leaning forward. The snapshot is folded and tucked away in my wallet, and the date is stamped along the back by the camera business that did the developing and I remember that it was not very long ago, so I am quick to say, in a familiar manner, "How was your grad?"

The girl stands away from the wall and steps closer, squinting to get a better look at my face, then she leans to one side, slips her hands into the back pockets of her jeans and gives me this "oh-yeah, how the hell do you know?" kind of look.

"I recognize you from a friend of mine," I say, casually watching the traffic pass, then plainly glancing at her. "Saw you with him."

"Who?" she asks, smiling now, but still holding back as she bends her fingers, hooking a strand of blonde hair back away from her mouth.

"Can't say." I place a finger to my lips. I tell her, "Secret." and her expression rises as if it is a game. She smiles widely and shakes her head, then she stares down into my tobacco can, eyeing the copper and the silver and even a few bills. Inching her foot forward, she nudges the can with the toe of her brown sandal.

"I've got a few dollars there," I tell her. "You look a little hungry."

Her eyes meet mine and she searches around there, trying to snatch the next move from what I am thinking. A large delivery truck passes by, blowing up a wind and her hair swirls around, but she does not touch it.

"Want to go for a bite?" I ask.

She twists her mouth, considering, then looks at me with one eye closed. "I don't know. Are you okay?"

"Sure I'm okay." My smile is natural. I have made it so. I even toss a quick wink her way, then raise my eyebrows. "I'm the proverbial cat's meow."

The girl laughs and scratches the tip of her nose, then says, holding her hand up to the side of her mouth, "Let's go for a toke instead. I need someone to give me a brainer."

A brainer, I think, no doubt. I'll make certain I give you one of those. One slow-streaming, soft-sell, mind-warming brainer.

The girl sits at the kitchen table across from me, watching as I play with the small flame on the candle. Her eyes are blood-

shot and the candlelight gives her lids an even heavier look.
She is slouched forward slightly and her hair hangs at the sides
of her face. She licks her lips and smiles, unable to force the
expression from her face so that she rubs her jaws, shakes her
head, then sniffs and straightens in her chair.

"You don't say much," she says, the corners of her lips
pointed with that undefeatable smile.

I look at her and I see that she is very young and very beautiful and I do not think there are any words that I can say to tell
her about the needlessness to say words to explain this. I have
to chuckle because I do not remember what it was I was just
thinking and I cannot make any fucking sense out of it at all.
It is lost and I can only laugh, dismissing it this way. Not one
single speck of understanding. Yet it seems to make me happy,
the warmly radical idea of simple acceptance of anything. No
matter what might happen, in my mind, or cast from the fingers of my body.

"What're you laughing at?" asks the girl, having to laugh
herself.

"I was just thinking," I tell her, sluggishly licking my lips
and gently moving my fingers above the flame. "About you."
I look at her, but only for a moment before staring at the flame
again, kindly tempting its orangey-yellow height.

"What *about* me?" She coughs with one loose fist up to her
mouth. Then she straightens again, attempting to be serious.
But her eyes are smiling fiercely as she pushes her back against
the chair.

"I was thinking about the type of person you are and where
you live and where you come from." I will not regard her this
time. I speak slowly and clearly, as if I am divining knowledge
from the flame in a way that will make certain she believes in me.

"It doesn't matter," she says.

"I can tell you. You want me to?" I shift my attention, stare
into her eyes because the time is right, and I see her eyes and
her face, and the dim orange light blending into the darkness
behind her, making me think of nothing else, other than intimacy and love. Absolutely. The only warm and shadowed
shades of emotion that can rise from such closeness, such subdued and personal light.

"Tell me what?" she asks.

"About the type of house you live in. The cream-coloured furniture and the matching carpet and how everything is in its place."

The girl shifts in her chair, a shallow line creasing along her brow as she reaches down with both hands and absent-mindedly holds the seat.

"I can see it."

"Yes," she says in a quiet way.

"Your folks' bedroom probably has old furniture in there, all done up to look in perfect condition, preserved, and your mother's closets are filled with expensive clothes and you probably have a cute little dog, white and furry with a pink bow in its hair. Something like that."

The girl's eyes are fixed on mine and I realize that she has not even told me her name and I have not told her mine and it does not matter, because I am seeing now, knowing more than her name, knowing beyond that alphabetic camouflage. She is seeing too as she shakes her head slightly as if to say she cannot believe in such vision, the accuracy of how I gaze into the treasureless teenage hollow that is her heart. Nothing there, except the vacancy that my understanding promptly occupies, filling her with charm and magic and the memory of adolescent longing.

"Am I close?" I ask.

"It's scary," she says, her head twitching against her own thoughts, something in her wanting to refuse, her face changing as she throws up the barriers. "Stop now, okay, because you're starting to freak me out." She reaches for one of her ear lobes and takes it between her fingers, rubbing and pinching it.

"And your bedroom has frilly curtains and stuffed toys everywhere because you probably collect them and there's a picture of someone you really care for on your dresser, a man, maybe a teacher, maybe an uncle. You need that. Someone close you've never had."

The girl stands abruptly, the legs of the chair scraping along the linoleum. She stares down at me, her hands hanging by her sides, her legs perfectly straight. "I'm freaking out now," she says. "Just stop it," slowly holding up her hands, "because I'm freaking out. Okay, so stop."

"I know what you want," I say to her as clearly as I can and with all of the feeling I can summon in my voice. "I know where you've come from. We didn't meet by accident. You understood my sign on the street. Everything that it implied. I know the pale blue dress you wore to your graduation. Blue, with little white flowers in your hair. The image that your mother hoped for. The prettiness, but that's not you. This is you."

"Stop it," she says, her lips trembling. She draws in a deep breath, tears blurring this breathless image of me from her eyes.

I lift a fresh joint from the table, wet it in my mouth and lean toward the candle flame, puffing, then lean back, blow out the fire that crackles at the tip. I take a draw, pass it up to her, holding the smoke in my lungs. The girl stares at the hot tip, then quietly takes the joint from my fingers, looking at it, waiting, before she sniffs and sits again, coming closer, settling closer, watching me in awe as she wipes at her eyes.

A thought comes to me while I lie in bed with the girl's cheek resting against my bare chest. I have been so busy with the events of the day that I forgot to send flowers to Patsy. I had forgotten all about her. Stroking the girl's hair, touching her bare shoulder, I look at her face, her opened eyes thoughtfully staring at the wall not far from the side of the bed. I pull the photograph of her from memory and remind myself how I should remove the real thing from my wallet, at the earliest possible convenience, and destroy it in the bathroom, tear it into tiny pieces and flush it down the toilet. I imagine the sound of the flush and when the telephone rings it seems as if I am expecting it. The girl lifts her head away from my chest and looks at me, smiling nicely with her lips closed and her head tilted slightly so that her hair hangs to the side. She glances at my chest and quietly moves her fingers around there.

I reach down by the side of the bed and lift the receiver.

"Hello," I say.

"Hi," says the voice that I recognize as Patsy's. "I've been thinking," she says and I know by the sound of her voice and by those very words she has just spoken that I have been forgiven, the broken chain of flower deliveries prompting her to step into the blankness and take inventory, knowing now what she is really missing. She has been thinking, she says, so I hang up before she explains any further, knowing where she is — in her apartment and that she is alone.

"Wrong number?" asks the girl.

"No." I sadly shake my head. "Just nobody there." I do not say another word. I simply watch the girl and smile my special kind of smile, believing now that it may, in fact, mean something. She returns my smile, and I am pleased to see that it is a loving one, drawing me in as she sweetly closes her eyes against the feel of my fingertips, my touch, willing it elsewhere, inside, willing it along the clean length of soul that makes her gasp euphorically for breath as I stroke her. But I must lift my fingers away to see what I have done, to sight the possibilities. When her eyelids slowly rise and she stares at me with a look that softly bids the deepest kind of entry, I know that I am in there, I am home free. Leaning forward, I close my eyes, and gently press my lips to hers.

Mime

I

When I walk through the door, I see Vicky is practicing her art, standing in the hallway wearing her white face. I'm half an hour late for supper, but I can't tell if she's mad. She just stares into space, stiff hands out in front of her chest, lips slightly opened and her head tilted.

I step past, but her eyes don't follow me. They don't even blink. I want to ask, What're you watching? What's so interesting in thin air? I've got real troubles that she should know about, troubles that I need to share with someone. Not to mention the car. The side of the car and the hundreds of scratches that the adopted kid from next door cut into the paint job. I didn't see him do it, but I know. His mother is an older woman, quiet and gentle. Controlled. She only whispers at the little savage while he steps to the side of her, carefully setting his sights on her thin ankle before kicking it.

I stare back at Vicky to try and detect the slightest movement. Not a flutter. Her fingers don't even tremble inside those white gloves. Watching her like that, I think of the Indian. That's who I have to tell Vicky about. Here's where the trouble's coming from. Slaney's Mill outside of Blaketown. The Indians just blocked the road so we can't work tomorrow. The Indians showed us their rifles — the stocks pressed into their hips — while we drove back into town from the mill. They said they'd let us go home, but we couldn't come back to work.

I heard on the radio how the police were sent in, and gunfire broke out — as if by mistake — and one of the policemen was dead. A dead policeman is not a good thing. It brings certain issues to mind that question the whole notion of justice.

This one Indian — who I watched in my rearview while I was pulling away — just stood there without moving an inch, just like Vicky. He had on a blue plaid shirt with the sleeves torn off and black denims on his thin legs. The empty arms of a brown vinyl jacket were tied around his scrawny waist. Like most of the Indians his hair was black and straggly. What really set him out from the others were the big pilot sunglasses on his face. Every now and then the sun would flash in them as he held the rifle firmly against his hip; the barrel aimed into the sky. By the looks of him, he had no plans of moving, ever. I could tell by the way he was standing there; he had no intentions of saying a word. He'd said enough. Talking for decades. Speaking white man's words that no white man was listening to.

I drove off, watching him, and then about fifteen minutes later in town I heard the news of them shooting a policeman. I knew it was this Indian who had done it. I just had a feeling. It was one of the surest feelings I ever had. The reporters were already there with their cordless telephones and cameras, waiting for something to erupt — something that would make them seem more alive; the prospect of people dying.

The smell of pot roast and gravy brings my thoughts back to the issue presently at hand. Supper. I move down the hallway to the kitchen and wash my hands in the sink. Glancing out the big window, I see the kid from next door throwing a kitten up into the air, swinging it by its tail and letting it fly. The kitten twirls with its paws spread, frantically scrambling, then they're still. When it comes down, it doesn't land on its feet. It slams the grass on its side. The kid scoops it up without a moment's hesitation and lets it rip into the sky. This time, it whacks the ground face-first. It happens fast. I can't believe what I'm seeing. The kid keeps picking up the kitten and twirling it through the air. Dipping his blonde head back, he watches the kitten rise, then drop. His face doesn't change, except for the widening grin.

At first, I can't even move. I feel stunned. Then the pure anger comes to me and I rush to dry off my hands in the towel hung over the stove handle. I lunge forward, sliding open the window.

"Hey," I shout.

The kid looks over, startled. He just stands there. That's all he does. His smile comes back and he takes great pleasure in showing me his teeth. He can't be more than seven or eight. Blonde hair. Blue eyes. Handsome as any kid can be. I don't understand where he gets all the meanness from, or what sets that creepy stare in his eyes.

"What're you doing to that cat?" I bawl at him.

"They land on their feet," the kid calls, glancing at the kitten on the ground. "Always."

"No, they do not. That one doesn't. Don't touch him anymore."

"He's my kitten. Mine." The child grabs up the fur-ball and holds it close to his white, button-up shirt. When he moves the kitten away, I see small splotches of blood staining the front of his little pocket.

"Always mine, no matter what."

"Put down that kitten," I scream. "Now!" My hands and arms start shaking where they're pressed against the countertop. "Or I'll go out there and crack you in two."

The kid drops the fur-ball. First thing it does is lick itself in a sloppy way before trying to scamper off, but it keeps tumbling to the side as if one of its little paws is broken.

"Don't let me see you do that again," I call after him. Leaning further out the window, I feel my belly pressing into the edge of the counter. "You hear me, you little prick."

"I'm telling," he shouts, instantly turning and running toward his back door. "I'm telling my momma what you said to me."

I pull the big knife from its rack on the wall and slice through the roast. Chunks of garlic lie on top, their smell filling my nostrils in a satisfying way. The meat is dark on the outside but pink and pinker as I cut deeper. The baked potatoes are soft when I poke the fork into them. I lay out a placemat and a plate on the table. I even put down a setting for Vicky, but I know she won't be eating. She always practices her art around suppertime. Says her concentration is best after she has everything done; the washing and ironing and cleaning and cooking. This is what she says, like it's one big word — the-washing-and-ironing-and-cleaning-and-cooking. And shopping, I add. I don't shop much, she says, not like I used to. I don't argue with her, or she puts on her white face right away and sits around for hours, holding an apple in one hand, a bunch of grapes in the other.

I take my place at the table and cut the slices of roast into chewable pieces. The sections are tender and juicy and I swallow easily. The baked potatoes split open with a quick stroke of the knife. The butter turns them yellow. I like lots of butter; what it does to the taste.

When I'm almost half way through eating, someone fingers the doorbell. I have an idea who it is as I push myself away from my meal with a sigh. I can see a woman in the glass down the center of the front door. Stopping for a second, I tilt my head into the living room to see Vicky sitting on the beige L-shaped couch. Her legs are crossed like some kind of statue from another country, and she's sitting perfectly straight. White pants. White shirt. White face. Her eyes are opened extra wide and she's facing the television. The television is on. Vicky stares, but her expression doesn't change.

"Hey, don't bother getting up," I say, trying to sound as bothered as possible before leaning back out into the hallway.

"Yes, Mrs. Kent? What can I do for you?"

"Mr. Fagan," she says, her face too humble-looking for my liking. "I find it to be quite an unpleasant task. Knocking on your door like this." She stops for a second as if that's enough to get an apology from me. But when she sees that I'm just waiting for more, she goes on: "My husband and I prefer to remain at home. We try to live the only true life. With Christ, you understand? As a family giving extreme care to Joseph's raising."

"Joseph?" I say.

"Joey," she says, smiling as if to let me know that she

forgives me for not catching on. "You see, our son."

"Yes, I understand, Mrs. Kent. The Joseph who was just throwing a tiny little kitten up into the air and watching it smash its face on the ground. That Joseph, you mean."

Mrs. Kent winces. She covers her ears, but quickly lowers her hands again. She seems confused as her face closes up like someone just punched her in the stomach, her lips wrinkling and puckering. She turns away for a moment as if wanting to escape a foul smell that's crept into her nostrils. Her eyes stay off me for a while, so I glance past her head at the houses behind their trees on the darkening block. I see Mr. Stone's big car curving into his drive across the otherwise still, dim street.

"Not only that," I say, raising my voice and setting my eyes back on Mrs. Kent, "he scratched the shit out of my car. The side of my car. Have you had a look at that?"

"No, Mr. Fagan!" Mrs. Kent is shocked beyond belief. She moves her lips from side to side. I hear her breath turning heavy. "There is no need to be vulgar." Her chest begins to tremble, but in a powerful, almost frightening way. "I am a Christian woman. My husband and I. And I do not appreciate your filthy words. I do not want filthy words to traumatize Joseph. I have to say this, to tell you. I simply have to."

The sound of a car door closing draws my attention away from Mrs. Kent. Across the street, Mr. Stone is standing in his driveway, watching us. He looks kind of tired; always working late at his antique shop in town. The same beige raglan that he's been wearing for years hangs straight off his body. I reach up and give him a cordial wave.

"Evening," he calls, his voice dull and far off. The good Mrs. Kent turns, but she does not say anything. I see the side of her face and it tells me nothing. When she looks at me again, she is stern and ready. Mr. Stone moves off. He walks toward his house, shaking his grey-haired head and calling to his dog in a playful way. The dog comes out to meet him, barks once or twice as it jumps up with its big paws, then gladly follows Mr. Stone inside.

"You cannot threaten a child, Mr. Fagan. What will happen to Joseph? He'll carry your meanness, your horrible anger around with him for the rest of his life. And I can't have that for *my* little boy." That's about as much as she can get out before the tears take over. She begins crying, weakly lifting a cupped hand to her eyes, her shoulders jittering back and forth.

For some reason, I think of the Indian shooting the cop. The policeman slowly, soundlessly, dropping out of sight. The Indian's face unchanged behind his big sunglasses and through the dust that's been stirred by the fallen body. Haze rising like in slow motion. I don't know why the image comes to me, but it does. Just like that; as quick as snapping my fingers.

"Mrs. Kent, your son's spoiled rotten and I've got no time to waste talking about it. I have other things to do. But if I ever catch him harming any animal again I'm calling in the Humane Society."

"No, Mr. Fagan!" Mrs. Kent grits her teeth and stomps a foot, anger washing clean her teary eyes. "You cannot do that. They have no right to interfere, no one, in our lives. I pray you would be Christian toward Joseph. A small helpless child having gone through such great misfortune. Trauma. Abuse. If there was any other way I would not be telling you this." Her eyes dart from side to side as she fingers a button on her peach-coloured blouse. "But I see you need to know. You need that more than anything, because your knowledge of the matter is slim." Lowering her voice, she speaks with her eyes opening wider, "His biological parents carried out unspeakable..."

I cut her off. "I'm not interested, Mrs. Kent. My supper's getting cold."

Straightening her back, Mrs. Kent blushes and tilts back her head, carefully watching me: "I must ask you for the good of God, please consider..."

"For the good of God!" I can't help but chuckle in a surprised kind of way. "I'm not a Christian, Mrs. Kent. I wouldn't want that kind of torture." Edging the door closed, I say, "Goodnight." Then I press firmly against the wood and shut it all the way. I even take the time to make sure it's locked.

Before I know what I'm doing I find myself back in the kitchen, but I can't eat. Mrs. Kent has made me angry and anger has snatched away my appetite. I just look at my plate and wonder about work and where the money will be coming from. Slaney's Mill sure as hell won't be paying us if the road stays blocked. We aren't working. And the Indians aren't saying anything. They have nothing to say. Everyone around here knows about their land claims and how the Mill is run on lumber cut from their land — stolen from their land if you listen to their point of view. They have nothing more to say. They've said enough. Now, they're standing strong and silent. Talk means zero once you've reached a certain point. It means less than the bonds that pretend to link us all.

I'm lying in bed for an hour or more before Vicky lays down the book she's reading and switches off the light that's clipped onto the headboard. My eyes are open and there's not even a trace of fatigue in me. Vicky sighs — so I can barely hear her — and rolls onto her side, facing the window that looks out over the field behind the house. You can see the round moon from here at this time of night. Its calm light rests on the grass that the breeze gently leans to one side. Further on, the river stirs and the moonlight is on that too, flashing in tiny spots so that you know the water's moving. It seems like everything is moving tenderly in the night.

I turn my attention to Vicky's back, take delight in studying the length of her blonde hair. She's the prettiest in Blaketown. Right from the start everyone always wondered why she ended up with me. And I guess she's started wondering that exact same thing.

I wait for a little while, then reach for her shoulder, try to turn her close to me. I'm as gentle as I can be, and she rolls onto her back. Her eyes are closed, her face toward the ceiling. I watch her lips and the way they're almost set in a pout. They're beautiful lips and I want to kiss the sadness out of them.

"Vicky," I say.

She doesn't answer, but her eyelids tremble, like she's pretending that I'm not here.

"I know you're awake, sweetheart." I hear her breathe, but that's all she'll let me know. "It's been a while. Too long." My fingers slip along her bare arm and tingles run through me. I hold my breath, then slowly slide my hand onto her breast. The cotton material of her nightdress is warm and she feels so soft. I want to tell her certain things, but I can't. She won't hear me. She's not listening. I want to bring her back to me. I just need to see something move in her face; an expression of how I can still give her that wild smiling joy.

Edging down my pajama pants, I take hold of her hand, carefully pry it away from where it's joined with her other fingers, and place it between my legs. But her hand just rests there. Her fingers don't give me the pleasure of movement.

"Vicky," I say, tossing back the covers. "Vicky, please." I inch her nightdress up above her thighs, over her underwear, and higher still, until I see her smooth waist. She won't move her legs for me. I have to do that. "Please, Vicky," I say, slipping my fingers beneath the elastic of her underwear, sensing the heat as I press my fingers against the tangle of soft hair and the warm flesh between her legs. "Say anything." I kiss her pouting lips, but they're parched and don't respond. Edging closer, I gently move on top. I tell myself, Be careful, be gentle. I take my time trying to enter her, but she is dry. Moaning, I kiss her neck and breasts and try to press into the place beneath her belly, but I feel I will hurt Vicky, so I stop and rest, sadly look at her and touch both sides of her pretty face.

She lies there without recognizing my touch and I notice something creeping from the corner of her closed eye, something that's stronger than any words — a full tear, running along the side of her face and catching in a few soft strands of her honey-coloured hair.

II

I go to work, just like every other day since they put up the blockade. I'm trying to pretend, and hoping that the road is re-opened. On the way out of town I stop at Whalen's General Store for a small bottle of orange-pineapple juice and an apple flip. Old Man Whalen looks down at what I've got. It takes him a long time to figure things out. Both his blue-veined, wrinkled hands are leaning on the counter and he looks like he's trying to muster up enough strength to turn for the cash register. Glancing up at me, he smiles half-heartedly and nods, proudly showing me his pink gums. Then he pokes at the apple flip.

"Old one," he says.

I look down and see the green spots growing inside the plastic wrapper.

"New ones there." Pointing to the rack beside the counter, he laughs — once, fast. "Go ahead. Change it up."

I toss back the old apple flip and grab a fresh one.

"Working," says Whalen, in no hurry to punch in the price of my snack. "The Indians. Pow wow." His crackling, weary voice fades off, "Give 'em something to..." Staring at the dark hardwood floor, he presses his lips together.

"Road still blocked?" I ask him.

Old Man Whalen sucks on his gums and shakes his head. He doesn't say anything, and I know exactly what he's trying to say. Silence sometimes has its own meaning; more accurate than any kind of talking. Silence like its own complex language.

"I'll go up and have a look anyway. Maybe something's changed." I give him a comforting smile. "Let's hope, hey." Glancing toward the front of the store, I see a pick-up truck through the plate glass window to the left of the double doors. It's pulling out of Old Man Whalen's lumberyard behind the shop, making off with the old man's lumber. I turn my attention back on Whalen and start to tell him what's up, but he looks like he already knows and doesn't give a damn. He's way past caring. This is what he keeps telling me. For as long as I've lived in Blaketown, he's always insisted that he couldn't care less about what goes on around him; what people do, or say.

"They're all dead," he's always insisted, carefully pointing at the customers in the corners of his store, leaning toward me and whispering, "Dead. Not like you and me." Tapping his fingers against the side of his head and widening his eyes to hit home the point: "They're dead up here."

He stands there now. Nervously licking his lips, he smiles, then winks at me, laughing with an open mouth.

"It's war," he says, triumphant memories glossing in his eyes. "Jesus, friend! Just like before. The Indians. They're not out of the picture at all." His lips take up trembling, then his whole head starts quivering and he hopelessly stares at me, tears spilling down his ancient cheeks, coming freely like rainwater running off a roof.

"I don't know," I say. "How do you ever know who's right?"

"No one's right," insists Old Man Whalen, squinting as his sadness turns to anger. "Right?!!" He looks at me as if I'm crazy and swipes the tears away as if they're nothing more than a bother to him. "I thought you were one of us; alive, like me. So listen." He lifts his jittery hand, points one shrivelled finger straight at me, jabbing it in the air, "No one's ever right." He pauses, thinking hard on something, needing to remember my name. A few seconds later, he gives up trying, and sweeps his hand through the air. "Don't be such a bloody fool."

The Indians are wearing red or blue bandanas tied around their faces. The material covers their mouths and rides up over their noses. I recognize the Indian from days ago because you remember the shape and ways of a body without having to see the face. Besides, he's also got those big pilot sunglasses on. From where I'm standing behind the police barricade, I can see the line of Indians in the distance. Must be a hundred feet or more. Slaney's Mill is silent behind them, like a painting you see in one of the tourist shops. The big brown building. The big blue country sky. Still and not a sound. Green trees. Colours. But they've shut the mill up. And stopped it from eating their land.

A helicopter tilts out from behind Hawk Mountain and chops through the air toward us. It stays up high and I see the signature shade of brown, and the symbol of the national police on its side.

"What's going on?" I ask one of the policemen.

"You can see," he says without looking at me. "Can you see them over there?" He's a tall man with a bony face and dark eyes that glance down at his holster, then dart my way to see if I caught where he was looking. His fingers play with something in his left pocket. Slivers of metal, rattling. A ring of keys.

"Nothing changed?" I ask.

"Changed?!" He shakes his head like I just told him something way out of line. "Go on now. It'd be safer if you went home. Don't cause any trouble here." Taking his hand out of his pocket, he wipes the palm against his dark blue shirt.

"I'm not here to cause trouble," I tell him.

The sun is harsh and bright and the air is empty. It offers nothing. You can smell the dust from the dirt road and it seems strange for me to be here and not going to work. It seems like

I'm on vacation, but I'm not supposed to be, and there's nothing to do, nothing planned. Everything feels a tiny bit out of whack and I don't like the creepy feeling that starts going through my body. I don't recognize it, and it scares me for a second.

"I'm just going," I say when the policeman tilts his head at me to leave. I watch the Indians as I walk away. They're shouting something from behind their barricade, but it's just a small distant sound, as if they're only two inches high and we're standing, looking down at them, wondering what the hell their teeny-weeny problem could possibly be.

The kid from next door is piling up dirt in my driveway when I pull in. He stands there in front of my garage door and shows me his teeth. His blonde hair is combed perfectly and his handsome face is cut with the mean intentions of that horrible grin of his.

I shut off the Tornado and lean out. When I slam the heavy door, the sun catches the red paint job and I see the scribblings of scratches all along the side.

"Clean up that dirt," I warn the kid, "or you'll be in for it."

Pushing his face forward, and smiling through perfect white teeth, he says, "Fuck off, you shit."

I lurch forward, but hold myself, my muscles going tight, wanting to snap open and beat a lesson into the spoiled little brat.

"Put that clay back where you got it."

"From your backyard," he says, quickly pointing — with the steel prongs in his hand — to the rear of my house. "Dug it all up. All. All. All." He wipes his dirty little fingers against the side of his green pleated pants, then he drops the steel prongs and claps his hands together, getting ready to run.

"Come on," I say, chasing after him and snatching hold of his arm. I squeeze into his flesh until my fingertips touch close to bone.

"Owwwww. Let go." He tries to kick and bite me but I hold him at arm's length, pull his stumbling body along the side of the house. "My hair," he shouts, "is messed up."

When we get to the backyard, I see the hole he's dug in Vicky's rock garden alongside the patio that I built. She had just planted the purple, orange and yellow flowers a few weeks ago and now they're slumped over or cracked in half, leaning on the ground.

"WHAT THE FUCK ARE YOU DOING?!" I scream, shaking him so that his head snaps back and forth like a rag doll. "You stupid little shit! Bastard!" I shove him away and he tumbles backward, landing with his hands behind him on the ground, and I see fear freeze and clear his eyes.

"MOMMA! MOMMA!"

"Come here." I'm quick to grab him when he tries to make a break for it. Bending him over my knee, I pick up a piece of one-by-two that was left over from the patio and whack him across the backside.

"You stay away from my car." Whack! "You stay away from my house." Whack! "You respect your parents." Whack!

Whack!

Whack!

Whack!

Someone has their hands on me. I look up and my eyes are burning with fury. Mrs. Kent is white as a ghost. In fact, she could be a ghost for all I care or am able to realize. I hear nothing but the blood booming in my throat and ears.

Her mouth is open and she's trying to say my name but nothing comes. She can't speak. She grabs Joseph away from me and holds his wailing body close to her breast, protectively pushes the side of her precious boy's face into her cheek.

Then the sound comes to me: "No, no, no," Joey screams, his high-pitched voice filled with terror. He shrieks and yelps. "Hurt, hurt, no, no, no." His head lashes back and forth and I can hear his teeth clicking as he crazily opens and closes his jaws, like he's trying to bite someone. "Hurt, hurt, hurt."

Standing there, struggling with what's shocked her body into silence, Mrs. Kent finally manages to get one word out, one big word — the one she's been longing to hurl from between her clamped-shut Christian teeth — "EVIL!" she says, stabbing a finger at me, stabbing and stabbing as she backs away, her stiff finger wanting to split open and blast me with mighty shoots of fiery condemnation.

I hear water splashing from the bathroom and I know that Vicky is taking a bath. She hasn't heard a thing with regards to the trouble out back. The water must've been running. Either that, or she just decided — as she has been doing lately — to ignore absolutely everything around her.

I creep in closer to the door. It's opened a crack and I press my eye in to view her. What I see is so perfect. She's in the tub, soaping her shoulders, moving the suds down over her full loose breasts. She has her hair pinned up and two stray strands hang loose and wet at the sides of her neck.

Tilting back her head, she squeezes the sponge, loving the feel of warm water rushing down the front of her body. A smile comes to her lips as she lifts her leg to wash each toe, taking her time and smiling like the sight of them makes her happy. Her smile grows even bigger when she moves the sponge up the length of one shiny leg, then along the inside thigh of the second. Bobbing her legs in the water, she watches them float close to the surface, so the cool air can touch her wet skin.

Vicky sits still, thinking. She takes a good look at her body and whispers, "All this water around a barren island." As if the words have somehow offended her, she shoves her behind along the bottom of the tub, slipping back and quickly holding her breath before going under. She stays down there with her eyes closed. Then — when I am about to leap forward and pull her out — she rushes up, frantically wiping at her face.

"Island," she gasps, spitting the water from her lips. She sits there in stillness and silence. Her face looks like she's in a daze. She just stares at the tile wall, then leans forward, soaping her face, slowly and carefully scrubbing each spot. With her eyes closed like that, I think of stepping in and touching her body, washing her skin like I used to do all the time, pretending my fingers were hers the way she wanted me to do. But I hold myself and watch her, not wanting to lose the emotions that're rising inside of me, glazing my eyes and giving me a sad kind of pleasure.

Vicky lowers her arms, letting the sponge float on the surface before rinsing her face with the water from her hands held like a cup. I hear her moan as she pours the water down over her head. She does it again — keeping her eyes closed and moaning like something else is going on — until almost all the soap has been washed away, only a few traces of lather clinging to the hair along her forehead.

She opens her eyes, carefully looks at her body again before leaning forward and pulling the plug. One of her hands grips the edge of the bathtub, the other pushes against the pink tile wall. Standing, she sighs as the water rushes from her skin. The liquid sounds strangely like the tiny laughter of a child as it splashes back into the cloudy bath water. Vicky's expression seems happy, but there's more to it than that. Even though her happiness is inside her, it seems not to be a part of her at all, like she's looking at it from far away. The water drains from the tub. Vicky watches it go down. Then, turning, she sees me in the doorway. The water level sinks past her calves, then down below her ankles. The liquid pulls away from her skin until the bathtub is empty and Vicky is standing there, shivering and pale, unable to move because I'm watching her.

I'm sitting in the kitchen when I hear the knocking on my back door. Mr. Kent has pulled himself out of his house to take over the cause. Tag-team Christians in a bout to rid the world of evil. He is a tall, thin man — with long fingers — who constantly dresses in green workman's clothes. Since moving in next door several years ago, he hasn't said a word to me, only nodded a hello every so often when we came so close in our adjoining driveways that it was necessary to pass some kind of comment.

"What've you done?" he asks plainly. I watch his fingers as his heavy boots step up, into my house, "To Joseph — what have you done to him?"

"Hey," I say, pointing down at the threshold, like he's crossed a line he had no right to, then I say it again, "Hey."

"Do you know what you've done?" Mr. Kent stares at me with lost-looking eyes. "Do you understand what the boy has been through? What you have done to him. What was done to him before. What this world has put him through." Mr. Kent swallows and his eyes shut as if a light has suddenly turned too bright. The muscles in his neck tighten. When he lifts his hands, I step back, but he only squeezes them into fists and stands there, his eyes so narrow I wonder if he can see me at all. "People not of the Lord. Always people not of the Lord. People like you in this old, old mortal world."

"That boy needs some discipline," I say, coughing to clear my throat.

Mr. Kent looks at me with the weary fullness of his eyes
suddenly revealed, then he turns, steps down and out of the
house. Shoving his hands into the pockets of his workpants, he
wanders around in circles on the grass in my backyard. He
stares at the ground, but I know he's not seeing anything. What
he's thinking about is the only thing that holds his attention.

Dusk is starting to do its work, dimming the shapes of everything. I flick on the light over the back door. Mr. Kent stops
instantly. His grey face seems wounded, lined with the markings of illness or fatigue.

"I'm sorry," he says, staring off to where my yard ends by a
grove of evergreens. "My anger — a curse — ask only for forgiveness," but he's not saying it to me. His apologies are
directed elsewhere. Bowing his head, he says a bunch of quick
sentences under his breath, the words all running together as
smooth as anything. He repeats things three or four times,
then, without offering another word to me, he wanders toward
my open gate and moves out, over, and in through his own
gate.

I turn in the doorway — deciding to leave the light on out
there — and I see Vicky standing behind me. Her white face
glows in the dimness and the black tears that she's painted on
her cheeks make me flinch because I've never seen them before. Strangely enough, they remind me of the children her
body's not capable of having. The children I can't have because
of her.

I walk sideways so as not to brush against her where she's
standing still. I move in through the kitchen and pause before
going through the archway. Glancing back, I see that Vicky's
still standing there, staring out through the screen door as if
there's something lingering in the coming darkness that she
longs for, something that belongs to her, and no other person in
this world. Least of all to me.

The army has been sent in to drive the Indians from their road
block. Over two thousand soldiers are on their way to keep
peace because people from all around Blaketown are getting
angry and forming violent mobs that rush into the nearby res-
ervations and beat Indians in the night. They killed two
Indians already. An old woman and her grandson. Helpless peo-

ple. The army is sending armoured personnel carriers, earth movers and other equipment. Maybe they're going to cut new roads. The Indians aren't saying much. They issue statements on the news, but they refuse to negotiate with anyone with a mouthful of the whitest lies.

The people from this community are losing wages. Not only that, a second band of Indians has blocked a road that cuts off a few other towns from the main highway. And these towns are tourist towns that count on road traffic to make a buck. The Indians just stand there with their weapons and masks, occasionally firing their rifles into the sky.

The other day, I heard from Old Man Whalen that these Indians are trained soldiers, some of them from the American and Canadian armies. They have a complex system of signals and codes, so they don't even need to talk to understand each other. They use natural signs they've learned from animals, things they've been passing on for generations. Old Man Whalen told me that it's a way of thinking that would take us centuries to set into our brains. Our own smart brains, he said. Us. And we're not even as stupid as the dead ones.

I get a letter in my mailbox from Mrs. Kent. She explains that they will not be pressing charges against me for assaulting their disturbed little boy. Even though I am an evil man, God will deal with me when the day of judgement comes.

They do not want the courts involved. The note doesn't say this, but I assume what I assume. The note says this: We, the Kents, are simple people. Christian people with high ideals. Nothing must interfere with us living a sacred and peaceful life.

The next day I'm amazed to see an ambulance and police car parked in front of the Kents' house. Two men carry out a body in a black bag, zipped right up. A policeman carefully carries a shotgun from the Kents' basement, out through the opened garage door. He tries not to touch certain parts of the shotgun and his hold is awkward. Mrs. Kent and Joseph stand in their driveway, staring at the movements in front of them. Mrs. Kent has no expression on her face, as if any kind of sadness or joy has just been carried away in the big black bag that moves away from their house. The boy seems weak and stunned, but then he stares up at Mrs. Kent and I see him watching her misery, sucking in her grief and — slowly — a sickening type of sneer takes over his face and holds him like something poisonous, something with a terrible kind of sharpness that's waiting to sting, or bite a nasty hole clean through his new mother's skin.

III

Down at Whalen's General Store, I buy lumber from the yard, and nails from inside, and I load the planks into the trunk of the Tornado. At the cash register, I wait politely while Old Man Whalen takes his time telling me that Mrs. Kent claims it was all an accident. But the police are saying other things. They ruled out suicide because of the direction and impact of the blast; the way the spray of lead tore through the side of Mr. Kent's face. It was from a distance and on an angle. They say the boy shot Mr. Kent. The boy shot Mr. Kent because he wanted a new bicycle, and Mr. Kent couldn't afford one. Old Man Whalen tells me he saw the boy and Mr. Kent in Piper's on Water Street, and the boy was shouting for a bicycle, screaming with his face gone all hot and red.

   Old Man Whalen tells me things, and he knows that they're for real. His nephew is one of the local policemen, the partner of the officer who was shot by the Indian up at Slaney's Mill, so he's a little upset and doesn't mind offering Old Man Whalen the whole truth about how everything that's fair and just has suddenly gone all wrong.

The Indians are banding together. Thousands are moving in from the northern areas of the country. It's on the television news. I see footage of them sweeping through the shadowed woods and shooting at what gets in their way. They want their land back and who in their right mind could possibly argue with them? I know they're right. No question. But that doesn't stop me from taking the lumber from the trunk of my Tornado and boarding up my windows and front door, keeping only the back door clear.

   Vicky sits in the living room without making a sound while I hammer the planks of wood into place, blocking out the light, blocking out my wife's staring image on this side of the win-

dow with me. The Indians will all be here soon; they've taken
over two towns further up the highway and word has it that
Indians have done the same in lots of other parts of the country. They killed twenty-seven white people: twenty-one
soldiers, six civilians. The television has the numbers up on
the screen. Twenty-seven and counting, it says — the numbers
flashing white against red on a special emergency channel.

Old Man Whalen tried to explain about the Indians' signals
and codes. I know I'll never understand what any of them
mean, but I'll see the movements of their hands and listen all
the same, wanting to hear, needing a sign myself.

When the fighting backs up into this town, I'll be ready.
They'll think no one would be living in a boarded-up house.
But there's a little peephole in one of the planks where a knot
used to be, and I'll learn not to make a sound, just like my
wife. I'll sit here and watch the Indians reclaim what was
theirs all along. They'll never know about us, but I'll be sure to
see them when their gunfire makes its way down our street.
I'll rush for the peephole, lean over the back of our couch,
alongside of Vicky, and I'll see the whole scene, just like I see
Mrs. Kent now, standing on my front lawn. I haven't seen her
for a few days and it looks like her face has lost all its colour.
Her hair is unclipped and seeming straw-like and wild. She's
staring right at me with her fixed eyes and she keeps crossing
her heart, crossing her heart with her finger and nodding toward the grass.

Taking the hint, I look down to where Joseph is kneeling to
the right of Mrs. Kent, his blonde hair shaved flush to the
white skin on his head. I notice how his hands are still, holding a black book with gold-edged pages, his fingers out straight
and looking weird, like they've been glued to the covers.

Mrs. Kent leads Joey closer by pressing his shoulder, and he
has real trouble walking the way she wants him to — on his
knees.

I lift my hands and hold them flat to the wooden planks,
press closer to get a better look at the boy, to make out the
black marks criss-crossed along his lips, which are all swollen
out of shape. Closer and closer, into the peep hole, I catch the
deafening sight of his mouth stitched shut with sewing thread.

I listen, but everything is calm and seems in its place. A

fresh breeze from the open back door moves in to touch my skin. It makes me feel kind of good, but soon it makes me wonder how the door got open in the first place. Then there is a sound that makes me turn: a fast-moving type of noise like a struggle and Vicky's muffled scream as the face with the straggly black hair and big pilot sunglasses looks up at me from where he's crouched beside my wide-eyed wife. He doesn't move a muscle. He just waits, staring, then tips down his sunglasses so I can see what's in his eyes. Cautiously, he lifts one straight finger, setting it to his lips, "shhhhhh."

The Law

The shack was weather-beaten, its planks worn soft and paintless grey. From the branches of the trees surrounding it, insects hung on fine threads catching the rays of sunlight sifting down and through. The spruce trees were a dull and distant green as if seen beyond mist, their branches half dead and spotted with illness. Ches Coombs stood beneath the tree closest to the open door of his shack and shoved the trunk with both hands, feeling the needles fall against his bare arms and bare shoulders and in his grey and white hair, which was trimmed so close to his head that the needles touched his scalp. He quickly brushed them free with a sweep of his palm, then shook the trunk again, stood straight, listened to the needles softly hitting the forest ground like far-off rain, falling where he could barely see it higher across the westward rise of the valley.

Ches did not hear the truck coming because it was rolling slowly over the narrow road, the thin tire tracks were riddled with humps and clotted with patches of grass. He turned to watch the bugs spinning on their fine web-threads. They were curled like caterpillars struck by fire, hanging without intention; done with their gluttonous chore. Ches's eyes caught sight of the truck with Wigs Bisell rocking behind the wheel. He thought he heard the cry of a baby above the sound of the truck bouncing on its springs, then coming to a stop, the low cry disappearing into the silence that was held at bay only by the vague churning of the engine.

Wigs turned down his window and spat, settling with his elbow out and waiting for Ches to step up. He wiped a sleeve over his wrinkled sunken face, down across the sharp cut of his chin. His blinking eyes were quick with the humour that was easily coaxed from him.

"Nar tell'n wha's com'n," Wigs said, watching the sky and hoarsely cackling. " 'N here ya can't tell nut'n. Da light comes strange down. W'aw's block'n w'aw? Rain'n maybe furder off up da valley. Lees'n ta it."

Paying little mind to Wigs, Ches stepped alongside the side of the truck and leaned with his elbows on the metal edge, watching the goat; interested in its big eyes, which looked ugly and wrong by how they were set across its face.

"Dey bounc'n reet good fer da ride. Saw 'm in da rearview tumbl'n sideways." Wigs leaned further out of his window, then struggled for the cracked handle inside his door, the half arm left in place, but hard to grip with his fingers, the edges prying into his skin. He held it with both hands and yanked the lever upward, his face scrunching with the effort, then suddenly refreshed when the door swung open. Climbing down, his boots hit the ground, bending and cracking the dead yellow grass. His eyes caught sight of something moving over across the thirty feet fronting of dry tangled brush and rust-coloured blueberry shrub that led to the open doorway of Ches's shack. Wigs stared to see a girl standing there. She was husky with a round head, dark hair cropped unevenly along her thick forehead and along the side of her face of flat plain features. Her feet were set close together, as if she was intent on guarding something and her hands were playing with each other, then pulling on the skirt of her dress, pulling with her fists clutched and letting go. She watched Wigs, her face struck by fear and delight, changing easily from one extreme to the other as she turned and ran back into the shack, calling in a way that made no sense.

Ches ignored the sound and leaned forward, poking at one of the two kids, its hooves clumsily striking and sliding against the steel.

"Take 'm out," said Ches, sloppily pointing as he stepped back, not noticing the wide stripes of dust that had rubbed from the side of the truck onto his green work shirt and pants. "Down from da tail."

"Ye's," Wigs confirmed, nodding twice and laughing, scampering forward, his breath heavy with the intention of the idea, his eyes blinking furiously. "Pulls da rope and dey come wit 'er, da young tings. Just grab'er 'n pull." He popped the latch and let the tail drop with a clang. The braided rope was close and so he took it in his hands and dragged the goat across the steel on its stiff legs until it came to the edge and Wigs pulled harder, the rope burning his palms as he rocked back on his heels so the goat had nowhere else to go, except to jump, landing heavy on its thin legs. The kids waited, bleated, leaned to jump several times, hooves closer to the edge, before leaping high and clear.

"Won't go nowhere," Wigs insisted, making a point of throwing down the rope and stomping it. Laughter in his eyes as he spat close to his own feet. "Stun'd lot of 'm. Leettle suck'n close. Stand'n 'n eat'n dere. Dats all. Won't budge."

The girl appeared in the doorway again, expecting a sign from someone. A command for obedience. Her shoulders were hunched and her fingers worked carefully as if she was shaping a tiny ball from material that constantly escaped her. Wigs waved, sweeping his arm above his head, cupping his other hand to cover his mouth and giggling as he anxiously bent forward, then straightened, the heels of his boots gleefully drumming against the hollow-sounding earth.

"Rayna," he called. "Me duckie."

The girl remained in the center of the doorway, her fingers now pulling at her dress. She laughed at what she was doing, and laughed again with her tongue coming out. Grunting, she slowly licked her chin.

"Where's da missus?" The smile was still on Wig's face as he turned to Ches.

"Drove ta Cutland. See 'er brudder."

"At da jail?" Chuckling, Wigs clapped his hands together and held them that way, lifting them close to his face and shyly offering, "Lock'd up, reet?"

Ches nodded and watched the goat, the kids pushing underneath to suck away a taste of milk.

"Dey got 'im for do'n it ta 'er." Wigs pointed at Rayna, trying his best to contain himself, bobbing on his feet as if needing to relieve his bladder. Ches did not nod this time. He watched the goat and the kids, which nervously swayed around, stirring with each slight movement of the mother. The goat backed away and the kids scurried closer when Wigs swung back his leg and looked at Ches, but Ches was not interested in Wigs. He was watching the goats, his eyes set with an understanding as if their presence here had suddenly confirmed something he had thought for quite some time. Rubbing the sharp cut of his chin, Wigs nodded with the laughter glazing his eyes, bringing tears so that he wiped them away with both hands.

"Stun'd," he said, swinging his leg forward at the goats and watching them flinch. "Stun'd." Swinging back his leg again and repeating the word, until Ches wandered off and Wigs felt he must stop speaking to watch what could possibly be leading his friend away from this.

Arlene saw Ches sitting in the window as she pulled up in the pale green Pinto. He was in his wooden chair with his elbow on the sill and his palm resting flat against the top of his head. It had begun to drizzle, and he was watching the trees and did not notice Arlene until the car door slammed and he turned his head only slightly, his greyish-blue eyes empty of expression, watching her stepping toward the shack without giving him a look.

The front door opened and Ches heard Arlene set a bag on the heat-cracked wooden shelf nailed to the wall alongside the wood stove. She said something but Ches was not listening. He watched the trees. The fading light made them seem darker than possible, darker than at night.

Rayna sat in the corner in her short-legged child's chair with her knees up high. Arlene watched Rayna and heard what the child said and how the child said it and Arlene held her anger as she lifted the head of cabbage and fresh carrots from the bag. The brace of rabbits with their stiff ears slapping the counter.

Rayna laughed at her mother, her hands flicking up into the air and dancing around like antennae.

"Hap-ee hap-eeee eat," she abruptly screeched, forcing out the words as if to get clear of them. "Kisses isss all." Her lips were wet and heavy with a dull smile. She swiped at them with the back of her bare arm.

Arlene slammed two tins onto the counter, then drilled her fist against the wood.

"Nuff," said Ches, watching the trees. "Leave 'er."

Arlene stomped her boots as if to let the flakes of mud fall away, but her eyes were shut and her face held in the truth. She placed a hand over both eyes and squeezed hard, her fingertips pressing into the side of her face.

"Me brudder," she said, swallowing a sob. "Me own brudder lock'd in der like a fuh'k'n dog come sick and crazy. For dis."

Ches stood and went out the door that was left open. He remembered Wig's delight when Ches told him about the woman he'd seen standing far off in the trees, watching him and coiling a length of rope around her fist. She had a ring of flowers in her hair and her skin was yellow and light brown in the creases and along her bare curves. At the end of the rope coiled around her fist was a goat. He'd seen that the goat was giving birth, but the head was round and pink and clean of fur. It was as pink as a woman's knuckle, and he thought it was the head of a baby. What was coming out of the goat and how the woman was telling him that it would complete the forest and what was happening to the trees. How they were meant to be eating and taking and growing to die, and everything would be eaten and stripped. That's when he'd gone into Cutland Junction and bought the goat from Wigs and had him deliver it as soon as was possible.

Ches had seen the woman just past where the goat was eating now, the mist settling in its coarse fur, using its teeth to scrape the dead bark off two lone birch trees set away from the dense evergreens.

When the goat had nuzzled close enough and pried its head into the woman's naked buttocks, the woman had dropped the rope and lifted her fingers, spinning the threads that the budworms hung from. The threads that glistened in the red and orange sunset lights that spilled from the west, rushing down across the valley, through the trees and onto him. His skin like hers, all of them the same in the light that came to them without calling. The light changing the woman's skin and, in this light, the goat dropping what was in it, as if the light was all that was needed to finger it loose, and the woman lifting the child, holding it to her breast, tossing the ring of flowers from her head around the goat's neck and the goat with its eyes, full and evil, but empty. He did not think of Rayna. No matter what the woman was trying to tell him, he would not think of his daughter, or what was coming. He could not. He would not think of children and the faults they carried, the possibilities of breeding, the wrongful ease of passing on what was inside of them; the workings that had been deceived, as if the wrong seeds had been shot inside ready flesh to find the wrong egg, and it was impossible for the body to put a stop to this, to not detect the mismatching.

Ches watched the drizzle bead along the budworm threads, collect and trickle toward the worm, until the weight was too much and the water and worm dropped. He looked back and saw Arlene standing in the yard at the chopping block, lopping the heads off the rabbits and throwing them with a vengeance at the goat and kids that were picking at the grass a few feet from Ches.

"She do'n dat 'cause dey're goats 'a mine," Ches said to himself. But he did not let the thought torment him. He forgot it and stared back into the trees where he had seen the woman with the yellow and light brown skin. He believed he knew the woman's name. He'd heard it in the way he saw her. It was coming to him for a while, then going when she walked off with her head staring down at the ground like someone had disappointed the intention that directed her to this place, the understanding being misunderstood, but misunderstood with such complete clarity that it was made to be an ever-greater truth; a truth all unto itself, and the goat was close behind with its head pressed in between her yellow buttocks and the bald, pink head pushing out again, coming, about to cry. The blind eyes, the flat nose, the mouth, coughing like a dog with a bone caught in its throat. It dropped.

Her name was forgotten now. Ches shook a tree and stared up. The needles fell into his eyes, stinging. He blinked them away, pulled one loose from where it was stuck in the corner of his lid.

"Dem goats," he said to himself. "Be eat'n da whole place. Gut it clear. W'aw she be affer. The nuh'k'd womb'n spinning worms on der strings. We be all gone, she tell'n by dis. Nut'n left any us. We be jus' animals com'n ow't eachudder, com'n ow't animals 'n animals com'n ow't us, eat'n evert'n dat was flesh 'n plant. Chew'n up all dat rises up from da ground 'n eat'n eachudder 'n wha' comes outta eachudder. No diff'runts. No diff'runts t'ween 's."

Rayna collected a handful of mud and fed it to the goat. She rubbed her hands together and looked at the smooth brown coating, then bent to scoop more muck. Ches watched from the window. The rain blowing against the glass, making him feel confident; safe and warm.

Arlene circled the wooden spoon in the big black pot. She sipped a taste of the broth and smiled to herself. Placed the cover back on and pressed down as if to seal the contents. She wiped her hands in her apron and turned — standing beside Ches — to glance out the window. Rayna wore a rain bonnet, clear plastic with a thin black trim. She had on her yellow and white striped dress with short sleeves, which was soaked through so that her heavy body could be seen, moving just as she was moving. Her skin was pink and clean except for her hands, bare feet and knees, which were brown from kneeling in the mud.

The goat ate the mud, but the kids only sniffed. They were slightly nervous, growing calmer and affectionate, not stirring, not backing away when Rayna leaned close to laugh and cough in their ears.

"SCHOOL BUS," Arlene shouted, shaking Rayna from her sleep in the smaller bed across from her parent's big bed; its iron head-railing set flush against the back wall of the cabin and next to the dark wooden three-legged table that separated the two beds.

Rayna's eyes opened and stared at her mother without blinking. She seemed not to realize where she was, until her mouth opened and her loose smile widened with complete sincerity.

"School." Arlene poked Rayna in her left side, touching the flesh of her breast by mistake when she had meant to strike the girl's ribs.

"UP," she shouted, furious at her miscalculation.

Rayna began to cry with her lips shivering, her legs twisting from side to side, tangling in the bedsheets. Arlene stopped and stood still, suddenly worried. She reached down and touched her daughter's hair.

"Okay," she whispered. "Okay, baby."

Rayna's hand had found its place between her legs where it rubbed at the grief that was bothering her, forcing her fingers into the place that made the anguish change, always change itself into something more pleasant, less barbed and confused. She moaned with her mouth open, her forgetful eyes intent on staring at the ceiling.

Arlene stood and watched patiently, remembering the words of the doctor who explained what was necessary and how this was particularly necessary as a release. As plainly explained as that.

Ches stepped into the room and Arlene looked at him and at the dead twigs — dried by the morning sun — in his hand for the wood stove, and he was stopped by the force of his wife's unexpected stare. He looked at Arlene, then at Rayna, and understood. Bending in front of the stove, he opened the hatch and stuffed the branches in. A blaze widened his eyes as the fire rose and pushed against his face. He heard Rayna's grunting growing louder above the noise of crackling, the harsh sound catching in her throat, bucking like a mule, until there came a pleasant silence.

Fire ebbing, Ches added more kindling. He heard Arlene whispering, "School," and the sound of Rayna's heavy feet softly, solidly, landing against the floor.

Yesterday's rain had cut the budworms from their strings. Ches took out what they had left behind, chopping down the dead trees and throwing them in a pile beside the goat and kids, where the goat nibbled the tips of the branches and scraped off the bark while the kids struggled under the goat, pushing for milk.

Ches swung blindly, not looking, feeling the blade catch and stick. He pulled it free and swung again. The edge lodging deeper in the pulp. He tugged it loose, feeling his breath rush out of his body like the sweat that soaked him, clean air made cleaner and fierce by the toil of his labour, its purity burning his lungs.

Arlene called to him from the doorway. She had called several times, but he only heard her now above the pounding of his blood in his ears and his chest rocking and punching. He stared at the sweat on the back of his hands and the veins that had risen, the sweat in the creases of his wrists.

When he turned, Arlene called that lunch was ready. She was small and far away and her voice was smaller than the hole in his ear, barely settling in without getting lost. He left the axe stuck where it was and purposefully walked close to the goat and its kids. The goat nipped at the leg of his green work pants when he passed, but he pulled away before it had time to chew. He kicked its hollow side, making a noise like a box packed with feathers. The kids scurried back. They were afraid of what was coming, what they were desperately growing toward.

"Few w'rds ta be said 'bout it," Arlene insisted from her chair. Even though she had laid out a bowl of stew for herself, she had not touched it. Her hard face was watching Ches eat. Waiting for reaction, her eyes looked from his bowl to his mouth and back again. She turned her head to glance out the window and Ches saw her ear and the hole that was sunk through the lobe. He realized that she had had her brown hair cut when she was in Cutland Junction. Cut and set in a loose perm that made her face seem more severe when she turned her attention back on him. "Me own brudder 'n da law com'n when dey tell me in dis school Rayna go'n to dat dey pulls Rayna off da boys in da closet dere 'cause she be want'n da screw'n all da time."

Ches looked up with seriousness in his eyes. He held his empty spoon in the air for a moment but did not say a word.

He just stared at Arlene, studied her beige short-sleeved shirt, then lowered the spoon.

"Own'y da troot. Dey tell me is da troot. She clamped onto da boys 'n hav'n ta pull 'er off 'n 'er ball'n 'er 'ead off ta 'av 'em put it back in 'er. Da bus comin' 'n av'n ta take 'er 'cause dey say she des'rves educat'n she be 'n'titled ta. So dey come in 'ere 'n take 'er ta school 'n squeeze t'ings outta 'er so dey c'n come 'ear ag'in wit da law 'n a'rest me brudder fur lies dey pull'n out 'a Rayna. Lies from a 'ed dat don't t'ink da way 'spose ta. 'Er 'ed don't know lies. Diff'runt troot dat she t'inks."

Ches drank his stew broth, his head bent over the bowl, slow steady spoonfuls. The heat in the shack made the situation feel all the more urgent, bringing colour to their cheeks. Arlene gave a long look at the stew in her bowl, the wedges of potato, turnip and carrot, the dark stringy grain of the rabbit meat, then leaned close across the table to make it easier to touch Ches with her words.

"Da law com'n firs' ta say dat she got ta be in school now. Da way t'is. Tak'n 'er, dem fuh'kers." She slammed her fist against the table and Ches's bowl edged away from him. He did not look up as he pulled it closer with both hands and dipped in his spoon. His eyes did not watch Arlene, but he listened and heard as clearly as if her voice was in his own head.

Ches was facing the humped road, cutting into the trees when he saw Rayna wandering down the road with Arlene leading her by the arm. He hadn't seen Arlene leave to meet the bus, but there they were. Arlene's face was tight with fury, staring straight ahead as she dragged Rayna by the arm. Rayna stumbling to keep up, dropping her red plastic lunch pail and stopping to pick it up, stumbling forward when Arlene pulled her, dropping the lunch pail until she dropped too, on her knees with her cheek flat against a hump of grass in the road. Sobs bucking in her chest.

Ches watched as Arlene waited and stopped with her small hands in the back pockets of her jeans, staring at Rayna, the fury calming as she licked her lips and shifted from one foot to the other. Calming and calming, she bent and gently took Rayna by her wrists to guide her to her feet. She hugged Rayna, and Rayna was bigger, like a big doll, Ches thought, dressed

that way too. Appearing to be so much like a doll that when
Rayna stepped back Ches was surprised for an instant. He was
amazed that they did not see him through the trees that lined
the road, seeming more alive than ever by how he saw them
and could watch this way without actually being a part of anything. He was going to call out but that would only injure the
situation; make everything worse than it already seemed to be
and cancel whatever kind of intimacy was moving between
mother and daughter. They wandered off, Arlene pulling again,
but not as violently as before.

Ches held the axe and breathed, thought of the shack that
Arlene's brother had lived in further back in the woods. There
were things in there that he could use. The extra chair from
her brother's table. The big one that he could put out in front
in his own yard and sit in to watch the trees and the light slant-
ing down onto the grey and brittle sticks of branches. He could
snap them with his fingers, but he liked to watch them anyway, imagine the sound the branches made when they snapped
and how the budworms slowly spun on their threads, bloated
from eating the evergreen needles and running slow from their
insides when he stuck them with the point of his buck knife
and watched them drip down the blade. Collecting the fluid in
a small salt meat pail. The juice of the forest that he could pour
back onto the earth. Trees growing when he felt the time for
growth was right. Not now. Not this way. The juice poured
into thick glass jars that he kept on the high shelf above his bed.

The goat watched him, its closed jaw moving from side to side,
its misplaced eyes set the wrong way with a black line down
the middle. Ches came with the axe and a plastic bag of tin
cans that he'd collected in the woods, the faded names on the
tins washed away by sunlight and rain. The plastic bag feels
strange from how it had been sitting on the forest floor. He
dropped it in front of the goat. It bent its coarse head forward
and was drawing the plastic bag into its mouth when Ches
stepped inside the shack.

Arlene's stout face was red and she was staring at Rayna as
if she had already said everything she could say and only the
striking of her hands could punctuate or push the statement
further.

"W'as?" Ches asked, leaning the axe handle in the corner while he kept his eyes on Rayna. She was naked and standing by the woodstove in the faint light of a late dim afternoon. He looked where Arlene was looking and saw what it was.

"G'wan 'n set yer 'and ta 'er belly," Arlene commanded. She stepped toward Ches and shoved him. "G'wan 'n feel w'as in dere. 'Ow 'ard t'is."

Ches stumbled forward and looked back at Arlene with aggravation tightening his eyes.

"Lees'n," he said, raising a finger. "Take 'er easy, womb'n."

Arlene turned away and stared out the window. She touched her lips with her fingers and pushed the top one into her mouth to nibble the dried skin.

Ches did not want to look at Rayna standing the way she was, but he knew that he had to turn because it was his duty as her father to see what had happened and to understand its appearance. He was struck by Rayna's nakedness and her child-like opened lips, which knew no word for this. The stricken expanse of her eyes. Her long, pale arms hung by her sides. Her thick hips and stunted breasts and the unexpected sparseness of her pubic hair, which showed the crack straight through. She looked like a child, stretched and stuffed to appear larger.

Ches did not touch his daughter's belly. He saw what was there in the hardness and sheen; how it had risen so slightly and he looked into Rayna's unknowing eyes. He smiled at her and she smiled at him and laughed with her tongue until a trembling blow struck the back of Ches's head and he turned to see Arlene glaring at him with her hand raised, ready to strike again for giving in.

When the time came so it was impossible to hide Rayna's condition, she was kept home from school and the law came telling Ches and Arlene that Rayna would be taken to school by a policeman from Cutland Junction if she did not go on her own. So she was taken on the bus and the children laughed and whispered things to Rayna that she did not understand, but words that frightened her. She understood the anger and the malice of how the words were built and she cried the tears she had been saving for what was changing in her body, what was becoming of her, what was pushing her belly out so far that she was leaning back and could not see her toes when she wiggled them bare on the shack floor in the cool fall. She was frightened to press against anything sharp, for fear she would disappear with a bang like a balloon she had seen disappear when her father brought it home to her and it blew from the shack and she chased it until it touched against a branch and vanished with a noise that made Rayna shriek.

The leaves were dropping from the trees and mingling with the rotting needles from the evergreens and the goat and her kids ate the leaves and the trees that had been cleared for a quarter mile around the shack. Stumps everywhere, flatly dotting the land. The goats were chewing the stumps too, peeling the wood with their teeth, and trying to eat Ches when he came close to them. Trying to eat Arlene, but leaving Rayna alone. Leaving Rayna to stand in their presence, to look out at what was being cleared, a wider space to watch what was becoming of the little that was left for them.

Arlene's brother swore he'd kill Rayna when he got out of prison, but that did not stop them from releasing him. It was only talk because he did not plan to kill her, rather to do something else that would fix her just as well. He took her one day when she was almost due with the baby. In her own shack filled with sharp winter air while Ches was chopping trees, his breath puffing in the air, and the budworms had stopped spinning on their web-threads because the snow was coming. Arlene was at the store in Cutland Junction and her brother had been released early for good behaviour, having been alone with the plan of what was to be done keeping him happy and content in his head. Arlene's brother seeing Rayna on his way down the road to his cabin and pushing into her now after she stood in the door bent forward with her hand reaching for the spot that he was in now. He went for her and shut the door, hearing the faint chopping in the distance and knowing it was Ches. The shack was quiet and he kissed Rayna first and took off her dress so that she shivered while she watched him, trying to remember.

Rayna moaned with her belly swaying as Arlene's brother grabbed for her small breasts and squeezed the whole of them in his palms. Pushing with less force and venom than the first time when he had cornered her two days after his wife's funeral where Rayna had been laughing mad the way she did while his wife's casket went down with what was left of her in it, what the cancer hadn't eaten for itself.

Rayna stared at the ceiling. "Hap-ee hap-eeee eat," she screeched, laughing once, her lips open and gleaming soft with saliva over her fingers, which were stuck in her mouth. She gently chewed them. Pointing with her other hand at Arlene's brother, her arm bobbing with recognition as she chewed her fingertips. Arlene's brother grinning through all the thoughts he had been thinking of Rayna while he was in prison, gently slapping her round belly, like a ball, while he rocked and tried to thrust the confusion out of himself, waiting for it to leap from him, up and into her.

When it was over, he stood and looked down at Rayna. He shivered in the chill as he pulled on his pants, staring at her face, studying her body, strangely feeling something like love for the way she quietly watched him with her eyes — her clear, full eyes — which he had no way of ever getting into.

Arlene's brother disappeared two days before the baby came. Ches and Arlene saw why he had disappeared because he had left himself inside of Rayna the first time, before he had been sent to prison, and was here now, crying up at them. Black-haired and with the unmistakable face.

Arlene left the shack and walked off into the trees, tearfully stepping over stumps until she found one that was flat enough to sit on. The goats were quick to find her and they pulled at her jeans and nipped at her boots and she let them have what they were after, being comforted by the sensation of being drawn away. Tugging on the curls of her hair. She understood that it was only possible for them to take so much.

Rayna sat the way she always had in the child's chair with her knees almost touching her chin, and Ches holding the baby in his arms, looking out across the stumps on either side of the humped road, everything cleared now and easy to see the police car coming from a distance, slowly bobbing around a corner that was cleared, rolling up with its blue and red lights on top and the policeman steady behind the windshield.

The goats had moved close to the door, hungry and sniffing, the mother goat clumping forward, awkwardly up with its front legs onto the floor inside, reaching with its head to chew on the wooden door handle.

The policeman parked the car and wasted no time in brushing past the goat to show Ches a piece of paper that explained why Rayna would have to go back to school. Authorizing him to take Rayna now. Her teacher was waiting and he carefully outlined — as he had done so many times in the past — the necessary course of action. What Rayna was entitled to and how no one could take it from her.

Ches held up the baby with its big head and flat nose as an explanation for his daughter's absence, and Rayna — hunched and rocking in the corner — laughed for what seemed like no reason, her arms flicking up and twitching above her head.

"Hap-eeeeee eat," she shrieked.

The policeman did not look at her, he did not see what she was offering him, but he was quick to accommodate the change in circumstances, the prospect of another child who would fall under the command of his jurisdiction, stating with authority that the infant would have to come, too, assuming that the baby was of the same ilk. He said, reading from the paper, "And therefore entitled to an equal stake in the possibilities this world has to offer."

Heber Peach

"Mailman here yet?" Darren called, his hand skimming loosely along the wooden railing as he lazily clunked down the stairs. Hearing the sound, the old man stared back from where he was standing behind the living room window. He tried to think, squinting at the ground with a pained expression as Darren stepped into the room. Speaking timidly, Heber moved his hands around in the loose pockets of his pale green trousers, as if his fingers were doing the talking, "Y'eh...Y'eh. I t'ink he by." His grey and white hair was slick and pressed flat to his head, the impression of the comb neatly raked into the surface. The old man's eyes flitted nervously to look at his son. He carefully shaped the words: "Y'eh... I t'ink so."

"You think, hey?" scoffed the lanky teenager. "Don't strain yourself now." His stare turned sour as he snatched his jacket from the worn arm of the brown and beige couch. It was a team jacket, burgundy with gold letters printed across the back spelling CELTICS.

"I'm waiting for something real important," Darren declared. "It ain't yours, like you always think. So don't let me catch you ripping it open."

Heber stared.

"You hear me?" The boy raised his voice, nearly shouting. Heber slowly nodded.

"I'll check the box myself." Glancing at his father's yellow shirt with the wide blue stripes and the long collar, he felt sickened by how the old man's right arm was bent in, set against his chest as if wounded. Lame. Useless and without purpose.

Heber nodded again and waited as Darren stomped from the room, then he shuffled, turning to face the window. He heard the door open and the clink of the mailbox top coming down. An instant later he saw Darren in the middle of the street, striding with his long legs hugged by new-blue denims, his black, unblemished cowboy boots (with elaborate red stitchings swirling along the sides) pulled up over his jeans.

Heber watched the boy shove his hands into the side pockets of his jacket. He listened to the boots striking the faded asphalt, the sound touching him through the window so that he swiped at his lips as if to brush away the closeness of the sensation.

Then Darren was gone. Out of view and utterly forgotten.

Heber kept watching. Cars passed on the street. He listened to the noises they softly made, like a purring stream, he told himself, but then louder, swishing, as the cars flowed before his pleasant, content eyes, showing him what was really making the sound. Sights drifting through his field of vision; few things staying put, only the row houses across from him and the parked cars, big and rusted along their sides, flat tires for as long as he could recall. He thought for a moment, wondered about where he was living. Progression and relapse. The time? He began to worry, believing he had to be somewhere, hearing a noise closer now, against the glass, or perhaps behind him; he turned to see his wife sitting on the couch with her knitting in her lap. She straightened her glasses but would not look at him. What had he done? Why, he asked himself, feeling shame and anger rising in his chest. He reasoned with himself, again and again, not to question the things he witnessed. They were fine as they were. *Relax, me son*, he told himself. But he continued to forget even his own words of reassurance, and he was vexed and shameful once more, squinting as he spotted a vague point of reference, glimpsed it and held on as if staring toward and through the clearing that was opening inside of him, into what he thought was new, only to find the old worn-out idea of who he was and how his wife was gone and the couch bare. His name.

"Dey tol' me," he quietly explained to the couch, "Me name. Me name's 'Eber. I n'ose it." Eyes glossing over with frail encouragement, he offered a quiet nod and stray toothless smile working to deny the embarrassingly impersonal sound of his own voice, " 'Eber Peach. Dey tol' me. I n'ose."

Come lunch time the street was filled with flashes of movement; sole colours passing, then several shades melding together as bright gatherings of loud, quick children stepped once, the first foot up, then down, the second foot rising, the body gone, vanishing like that, new ones appearing in the places of others as Heber blinked, thinking it was the most alive thing he had ever seen. The bright insistence of children's voices coming from far off, unseen, like chimes stirred by a breeze, rain in the air, smelling it, listening out of the quiet, and then the brilliant pouring wash of spirit and fabric and hair as the children swept into view, hordes of them skipping or walking backwards to face each other in groups, filling and occupying his eyes, not far from him at all, moving on parade, so that his dry rough lips smiled and he was encouraged by a sense of delight, until the crowd began to settle before him, focus filling in what he thought was a mere procession of merriment. The crowd carefully staring. Recognition as Heber viewed the teenager's face. It was familiar. Heber's face as a boy. He was remembering a look in the mirror. No, never as saucy as that. Not his own face. He would never act in such a way. He had no memories of this. The mean smile directed his way, defying him, challenging himself with his own youthful pride. Where were the eyes looking? Into what? It made no sense. He whispered, "Darren, it be me name." Then he carefully shook his head, saying, "I's right here," looking down at his feet, then up again, seeing the boy walking among the crowd, watching his father, always watching and wanting to steal what little peace had settled in his tired heart. Heber's buoyant smile twitched, snagged on itself, and flatly sank.

Breaking away from his friends, Darren shrugged, said a few

dull words, and stomped up the concrete steps, flipping the lid
of the mail box before opening the door. Heber studied
Darren's friends moving past the window. They surveyed the
old man on their way to the store at the end of the street where
they bought packaged egg sandwiches and sodas, small snack
cakes and chocolate bars. Sometimes, Heber would go down
there and stand outside, watching the young ones eat, the energy of their bodies, the anxious flashing of movements and
words. He would stare, one arm tucked in close to his chest,
his body tilted for balance, his right side numb and senseless,
having to lean that way to compensate. First, it was the stroke,
and then the years that took away his memory (instead of filling it in) and he would find himself standing in strange places,
patiently regarding people and neighbourhoods he could not
claim as familiar. He knew the outlines and the positioning of
the buildings, but his knowledge was far-off, and it was this
intimacy of blunt range that puzzled him, this lack of keen
identification, penetration beyond the pure shapes of things.
He squinted at the faces that passed, until he saw a face that
was his own. The dark, familiar eyes up close, glaring at him,
stung and offended by what he had let himself become, the red-
dish face scarred with acne. The thin boy would take him by
the arm and lead him back, pulling on his arm so that he had
to shuffle along, dragging one leg over the sidewalk, stumbling
from the edge of the curb and jolting down onto the asphalt.

"Stay here," the tall boy would shout at him when they
were in the house and the door was closed and Heber was
standing in the small porch, staring at the boy who seemed
filled with the punishment of the past, and slowly he would
remember, like grains of dust gathering to veil all areas surrounding the impression of what had been waxed out, the
confined clarity like the sound of shouting, lint found in his
pockets, pulling it loose to carefully draw it apart with his fingers, shapeless, holding it there, but nothing there at all, the
shouting with each rip. It was what he tried to remember; having been something, now lint. The boy was his son. But he
could not recall the name and was afraid to ask for fear of the
horrible reaction his words would invoke.

"In there, get in." The boy would point toward the living
room. "You go again and I'll bar you in your room. You stay the

fuck in here." And he would punch his father on the shoulder because he did not want to hit him in the face. He could not hit him in the face, no matter how angry he was.

Heber would limp into the living room, his dead arm in close to his chest, his leg dragging so that the shoe leather was worn apart on one side and frayed threads of his sock poked through.

"I'll put you away," Darren screamed, his straight brown hair hanging close to his eyes, his teenaged heart tightening against all the things he could not force himself to believe in, his heart not wanting to beat at all, hating itself, hating everything that made it feel the confusing heat that throbbed beneath his body's skin. Flicking back his head, "I'll have the nurse take you outta here, put you away in one of them fucking places." Darren stared at his father with troubled eyes. "You hear me?" he shouted, needing an answer more than anything, the simplest kind of reply, just this once, but the old man remaining silent and uncertain, always, watching the boy in a distant worried way.

Darren fixed himself a sandwich, slamming cupboard doors in the kitchen and kicking the chair away from the table so he could sit and bang the bottom of his glass against the table top.

Heber watched the street. His eyes moved slowly, of their own accord. There was no hurry. Things interested him and he took his time to study the tiniest of details, numbly connecting to other thoughts, forward and backward lines unbroken, whisking him here and there like a slide rule, to match the numbers — no, not numbers, pictures. The car that pulled up in front of his house had a sign and words on its door. He half-expected it to be backing off again when he blinked, but it stayed put and Heber knew right away who was in there before he even saw the nurse stepping out. She looked right at his window because she was expecting to see him there. First thing she did was wave and scrunch up her eyes with a smile, then she shut her door, walking and smiling at the ground, the sound of her knuckles tapping against the front door before she poked in her head and called in a merry sing-song, "Hiiiii."

Heber laughed in his throat, swallowed and laughed again as he struggled to turn. The nurse was a fine woman. He hurried to touch his hair with his fingers, grooming himself, then looked at the couch. His wife was not sitting there. What she did not know would not hurt her. Out of sight, out of mind. Phrases came to him without prompting and he nodded at their sense of easy agreement, smiling further, revealing his bald gums to the nurse as she stepped into the living room.

"Hi there," said Nurse Wells.

" 'Lo," said Heber, nodding and turning all the way around, having to lean and hop a little to accomplish the task.

"You're looking good."

The colour rose in Heber's cheeks. He laughed and touched the front of his shirt, then glanced at the couch. Taking this as a sign to sit, Nurse Wells settled on the edge of the couch with her spine perfectly straight. Crossing her legs, she tugged her pink skirt down over her knees, then rested her hands there. Her blouse was pale blue with a lacy design sewn into the material, and over the blouse she wore a short white uniform jacket with an insignia stitched onto the pocket.

"So everything is fine, Mr. Peach?"

Heber showed her his gums and nodded. "Y'ehs. Tis dat." He wiped at his lips with the back of his good arm and smiled again, offering a second, enthusiastic nod. "Y'ehs. D'light'd wid it all."

"Good, and how's your son doing?"

Heber listened for sounds from the kitchen, hearing quieted movements, faint stirrings, before the chunky-rhythm of boots sounded against the kitchen flooring, then the silent stride of steps onto the carpet.

Darren appeared in the living room.

"Hello," he said, offering the nurse a brisk smile. He held half a ham sandwich in his hand and raised it to her as a kind of salutation before biting into it.

"Hello, Darren. How's everything?" She levelled her head and smiled reasonably at him.

"Good. Everything's okay," he said, chewing. He looked at his father, a brief offering of attention. He even winked, but Heber was puzzled and looked for the nurse, wondering where she had gone, seeing his wife sitting there with her knitting, a young lovely woman, making a yellow sweater for the new baby, thinking of a name and deciding on Darren. He looked across the living room and saw a tall, thin boy standing there, eating a sandwich, chewing on his food without explanation or apology. A brazen boy invading the house.

"Oo're you?" Heber asked. "You." He pointed slowly with his good hand.

"You know, geeze b'y," the boy quietly replied, puffing out an indignant laugh. "Darren, right."

"I dun know ya." Heber's head shook nervously. He was confused but adamant, filled with growing rage, "I...I...nuh...nnn...n'ver saw ya 'for. Guh...guh...Git out."

"I've got to go, now," Darren loudly announced to his father. "I'll be back right after school, like always." He shoved the remaining crust of white bread into his mouth and started to turn.

The nurse drew her eyes from Heber to glance at Darren, "Can I have a word first," she called. Darren shrugged with his back to her, and left the room.

Standing, Nurse Wells gave a consoling smile to Heber. "Okay?" she asked. "I'll just be a sec."

Heber nodded, "Y'ehs, no sweat, me duckie. I knows you."

She touched the sides of her skirt, then followed Darren into the hallway where he was waiting, leaning against the stucco wall and moving his tongue along his teeth while he stared at the carpet.

"How's he doing?" she whispered. "Really doing, I mean."

"Okay." Darren shifted and frowned. He would not look at the nurse. A moment later he shrugged.

"Has he started wandering off yet?"

"No." Darren regarded her, his eyes defiant. "He doesn't do that kind of crap. He's no lunatic or nothing."

"But he forgets who you are?"

The boy waited. "But he's okay then." He glared at her. "Look, there's no problem here, right."

"He seems okay." Nurse Wells searched Darren's eyes.

"Nothing the matter with old Hebe."

"I don't much like the idea of him being here alone."

"He's not alone. He's always in that window and there's neighbours keeping an eye on him."

"Truthfully, he'd be better off in a nursing home." The

nurse watched Darren's face for reaction. "But there's a waiting list as long as a wet Sunday."

The boy stared at her, his splotched red face expressionless.

"You let me know, will you? If things get any worse."

"Sure." Listlessly, he shoved his hands into the side pockets of his jacket, then took them out again. He shifted against the wall, moving back a few inches as he quickly glanced at the nurse's chest.

"If he starts wandering off, it could be very dangerous for him. We'll have to have someone here when you're in school. Social services will pay for it. A sitter, if we can't get him into a home."

Darren was thinking, *I don't want no one here. No more fucking welfare.* He said, "Dad's no problem by himself. He has a look out the window, that's all. He don't want nothing fucking else."

"I don't want him hurting himself," said Nurse Wells, her voice turning stern and reasonable, as if defending herself against the harshness of the boy's vulgarity.

"I don't want him going away." The words blurted from Darren's mouth with such force and pained emotion that the nurse felt she should step forward to comfort him, but he had turned, striding and staring at the ground as he moved for the door. Nurse Wells called to him about the date of her next visit, and he grumbled agreement, then was out and down onto the steps, slamming the door with such force that the floor shook beneath the nurse's feet and dishes rattled against the cupboards in the kitchen behind her.

Heber watched the window shimmying, all things wavering as the boy blasted loose, out and into the world, disrupting the easy arrangement of the picture that had settled before the old man's eyes.

Heber smiled kindly at the children returning to school. The smaller ones stopped by his window and pressed their lips against the glass. He touched the glass with his fingers as if to capture their kisses. Smiling at the tiny faces, he lifted his fingers to rub them in his hair, wanting to look nice for all the young ones. He sometimes raised his good hand to wave but his knuckles would strike the glass, and he would remember that he was inside. He would look behind his back to see the room and how he was standing on the edge of it and he would wonder about what was beyond the room and where it led and who was waiting there for him. He remembered a woman he had seen in the bathroom upstairs, sitting on the toilet and laughing playfully up at him, saying words, a young woman he wanted to marry washing her hands in the sink and splashing water at him so that he saw the water, saw each drop and how his toothless face was centered in each wet curve before the drops exploded against his skin and he was gone. Wiping at his face, he heard the dry and rough sound of the stubble along his cheeks and jawline. He turned and saw an opening to the street and tried to step through it, but something stopped him, the glass rattling dully, and he fell backwards, striking the armrest of the couch and tumbling down onto the cushions, so that he laughed at how his body had been moved by invisible forces and he was lying down now. He was tired with all of these thoughts. His eyelids grew heavy and he let them close. People bent close to offer greetings. They touched him, carefully, as if to prompt him from his slumber. "What're you doing here?" they kindly, quietly asked. They said, "Come with us." Each of their names was inside of him. He wanted to address them with fondness but he could not remember how to speak, only to trust so openly in them and how they had passed on with such ease. They were all beautiful now. Happy tears filled his eyes. These people, his friends, were concerned for him and they were smiling gently. He believed he was sleeping, but there was no way of being absolutely certain. He wanted to open his eyes, but they kept opening and opening each time that he tried.

There was a boom. Something had fallen, or a cannon had gone off. Heber felt his eyes clearing. He saw his son standing by the couch and realized the boy was home from school and the sound he had heard was the closing of the door. He tried to sit up, but his legs were hanging over the arm of the couch and so Darren bent down and helped him turn to the side. He sat his father up, then stood there with his hands in the pockets of his team jacket, the tall boy staring down at his father's wet-gummed smile.

"T'anks, me son," he said, winking, feeling invigorated and hungry. "I cud eat a 'orse."

"I'll make you something," Darren remarked. He turned away without another word and Heber listened to the sounds from the kitchen. They were not as loud as usual and Heber smiled at the mercy and pushed his one good hand down into the cushion to stand, leaning to the side and almost falling, but straightening himself. On his feet, he looked toward the window to see that it was late afternoon. The light was fading with long, orange shadows stretching across the street and only a few children passed by. He fixed his eyes on the corner of the room. The television had once been there. He saw the dusty outline of where it had rested against the small table and he remembered watching Darren taking it away, struggling with it, and walking out into the street where a pick-up truck was waiting. He had loaded it on and came back inside without explaining where the pick-up truck was from or where it was going. A few days later a smaller television had been brought into the house, a tiny one that Darren could hold in his hand. He carried it in his pocket, the thin silver edge sticking out.

Heber smelled the cooking and called to his wife that he was hungry. He listened for the cries from the baby that always delighted and compelled him at once. Hearing it crying, he declared that his wife should bring the infant to him and he stared toward the living room doorway to see Darren step into the room with the tray of food. The boy laid it on the long coffee table with the veneer cracked off at the corners, exposing the pressed particleboard underneath.

"Eat the works," Darren said, pointing. "Got a sandwich and some of that soup you like from the tin."

Heber raised a wedge of the sandwich and began slowly chewing, his face half-numb. He watched the boy dubiously. Bits of egg hung from the old man's lips, then fell onto his shirt and onto his pants. Darren stood there, casually, and waited for his father to drink the soup. Unsteadily using his left hand, Heber dipped the spoon into the bowl and raised it on an angle.

The soup ran over the front of his shirt and down his sleeve, the hot fluid rushing along the inside of his wrist.

Darren stood rigid, disaster darkening his eyes.

"OKAY, OKAY!" he finally shouted, snatching away the spoon and plunking down beside his father. Heber's grateful eyes observed Darren. "Appreciate dis," he whispered while the boy raised the spoon, sliding it into the old man's mouth. Heber's eyes kept inspecting the face, wondering, but he knew it would be a mistake to call the boy Heber. It was not himself that he was seeing. How could his own younger hands be feeding himself like this? He watched the boy's untiring teenage face. *I love you*, he thought.

A wide bar of sunlight rose along the blanket, creeping across Heber's face until it touched his eyes. Lips opening, "Y'ehs," from sleep and he wiped at his mouth. His wrinkled eyelids twitched and rose and he was staring out the window, squinting, flat on the couch with a blanket laid over him. He was hot and kicked the woollen blanket away with his good foot and leaned up with a grunt.

He was needed somewhere. He was late. Waiting, he heard the slow sound of footsteps descending the stairs. His wife taking her time, her arms filled with the warm sweet-smelling bundle of the baby. Heber listened and watched the doorway. He was late for work at the high school; the garbage buckets in each room needing to be emptied. He had neglected doing the chore after mopping up yesterday, wanting to race home as soon as possible to be with his wife and new baby. He got up extra early, looked in on the infant, leaned by its crib and kissed the soft flesh that meant more to him than his own. But he was late now and there were footsteps on the stairs. He did not mean to wake his wife. He tried to push himself up, but one of his hands was not working and his leg was numb, so he waited for them to come to life. They were asleep, and he felt impatient, listening to the footsteps coming, suddenly clunking like they were footsteps of the principal coming to check the garbage pails, and so he punched his leg and arm, but they would not wake. He began shivering, the footsteps smearing the tears that bloated over the rims of his eyes. He swiped them away, and sniffed angrily.

"I 'ave ta," he tried to explain, weakly smacking at his arm and leg. "I 'ave ta clean 'er up. Me leg's shot. Me arm." He fell back onto the couch, sobbing with his chest rising and falling as his throat coughed out the anguish, calling his wife's name, lowly calling it, a useless cry for help, realizing he had been abandoned, not by her, or by God, or by the people who lived around him, but by the pure soulful function that permitted him to recognize himself. His own hands setting him down somewhere else, then rising away, leaving him there to find the plainest way back along the collapsed and scattered paths that were now his self.

Darren stepped down the last stair, bending with the weight of a large stereo speaker in his arms. He laid it flat onto the carpet beside the front porch, then stepped around it and out the door, checking the mailbox. A coloured sale flyer and an envelope. When he lifted out the envelope, he saw his name and address written on the front — and up in the corner, the U.S. postage stamp with an eagle perched on a mountain peak — and his heart kicked. He could not tear open the envelope fast enough. There was a letter in there. He yanked it out, his eyes flitting nervously across hand-written words, impossible to read all at once. He raced over the paragraphs, looked into the envelope once more to see a picture, printed like a postcard. A publicity shot of Wet Leather Noose, snarling with their chains and teased blonde hair, hell fire shooting loose behind them, a wall of fire that they had stepped through, unharmed, perfect, stronger, black and white flames licking the mouth-hole of a giant death-defying skull. He read the letter again, holding the page up to the light and turning it over to see the imprint of the words. It was not another printed message. It was a personal note, written by the collective hand of the group. He had been waiting for word. They would tell him what to do, and they did. They had answered his letter with all kinds of thoughts and, down at the bottom of the page, the lyrics of a new song: "Fuck your parents, they are a curse, they raised you up, all for the worse."

YES! His heart boomed in his chest. He could hear it; the punishing scratchy rip of the guitar, the beat, the bass drum pounding, solo, *YES!...YES!...YES!*

Darren folded the note and anxiously poked it into the back pocket of his jeans. The pocket was tight and so he strained to look back, using both hands, making sure not to wrinkle the letter. Then he studied the picture in awe. Wet Leather Noose was looking right at him. He said all of their names in his head, moving from one face to the next. They knew all about these things. Their fists were clenched and held up in defiance, their mouths twisted open, shaping his name, a mean championing shout: "DARREN." He slid the photograph back into the envelope and heard the noise from the living room. The sound of whimpering. His father. He tightened his fists and thought of the band. His father. His stupid, retarded father with his stupid, retarded eyes that didn't even recognize his own son. The lyrics playing over in his head, "A curse, all for the worse. A curse..."

Fucking right, yes b'y.

Darren could only carry one speaker at a time, impossible to take both of them at once. Two blocks across Maxie Street and over to Stabb Court. The welfare houses were all big yellow blocks, two stories high, their varying states of disrepair being the only thing setting them apart. A few were even boarded up completely, with sheets of bare plywood nailed over the windows. Groups of pigeons huddled on the roofs, their necks jilting. The houses were large and rectangular and set back from the winding street. Huge black and grey boulders lined the inner edge of the sidewalk to prevent cars from driving up onto the grass fronting. The units were arranged face-out in a circle, the backs around a park with a baseball diamond where the gang hung out at night, drinking beer and smoking joints, waiting for someone to cross into their park, listening and looking, alert with that special glow, trying to stay quiet, but laughing at the dangerous silence they were holding in their lungs, wanting to bust out as they punched at the chain link fence and smashed bottles to hear the noise of the glass exploding and jingling apart. Savage music, the roar of a rusty muffler from down the street. A group of girls screaming and laughing, taking turns screaming out sexy high-pitched curses, and screaming shrilly for attention, screeching, "Lick me crack," as the boys chased after them, grabbing and holding to punch at their chests or down lower so that it turned them on for later.

Darren hurried with the speaker, shuffling past a group of council workers leaning on shovels around a back-hoe and a large sloppy hole through the thick asphalt. The men watched him as he passed. One of them made a comment. Darren almost heard what it was but his mind was straining because of the weight in his arms as he walked the last ten feet toward the door he was so desperately wanting to rest against. He got there and let the speaker slide down, setting it on the chipped concrete landing.

He had to knock three times and was almost pounding before Hum finally answered the door in his underwear, his skin all white with his ribs sticking out. He stood looking at Darren, bothered by the sun as he weakly scratched his bare shoulder.

"The speakers," Darren said, blowing a drop of sweat from the tip of his nose.

"Yeah." Hum turned away with his eyes half-closed, leaving the door open and falling onto the couch. Darren bent and lifted the speaker from where it was set, stepped into the white-walled house. He gently laid the speaker on the floor and left right away without saying a word. Making his way back with the second speaker, his breath hot in his nostrils, his arms paining, he found the door still open and Hum asleep on the couch, facing in so that Darren could see the sweat on his white back and realize how hot it was in the room. Laying down the second speaker, he checked the thermostat, saw that it was up full blast. But when he stepped closer to Hum, he noticed that his friend was shivering and he heard him sniffing and understood that he was not asleep. Hum rolled over, looking up with clouded eyes. His crooked teeth were clicking together and his dark close-cropped hair made him look even paler.

"You sick, man?" Darren asked.

"I been..." The shivering overtook him, so that he had to wait to finish the sentence. He spoke quickly to force it out, "...puking. All... fucking night." He belched silently, moaning at the taste in his throat.

"You better get to the hospital, man."

"Something in... the fucking acid."

"The hospital, right."

"Can't."

Darren looked around the house. There was nothing on the walls and only a few scraps of furniture; a box used as a coffee table and a couch flush to the floor, no legs. A single medium-sized window was centered above the couch, giving a view of the flat patchy front lawn that led to the huge boulders and the curve of asphalt.

"I brang the speakers. Those ones you're after."

Hum laughed, as if agreeing, finding humour. His lips were a bluish-grey. His teeth chattered and he shook his head, not able to believe what he was hearing.

"So, what're ya saying?"

Hum laughed again, the trembling going with it. He let his legs slip over the side of the couch, the sides of his feet touching the floor, but he remained lying flat. "Feeling... better," he whispered. He tried to sit up, but had to hunch over immediately, hugging his chest and sluggishly rocking back and forth, staring at Darren's boots. "Nice...boots...man."

"Got 'em a few days ago." Darren looked down and smiled at the boots. They were new and perfect. Not a scratch.

Hum stood quickly, rushing up, then sitting back again. "I...don't know." His eyes unfocussed, he had trouble forming words, as if someone had just hit him hard in the face, "I got...is fucking pain." His chin drooped and he blinked, shaking his head and touching the right side of his body, just above his hip. He winced, his fingers shaky and cold. "Something swole up."

"Yeah." Darren stepped back to get a better view of the situation. "Yeah, you look fucking yellow."

Hum laughed, his shoulders jerking, lips seeming larger, "Yellow."

"So you want those speakers, or what?"

Hum nodded.

Darren was going to tell him about the letter from Wet Leather Noose, but he wanted to savour it first, keep the news to himself until he could find the best way to tell everyone, set up the words that would make him out to be the coolest. Maybe he'd tell them that the band delivered the letter them-

selves. Pulled up in a red and black van and slid the side door
open. A bunch of naked babes getting screwed in the back and
they didn't even care that he was watching. He maybe even
had a piece of it himself with the boys pushing at him and
growling out a tune in the background. How it had happened.
They had chosen him out of all their fans because he was the
best, because he knew every word of every song so perfectly
that his stomach felt a neediness that was not hunger but crazy
understanding all the way through to his aching bones.

"You got the cash?" Darren asked.

Hum shook his head.

"Well, fuck you, man." Darren pointed back at the speakers, sitting close to the door, their brown mesh facings turned
toward each other. "I carried them from my place. What'd'ya
fucking tell me for?"

Hum lay on his side, his knees pulled up, and held himself
tightly. His eyelids jammed shut and the sweat ran from his
brows, stinging his eyes, spilling down the sides of his nose,
over his lips, dripping onto the couch.

"I brang 'em here. You said you were buying, right. What's
your fucking problem?"

"Okay..." Hum whispered, his face flinching. He opened his
eyes, had to close them, fast, "okay later," he gasped.

"What's your fucking problem?" Darren kicked the couch
with the heel of his new boot, lifting it high and tilting back
the toe. Then he kicked it again, harder. The couch punched
against the wall. "The money, prick."

"Here," Hum said, staring straight ahead, his cheek pressed
into the cushion, his lips rounding out. "In...here."

"What?"

"Under." Hum pressed the tips of his fingers beneath the
cushion, but they were stuck there. He could not push further.
He waited, finally shoving his hand in with resolve, the fingers
remaining in there for a while, before gradually working themselves loose, holding a gun by the short barrel. It dropped onto
the carpet, landing with a dull thud.

Darren stepped back, whispering, "Fuck."

Hum turned his slow eyes to look up. "Neat, hey?" He tried
to smile.

"When'd you get that?"

"Had it."

"Wow, man."

"Take..."

Darren rushed forward and grabbed the gun. He felt the sleek heaviness against the skin along his fingers, weighed it in his palm. His face brightened as he shifted it from hand to hand. The gun was small and black, its wooden handle taped together with layers of dirty masking tape. He tightened both hands around the clumpy handle, spread his legs, and aimed at Hum.

"Hey!" Hum called, his pained eyes shrivelling. He sluggishly lifted one hand. "It's loaded, man." Moaning, he covered his face with his arms, "Get away...I'm...gonna die." He gagged and shoved his mouth into the cushion.

"So fucking what." Darren let the barrel dip toward the floor.

Hum took a deep breath. He mumbled into the couch, "You have that. Just...hook up them...'fore you go...Listen to some metal..." His shoulders jerked and his entire body bounced with a shiver. He made a trembling noise, but Darren was not paying attention. He was staring at the gun, feeling the completion of what he had suspected. The weight of the gun gave him perfect balance. It was obvious. The fiery skull, the shout of the band. The answer. His snarl back at them, which they accepted openly with a roar. The trigger. Boom. The lap of fire and metal making them one. Music's union. Drum beats. Explosions after the wild solo. A cheer with his hands thrown up over his head. Wet Leather Noose would hear about how he had made his own music that fit so well with theirs. They would send him letters of congratulations, dedicate a song to him. He would see himself in their latest video, his picture flashing up as the band sang a slow ballad lamenting his outlaw fame. The newspapers would be drooling after him, wanting his side of things. The television people needing him on their shows, so he could explain why he had done this. Maybe he'd tell them all to go fuck themselves, live on television, or break down and let them know what it was like growing up in a shit-hole with an old man who didn't recognize him. That's all he wanted, just a chance to tell everyone what was important. His father was a retard and so everyone

figured that he was the same. Now he could do away with that
part of him, and then be truly himself. They'd see him then.
He'd be a cool prison con. Get himself a tattoo and pump
weights, and the rest of the cons would treat him fine because
murder was something you respected. That was the greatest
show of strength and everyone paid attention to a murderer.
He saw them all the time on the television. Then, when he got
out, he could fuck over anyone who bothered him. The women
would be all hot and horny, looking to get banged by his new
prison meanness.

His heart was pumping fast for how it had all come together. What were the odds, he wondered, assuring himself, his
body feeling shaky with a happy kind of fright, what were the
odds of anything this perfect ever happening to anyone?

Wet Leather Noose had told him what to do, but as Darren
paced around the block, thinking with one hand holding the
gun in his pocket, his long legs working, he felt the confusion
weakening him, making him understand that there was more
to it than this. He did not want to understand anything, but
other thoughts presented themselves without coaxing. They
were puzzling thoughts, too. Once the rush of powerful ideas
had worn off, Darren seemed tired and out of spirits. A voice
told him that murdering his own father was impossible. He
could not do it. He thought of other people he could kill that
would make more sense, terrible people living brutal lives who
he would wipe out; the big stupid men who beat their women
and children. He remembered the panicky screaming sounds
he'd heard from the houses in his neighbourhood. The sounds
that frightened everyone. Killing one of them bastards would
make him a hero. The good boy to be praised, for once. One
thing for certain: someone needed killing.

The gun felt heavy in his pocket as he stopped circling
Stabb Court and pushed himself off, fearfully heading toward
his house. Nearing the foot of the long street, he saw his father
standing on the top step, staring across the asphalt at something in the neighbour's window. Heber was out again and who
knows what would happen, what people would say about the
old man.

The sight of his father made Darren's thought instantly

darken and shift. He slowed his pace. The idea of tearing free had been buried inside of him all along. The gun had made it magically clear, the steel connecting, powering him with a pure rush, like a high, but then the energy seemed muddied, drained. Darren felt let down, but growing stronger now as he watched his father standing there, staring at the window across from him. Everything had been too perfect. He had wanted it that way and it had come together like a dream. Perfect clarity had left him shaken because he knew it could not be true. He wondered why he had thought what he did because he now knew what was really true: his father was not his father anymore. A long time ago his father had changed into something not himself. He had lost himself in the past. It was not a question of getting back at his father, of hurting his father. It was more than that. Darren was thinking now, really thinking, *I never even knew my mom.* Really really thinking. Thinking hard, *She died on me and no one ever cared a shit for me, saw me,* forcing up the thoughts. His pain was lodged deeper, like the V of an arrowhead. He wanted to draw it up. He wanted to yank it out, to think it, but it was shoved too deeply away, and the hot tears that spilled from him only blurred the image of his father even more. He guessed; maybe it was this that mattered: *I'll make Dad find the parts of him that were gone missing. Force him to get a fucking grip for once.* He spoke to himself through gritted teeth. He would join the shabby remainder of his father with the pieces that had already broken away. Was it memories that made him forget? Was his father made of memories? Darren laughed, wanting to spit the tears away if it was possible. It would be a good thing he was doing. This way would make it better. A kind thing. His father was sick. He'd heard something about that. Sick people being killed because they were in pain. His father was in pain. Darren would blast loose the ghost of what was left of him. His breath seemed to free itself from where it was caught in his chest, the arrowhead out now, pointing elsewhere. He hurried his step. *That'll make people feel proud of me. I'm not stupid.* His legs swept him closer. He'd be famous for all the right reasons after all. Everyone would think he was the best. Brave and kind (and powerful). The best. He nodded and sniffled as he called "Dad," but the sound was nothing more than a sob as he lifted his hand from his pocket, his eyes squinting fiercely when the snarling roar was made.

Heber saw his thin reflection across the street. It was an old man and strangely pale and he thought it resembled himself, but he was uncertain. He raised a hand and waved and the image in the window raised a hand and waved. He laughed quickly, producing his gummy smile, but the reflection of the old man did not smile. It was the absence of the smile that convinced him. He recognized who it was and why he had looked so familiar. The reflection remembering: *there was a time when you could not smile so easily, a serious time. Full, warm-blooded life and reasoning.*

"C'mere," Heber whispered, waving as the reflection waved in perfect rhythm, but the morose image would not speak to him. "I n'ose yer name," he said with his eyes gone sad and staring, but needing to hold the smile, not to be ashamed of his happy forgetfulness. "'Eber. Ya can't fool me none." He stopped waving for a moment, taking his time to straighten his hair with his fingers, grooming himself. He swiped at his lips with the back of his good hand and laughed, the sound loud and sudden, crackling; his reflection laughing with him now. Finally. One quick jolt from its throat. So loud. Deafening. The laugh seeming to burn right through him.

"*I sees ya, 'Eber Peach. I sees ya.*"

Three Distant Lakes on Fire

for David Maher

I wish for nothing but landscape and highway. Elusiveness. Denial. It has come to this. A hundred miles or so beyond St. Shotts, I stop the car, open the door and step out into the dusky silence. I can hear my footsteps sifting along the loose gravel, the sound so clear it startles me into stopping. I am not moving now, but my thoughts have failed to settle, have not yet freed themselves from the momentum of the speeding car; images of asphalt and barrens still racing through my mind.

The sky is immense above me. Dark grey clouds hang thickly, with clear blue patches to either side and lighter areas of grey scattered here and there. A warm orange shading glows along the horizon like a radiant liquid vaguely moving within itself.

Leaning against my door, I see that no cars are coming in either direction. The expressive stillness intrigues me. I listen for the simple pleasure of hearing nothing. But soon I detect a distant warning, a faint insistent drilling, as a tiny fly nears, then buzzes fiercely into my ear, thrashing around, seeming stuck for a moment, before finding its way out again. Hurled free of me. Gone. Disconnected and in the air. I barely hear it moving away, and I have no sight of it at all. It becomes a mystery I cannot possibly solve.

A bird calls deeply from its throat, like a raspy gargling, not far across the brownish red stretch of shadow-covered barrens. I think of switching on the car radio. It seems the sensible thing to do, an electronic connection that will keep me informed (I want to hear the news, to learn if they have discovered my absence yet. It is a humorous thought. Who would care? Who would notice if I am gone? Why would the announcement be on the radio? I am no one of importance.) but then the notion of hearing another voice seems preposterous; it would blatantly disrupt and sever the concentration of wonder that contentedly presses around my body. The thought of this unsettling prospect forces me to step further away from the car, walking beyond its blue metallic outline, watching it gain distance in the fading light. It seems so vacant, abandoned. It cannot possibly be mine. How can it be? I am walking on my feet, and this automobile is made of a substance that has absolutely nothing to do with me. It is heavy and hard, like one of the huge boulders that randomly spots the sprawling barrens, only the car is completely out of place, as if from a remote steely veld of possibilities. It can come alive and glow from the inside with the insertion of a key. It can move me from one place to another. It has delivered me to this stillness. I laugh out loud. Unbelievable!

Holding the ring of keys in the palm of my hand, I let them drop onto the gravel beside my feet. How they land and settle convinces me that they belong in that exact spot. They have found their way home. I watch where they have fallen, and keep moving in reverse, blindly treading in the direction that I have already travelled. Regressing this way, I am assaulted by the possibility of what I am returning to. I counter the pull of my body. Stop myself. The sight of the car no more than fifteen feet away convinces me that I have not moved that far at all. It was not my body that was receding, but rather something inside of me.

Remaining steady on my feet, I glance to the right, see the dark amber light smoothly glazing three distant lakes far across the barrens. The bodies of water seem aglow, as if on fire beneath their calm surfaces. I open and close my mouth. A drink would be appreciated. I am thirsty, but I know I cannot drink from that water. It is too far away, and would burn my

lips because of what I have done. I recall the act, tell myself
that its specifics are of no consequence. The only prevalent
concern is the truth of being 'wrong.' I was wrong. It makes no
difference what I have done, if it was robbery, adultery, murder, or a simple lie. How many simple lies does it take to equal
the willful deliberateness of a murder? How can one discrimi-
nate between 'wrongs,' except through consideration of the
differing intensities of feeling? The unfitting acts vary, but the
prickles of wrongfulness, the degree of their weakness or
strength, are the only natural — and therefore true — gauges
that divide the lot. Self-analysis — regardless of violation —
offers the same ghost-like shadings of guilt. Always a face (no
matter what the wrong) present in your thoughts, always a face
haunting you.

Before the orange hue fades completely, I stare into its light.
The blazing colour sinks, restfully lowering itself behind the
distant treeline, flashing briefly between the trunks and
branches. A growth of dry flowers catches my attention in the
final warm light. I needn't bend far to reach their stems. When
I pull them out, I am startled by what I have done. They are not
dry at all. It was merely their appearance that deceived me.
They are fresh and alive, and the wetness from their broken
stems covers my fingers with a juice that smells strongly of
bitterness. Returning to the car, I open the door and hurl the
flowers in. Instantly, the dome light clicks on, revealing the
seats and the moulded dashboard and the fitted pieces of carpet
and the flowers that must stay here now to come to grips with
their new altered form. I close the door. The light vanishes,
leaving me. An act of forgiveness.

I move into the middle of the level highway. Nothing is coming either way, as if no one could possibly share an equal
interest in my retreat. Sitting on the cooling asphalt, I face the
direction from where I have come. This black strip of
unearthliness is what connects all of us, yet I have a feeling
that no one will be travelling here. The night thickens, like a
silenced confessor regaining life, as the clouds curdle and drift
lower to cover me. In time, a number of large dark birds fly
overhead. They make no sound, save for the smooth lifting and
settling of their wings. When they have gone, I hear dim

rustlings and snorts across the barrens to my left, the animals returning from their pleasant drink in the three distant lakes, their bellies filled by the quiet and harmless fire of communal faith.

I wait and stare toward the sky. It is a vague gesture on my part, and soon I look ahead. There were no stars in the sky to reconcile my distraught sense of longing. I am still thinking of things I have learned before coming to this place. It is wrong to think of things I have learned. Out here, it is very wrong; act only on instinct, and breathe the air that is changed in morning and night by the fragrances stirred to rise from the rootless ground. I hold my breath; a weak attempt at defiance, at humour, and listen to the rustling sounds growing stronger, the short and longer limbs of the animals making their ways to the edge of the barrens, labouring up the gravel embankment, only to halt, cleverly confirming my sense of hesitation. The smaller animals come first, carefully scouting for the bigger ones whose hard hooves soon test the pavement.

In the time that it takes for me to forget, all of the animals have found their way close to me, surrounding the space where I sit. They will not accept me into this place until they discover who I am. I see only their curious eyes, hear only the sounds of their nostrils, sniffing.

Into the Places of Those Lost

for Robert Rutherford

The bloodhound rushed to the side of the cabin, poking her nose beneath the garbage box lid and flicking it up, only to have it clunk down on her head. She barked and sniffed manically, pushing farther into the darkness, then jolting back an instant later, freezing on stiff legs as the raccoon leapt out. Running for twenty feet, with Sag in close pursuit, the raccoon stopped dead in its tracks, turning and lifting its tiny paws to the dog. Sag skidded to a halt, with a snort and a muddled "rhaaaa" sound that was more like a bad cough than a bark, before crouching low and backing off.

Cuz watched the scene with a smile on his swollen lips. He picked at his cheek, carefully pulling away a small piece of skin still coming off from the woodstove's flash fire that had rushed against his face after he had laced the junks with gasoline to keep things going. One match and his face changed with a furious roar licking his skin into a crumpled mess.

Carefully, most times absent-mindedly, he peeled away the skin, feeling a freshness that soon made him think of laughter. He called to his wife with words concerning the raccoon chase and Bridey looked up from the new red spinner she was fixing

to her trouting pole, and came to the door with an even, reasonable expression, leaning out to watch. But the raccoon was
gone, the bloodhound standing in the blueberry brush sadly
staring back at the cabin, as if nothing less than her life had
been taken away from her: Disappointment in herself and everything that led her to that spot. Bridey could not help but
laugh at the look on the bloodhound's face, glancing at Cuz
before turning back into the house, not knowing, not seeing
how she herself would be found dead in her car the next day, on
her way home from working for the Highways Department on
the road-widening project outside Cutland Junction, through
with standing in the dust all day, feeling the heat and the gritty
sweat beneath her hard hat, holding up the SLOW sign that
was turned around in the palm of one hand, again and again, to
the big white word against red — STOP.

Filling his duffle bag with one change of clothes, a few tins of
stew and soup, a sleeping bag, and an axe, Cuz wandered off
into the woods with Sag following close behind. The policeman had told him that his wife had died by accident, and Cuz
had merely nodded his head, understanding what that meant.
He climbed into the police car and was taken to the hospital,
which was, according to the green highway sign, twelve miles
away in St. Shotts. The room where he had seen his wife was
terribly bright and everything was made of cool silver, even the
table she was lying on. The room smelled sharp and seemed to
sting all the space inside his body. When the man pulled back
the sheet, he saw it was his wife. The man moved the blanket
down further to show Cuz that she was naked and seemingly
unmarked, her flesh the wrong colour — a polished greenish-
white — but he needed it all the same, seeing her still and
changed this way, feeling the final frightening rush of arousal
that made him want to climb on top, thinking he could bring
her back with his mouth and the warmth of his body and what
he would let loose inside her after he fit between her legs the
way he was meant to.

   The sheet was slowly pulled back up, and Cuz looked to see
the man with the brown-rimmed glasses nodding his head,
then carefully slipping a black strand of hair, hanging down the

side of the silver table, back under the white, shape-fitting blanket. Cuz stared at the man's hands, his fingernails, the white cleanness of them. He was startled by how the man stayed there with his wife when they left. Cuz glanced back and thought, "Wha' right's he 'av?" He jerked to get loose and say a thing or two to the man with the long white coat, but the policeman held his arm, saying confidently, "Come on, Cuz. She's gone now. Let's all of us try to be reasonable."

That evening, around dusk time, the raccoon came by again, lingering in the trees and watching, thinking it might be a trap because Cuz had dumped the garbage out of the bin at the side of the cabin, everything out from inside, to see what would come to claim the refuse, finding it necessary now for these things to be accepted by another. Both of his feet stepping and standing firmly in the dark rushing willfulness, his shaky limbs held defiantly stiff among the mad release of all that was tossed off and accepted into the wild order of more basic, but seemingly wiser, creatures. Faith. God. Animals that must eat, and shit out the stuff of biological communion that makes this world grow greener.

Cuz watched from behind the wall of the cabin, leaning close to the small square window, and fingering the tufts of moss stuck into the spaces between the stacked logs that made up the walls, thinking of other things; the brittleness of Bridey's cunny hairs. The tangle that his fingers caught in, searching for wetness. The wetness gone, drought hardening the once-sleek, fleshy, life-sucking hole.

Dead dry now, and black rubber hard.

The raccoon waddled closer, paying no attention to Sag lying fifteen feet away with her head resting on her outstretched paws. The raccoon approached the dog, but Sag only shuffled backward, mournfully slow, along the scratchy blueberry brush, not wanting to find fault in the presence of anything right now, knowing better, creature to creature. Acceptance of the spoils. A gift. A sad celebration that no one would speak into. Vacancy's momentary truce.

Cuz doused the cabin with gasoline, then scraped a match head across a torn piece of flint he fished from his pocket.

Without hesitation, he threw the match into the door, feeling the heat rush out at him so that he leaned away, the short patches of hair remaining on his head feeling alive and damp. He did not fear the fire, but called to it instead, asking questions in an off-hand way. Listening, he then said, "Go a'ed 'av it. No sus fuh'kin t'ing as excident." He sensed a corner of the skin on his face cracking away in the heat, and took the thin edge between his two fingers, pulling mindfully, hoping to snag a big piece, but the skin broke away and he was noticeably disappointed by the outcome, his fingers slipping over a smooth patch of hard pink skin. He called to the dog, not waiting to watch the cabin burn. No more to say than what that violent rush of heat was making plain. Everything said, but nothing explained in a grunt of human defeat. The cabin was useless to him now; his wife's presence branded along every square inch. Her smell, her laugh and her eyes in the dark, blinking white with thoughts that he could never understand. All over it. All over him. The wholeness of the place was just as much a part of her as what they would be putting in the ground. *Ashes*, he thought. *Steam rise'n frum 'er.* He wished he could smell the final scent. His cheek pressed against her naked belly, holding her hips, holding the easy shapeliness of her hips. Fingers forgetting. *Ashes*.

Moving into the darkening woods, Cuz could not help but imagine what the man in the hospital room was guilty of; how many bodies had he uncovered and touched? Bodies that did not belong to him. And why hadn't someone already stopped him from laying his fingers where he had no right? Touching all that flesh that was now beneath his hands; the man with the long white coat and glasses to help him see plainly in such wicked brightness. No such thing as one little squint out of him. All the bodies that had been mothers and fathers, daughters and sons. Naked and touched. Cuz's wife now. The man holding firmly onto flesh and cutting, alone in the room that seemed so alive with the buzz of confusion scrubbed unbelievably clean.

The axe had been sharpened only two weeks prior, and so Cuz had no trouble chipping away at the spruce boughs and placing them atop each other to form a lean-to. He did not feel like eating and so he built no fire, despite the fact that the summer heat was cooling off, pulling back to unpin the cool forest darkness that slowly rose and lingered. The walk through the black woods had made him tired, and so he turned from where he was sitting, staring into the featureless trees as if expecting to see the movements of what he was thinking, and crawled under the shield of boughs where he lay down on his sleeping bag. Sag followed in through the hole, her movements sounding loud and clear as she lumbered close to drop beside Cuz. Shifting several times, she blew out air and pressed nearer.

Wading through shallow sleep, Cuz saw a vision of the man in the dead room. He saw the man glance around the room before clicking off the lights. Silently the man left the hospital and bent into his car, staring straight through the windshield ahead. When the engine turned over, a raccoon's tail hanging from the rearview shivered slightly, and Cuz was vaguely aware of the fact, then mildly startled by the certainty that the raccoon from the shack was missing its tail; a detail from actual life that had reinvented itself in his dream. The idea troubled him and he rolled over, grumbling, and was concerned — though not yet awake — by the presence of open space beside him. Something had been there on the ground. In his dream, he saw the man turning the ignition again, needing to provoke the engine more than once, and as the engine made its catching rumble he saw his wife's eyes opening as if she was still dead and it was only the man with his fetish for biological mechanics that had triggered the sudden rise of her eyelids. She was lying across the back seat, one hand set against the naked coldness between her opened legs. Bolting up, she laughed and touched her chest with both her palms, before presenting the man with one of her breasts, jiggling in her cupped hands. "Yours," she said sweetly. "Take it home. Yours."

What was missing? Cuz wondered. Something had been there on the ground beside him. He woke up and was alone, knowing only the stinging taste of fright in his mouth and the brutal closeness of all he had been dreaming, hating the raccoon, knowing now that it was his enemy because his dream had purposefully spliced the connection.

Sag had left her place beside Cuz. Was that it? What was

missing now? Cuz listened in the darkness that seeped well beyond his startled eyes to hear the vague stirrings of the dog, her paws moving quickly against the forest ground, but in the same location, as if someone was exciting her, perhaps scratching her head. He heard a voice whispering low. It was a sweet sound coming to him through the trees, through the soft yet brittle wall of boughs that surrounded him, and he realized painfully that the low pleasant sound must be the voice of a woman.

There was no moon in the sky when Cuz ducked out and straightened, keenly aware of the dark, moist scent of the night earth. The movement he saw in the wall of black trees could have been anything. The movement was ten times blacker than he thought himself capable of seeing, the denseness full-bodied and leaking away from itself, and a voice seemed not to be moving with this mass shifting in the trees. The restless voice sang low and sugary, without words, only breathy sounds, all around him and the bulk of something that moved apprehensively, as if on its own, but trying to find the voice that surely belonged to it. Sag was there with her legs stumbling. Cuz could hear the paw-moving sounds of the dog, and her short bursts of whining, following the movement of whatever it was, but her dog ears confused by the voice that was coming from everywhere at once.

A lovely scent visited Cuz, a whiff of roses and lemons pleasing him, and he realized that he would be seeing someone soon, someone he did not expect to reach forward from the trees, a woman's stiff arm coming white through the branches, but he was wrong. There was no arm. The first thing that came was the pale slant of a naked leg, stepping forward, then the lower body and the black-red shading of glistening pubic hair, alive and stirring, fibers bending to blindly feel the skin they were fastened to. And then the second leg revealed beneath the spill of moonlight that bravely freed itself from behind a grey cloud. A corner of the moon uncovered and uncovering a section of the body, before the woman stepped freely from the trees and stood watching him, with Sag's wrinkled face looking up at Cuz, then at the woman, as if wanting to prompt acknowledgement.

The woman smiled, her hands beside her square naked hips,

her breasts full, their black-red nipples studded with seeds, like ripe berries about to drop from the veinwork of branches that stretched inside of her, needing to find root elsewhere. The nipples fell off, seed by seed with new ones pushing out. Bending slowly at the knees, the woman patted the dog. Cuz watched without comment, held only by the love that settled through every inch of him. He felt that he should speak and so he said, "Do ya wan' sum clo's?" The pleasant woman shook her head without a word, then opened her lips, but waited before she said, "What for? I'm not cold." Standing and stepping closer, the woman appeared familiar. She was not his wife, but Cuz thought there was a slight resemblance and he wondered what she was doing here, lost in the woods?

"I should be the one asking you. What're you doing lost in the woods?"

Cuz had not said a word and he wondered how the woman had known. Feeling frightened and angry, he retorted, "I'm naw laws'd."

"Come here," said the woman, and Cuz went closer until the woman kissed him and a rush of colour that was the colour of his dead wife raced through her skin.

"Ooow," the woman thrilled, with her eyes closed. She jerked her neck and carefully shook her wrists, as if trying to loosen something. Soon the colour of his dead wife left the woman and she was perfectly white again, as if her skin was thick and polished and beautifully clean.

The woman opened her eyes. "I can't touch you now, Cuz," she told him.

Cuz said his wife's name, but the woman did not seem to notice what he was saying. A moment later she shook her head. "I'm sorry you don't understand." Her smile so soft and becoming. "It's impossible to explain."

Cuz thought that she was someone very different, someone wild but holding back, tamed in a way that made her happy, and Sag stayed close to the woman's legs, knowing by the scent that she was who she was, no matter how she happened to appear.

"Do you want me?" the woman asked. Without answering, Cuz turned away and dropped to his knees, crawling into the lean-to. He lay down and shut his eyes, repeating the crying

word 'help' inside his head, but it was not so loud, more like a
prayer than a shout. He told himself to go to sleep, but he was
cold. When he opened his eyes again, the woman was lying
beside him, her green and brown and blue eyes watching him
up close, her body white and smelling warm and powdery. She
kissed his cheek and half of her face flushed green. She rubbed
it with her fingers, grimacing slightly, but in a way that made
Cuz think of pleasure.

"Wha're ya affer, womb'n?"

"Cuz." The woman smiled and reached between her legs,
yanking out a silent white baby and tossing it toward the low
roof of the lean-to, where it hovered weightlessly, glancing
down and fluttering its tiny fingers close to its face, before giggling and slowly drifting up through the boughs.

"Don't touch me," the woman whispered, shutting her eyes
cosily. "Just don't. Passion works instantly now. The mere
thought of such emotions brings on immediate conception.
The way it was meant to be."

Cuz understood that the woman was strangely mad, like
the village idiots he remembered seeing throughout the years
in Cutland Junction. Love melding with fear, he rolled away
from her, over on his side, but felt her warm breath against his
neck, prompting him to roll back again, to view her face gone
green, her eyes larger and her lips coming forward, soon on him
and they were blue like in the winter when the body stays out
too long against the elements that mean to take something
from you, something that belongs back with the woods and the
water and air, a scrap of vastness that was once part of a whole
but now wrongly set in one broken misdirected person.

"On top of me," she said. "Do what you intended, what you
thought would bring me back." Clutching him with her hands,
she easily lifted him on top of her and reached down to take
hold of his prick, to force entry. Cuz felt himself growing into
her, as if reaching into warm mud that was cooling. And he
knew that he must love her so fiercely that she would die, kill
her with the scalding semen that was sure to erase her, or do
something much different from killing, something well beyond killing for which there was no given name, for she was
already dead. But the idea of killing was close enough. It would

lead him toward whatever it was that he was really trying to do. The woman closed her thighs on him so that he could not pull himself free from where he was lodged inside her.

"Let it loose," she said. "Please, sweetheart." Her lips splitting and hardening. She could barely speak, her eyelids cracking, like the burnt skin across Cuz's face, small flakes falling against her yellowing eyeballs.

Both of them coming apart, and it was all by accident.

Cuz thought of the occurrences that had named themselves accidents — the unbalancing of objects wiping things out and replacing them with holes that were to be filled painfully by acceptance of the sorrow, or the repositioning of other, newer bodies into the places of those lost. Thinking such bold frightening thoughts, Cuz could not hold back any longer. He tried to draw away, tightening the muscles around his groin, shrinking back into himself, not wanting to make her pregnant, but really needing to more than anything. Punching free, the ejaculation tore something from him, an urge or an understanding not yet complete, and the woman smiled, saying, "Now, what does that prove?" before turning to dust beneath him. Unsupported, his body thudded to the ground, his face against the musky grass. When he rolled to his side and turned his head toward the opening of the lean-to, he saw Sag standing there in the narrow hole with her face hanging loose and horribly sad. A shadow was standing on the dog's back, and Cuz saw that it was the raccoon, its tiny claws in front of its face, sloppily rubbing against each other, as if clapping at the farcical outcome of what it had just been blessed enough to see.

Cuz took it as a dream. Although waking in the morning, he was uncertain if the dream still held him. With a lingering numb sense of detachment, he packed up his duffle bag, and wandered off. The sunlight through the green and grey branches was reassuring and he could see everything. In this expansiveness of clarity, there was no question whatsoever about things moving around him without being identified for what they truly were.

Walking all day, deeper and deeper into the woods, through brief clearings and back into the shadowed denseness of trees that tried to hold him, he trudged until dusk pulled those shadows from the woods across a new bigger clearing where he stopped, sighting a lake where Sag was bent to take a drink. Cuz decided that this would be a good place to camp for the night. The gentle lapping of the water was calming, reassuring. He was a man again, in the woods with his dog. It was as simple as that. A male body. Solid with the land. No dreams needed here.

Done with her sloppy drinking, Sag wandered off, lifting her head and staring into the trees, then sniffing the cool grass, lifting her gaze and shaking her head, her ears flapping back and forth, her nose soon low to the earth again, the skin along her mouth jiggling as she worked her way toward a bark.

Cuz took his axe from his duffle bag and purposefully strolled off across the green and yellow grass to the edge of the treeline, where he cut several boughs. When he returned to collect his duffle bag and call for Sag, he noticed how the light had retracted farther into the trees, the shadows so long they were almost spread along the entire stretch of space before and around him, but he could still stand in the narrow orange slants of light set between the shadows, the remaining tempered heat richly spilling across his face.

" 'Ey?" he called to Sag. Listening, he heard a crow cawing and the swooping flight of a bird overhead, before realizing the frantic sounds of paws racing through the woods, then the howling that Cuz had not heard in quite a while. It was a call of pursuit. He followed the sound. Eyes skimming the treeline, he saw Sag breaking through the tangled edge, flushing the creature that waddled quickly ahead, running to the edge of the lake and racing in. Sag strode close behind, making a lot of noise as she splashed toward the deeper water, then swam smoothly, but desperately, after the escaping raccoon.

Once closer to the water, Cuz saw by the wake of where it was swimming that the raccoon's tail was missing. It swam, as if with certain purpose, but lack of concern, toward the middle of the lake, before pausing, turning to face the bloodhound, waiting for the dog to find its way closer, waiting with a single idea suspending it in the water. Sag struggled to reach the center; she was old and determined and paddled with great effort toward the raccoon. Cuz smiled at the sight of Sag and the game she was playing, but he wondered why the raccoon had stopped now and was waiting in an almost friendly way as Sag laboured closer, directly toward the raccoon, which easily circled behind the dog and climbed onto her back. Expecting to see the raccoon brush its hands together like in his dream, Cuz stared with distant interest, sensing the tingling fear rise toward his mouth again, the matching of disaster with the brewing of sleepy suspicions. He drifted closer to the edge of the lake, seeing so clearly he was rendered immobile for an instant. A breath, then one insensible step into the shallowest part of the water.

The raccoon took its time wobbling up the length of the bloodhound's back as Sag turned in slow circles before frantically deciding to paddle clumsily toward the shore. The raccoon continued its slow jolly walk until it paused, resting on the top of Sag's head, the weight pressing the dog's muzzle beneath the surface of water. The raccoon remained in place until all the dog's movement ceased, then it slid into the water and swam effortlessly in the other direction, toward the farthest shore.

Cuz stood in disbelief, witnessing the heavy body of the dog slowly rolling over in the water. He realized that it was not a replay of his dream at all. It was something he had not expected, something he could not have anticipated. All of it was real and seemed physically attached to him, more frighteningly clear than any dream could ever be.

The following day, Cuz returned to the police station in Cutland Junction, confessing to the policeman that he had killed his wife two nights ago in the woods.

"I kill'd 'er 'cause I cud'nt bare ta see 'er da way she was so perfuk. It 'armed me eyes. It made me stumuk vomit. She turn ta dust. Was 'er all over a'gin. I try ta bring 'er back, but all I's did was kill 'er and kill 'er more."

The policeman took Cuz to the dead room and again showed him the body of his wife, which had been held for pickup. The body was white and drained and pure. A thick Y-shaped scar ran from her shoulders down across her breasts, connecting at the top of her belly before continuing down to the space between her legs. The ridges of the scar were neat and perfectly white with no pinkness. The pinkness gone. She was changed again, put back together and Cuz agreed that the woman he had killed did not look much like his wife, but he knew that it was his wife all the same. The woman had crumbled right out from under him, turned to dust in the blink of an eye, he told the two men.

"It's okay," said the policeman.

"We need to bury her soon," the man with the glasses calmly declared, pulling the sheet back up. "We never hold bodies here for so long. But I was..." He stretched his lips with a quiet, even gesture of resignation, "...waiting." And he nodded with relief as he straightened his glasses with two fingers.

"She aw'rady gone," Cuz said to them both. His left eye was almost swollen shut from the smooth fire scars on his face, but he could still blink away the tears. The two men looked at him, understanding the need to hold their expressions as plain as possible.

"Let's go," the policeman said. "It was an accident, Cuz. You didn't do anything."

"I di'nt," Cuz blurted out. "I dee'd."

"Come on outside," said the policeman, gently laying his hand against Cuz's solid back.

The man in the room watched the door swing closed as the two men slowly moved out. He waited for silence, stillness before telling himself that he had never seen such a display before. The woman's husband, the man named Cuz, had such a ghoulish face. It was frightening the way he looked and the way he talked, too, particularly when he cried. It was an absolutely terrifying sight. The man in the room shuddered, glad that Cuz was no longer present. He breathed a slow sigh of relief, using both hands to carefully push shut the shiny heavy drawer where the woman's body lay. Snapping off his plastic gloves, he stepped across the room, struck by a troubling sight as he observed the row of specimen jars along the cool silver ledge. Something was definitely wrong here. He stared beyond the glass, into its pinkish-white contents that rested there so

obligingly. He wondered until he was almost worried, then realized he was looking much too closely. What a gift to possess
the good grace that afforded one the most reasonable of conclu-
sions. He smiled to himself and took one step back, focusing
on the exact surfaces and edges. He saw what was important
now. Of course, the line of jars was merely out of order, one
crock of specimens crooked, simply in need of straightening.

The One

I

They ask me what kind of woman I could possibly be. I find it difficult to respond, never having thought this way. What kind of woman do they want me to be?

I tell myself I am simply an observer. A body in a lacy slip with a gun to her throat. Not a victim. It would be ridiculous to think so. I am the one staring out at the truer show of humility; the rows of intrigued faces watching from below the edge of the stage, crowds all the way back toward the rear wall.

I cannot see the fear in my eyes, but I see Num's angry lips only inches from mine, cursing violently, accusing me. He is close to my face. My head jerks to the side when he savagely tugs my hair, wrapping a length of the wig's strands around his fist, and shouting again. I play along. People stare from where they stand in the dim auditorium. They are poised expectantly, believing they will soon witness a revelation in the spotlight, but I am the one who sees the truth in their agitated expressions. I am the one mastering them with my leashed big-boned body. They have not wished me into this state. I have chosen it. I am the woman I want to be.

Num guides back the pistol's hammer with his thumb. His index finger curves and trembles slightly against the trigger, applying pressure. Realism and extremity are the two key features advertised for this production. The audience has paid its money, and the script has led to this; the final act is drawing to a close. The heavy curtain of luscious red velvet slowly, soundlessly begins its descent from high above. And the wall of shadow sweeps along with it.

The silence seems whole, but something trembles within it; constrained thoughts pull tighter like tangles of mating snakes unable to free themselves from the fanaticism of their biological incitement. Men breathe for me. Their bodies press closer to the lip of the stage.

Num hooks a row of bent fingers into the front of my slip, then digs down deeper between my cleavage, gathering the material. His hand thrusts away as cloth rips like the sharpening of a hundred knives. I hear the quiet grunts from the audience as my breasts' clumsy weight jolts loose. They are exposed to the cool air, my nipples alert, extending for the crowd. The breasts. Memorabilia. Infantile nostalgia.

The luxurious curtain is no more than six feet from touching the floor. Num empties three rapid shots into my face. The sound effects are synchronized perfectly. The curtain slides the remaining five feet and is down. Now masked from the audience, Num smiles, leans closer with his brutally sallow face and pecks me on the forehead. Beyond the curtain, slow footsteps sound across the wooden floor as the people begin to shuffle from the room. As usual, there is no applause. The audience offers no reply. They do not comment to each other. They are simply holding the image of me in their minds and I feel thrilled that they should carry this with them, now and for many weeks to come. Perhaps until the day of their deaths.

In a matter of moments, Enan appears from the off-stage shadows. He pats the fingertips of one hand against the palm of the other. The gesture makes little sound. It is only a signal; his casual acceptance of matters.

Num wipes a finger down the side of his nose. He stares at Enan, anxiously awaiting judgement.

"I think we should consider changing the ending," Enan says. "Too much of a con."

I watch him step closer, then I lift the front fabric of my slip back into place, press my forearms against my breasts so that they rise nicely for him.

"How do you mean?" asks Num, unconsciously running the tip of the gun up and down along his bare, hairless chest. He is a big man whose actual voice is soft, noticeably effeminate. His wife, a small woman, works at the ticket window. She is expecting a child and Num is very pleased. The recent string of full houses has ensured him extra money for the baby; a crib, sleepers, diapers. A few days ago, he told me he opened a bank account. He was very proud of the idea, never requiring the services of such an institution before.

"The red stuff," says Enan, glancing around the stage flooring and gesturing with his hand. "An abundance of the red stuff will make matters more authentic." Stepping in, he kisses me high on the cheek. I smell his scent; the heaviness of sweetened musk. There is a chemical coolness to the perfume, but also a murkiness that is so fragrant it stirs affection within me.

"What's that you're wearing?" I have to ask him.

He smiles and his narrow eyes lift; sensual hooks tugging deep into my groin, arousing me. His lips are small but not fine. I remember how soft they always feel against mine.

"The scent?" he asks, noticeably pleased with the response he has drawn from me.

I nod and laugh lightly, girlishly, the way he is fond of.

"Cute," he says, with just a hint of sarcasm. Pointing at my mouth, he suggests, "But bite your lip a little at the corner for fuller effect."

"Yes," I say, blushing, but smiling, agreeing with what he expects of me, just as his behaviour must fall in line with what I require of him. "But what is it? The scent?"

"It's the spunk from all those faithful ticket buyers." He flicks his fingers out in front of himself, "releasing onto me, like skunks, like spraying cats, like the blowholes of whales."

Num laughs sympathetically and nods his head.

Enan is the most intense of us all, but he can hold himself perfectly in character. He is totally believable, his sharp handsome features agreeing with such affectedness, his slim, tall body implying precise command. Each gesture is in perfect harmony with the notion he wishes to express. I find it difficult to respond to his replies, always peppered with such vigorous images. He holds me with his style, grasps me with his eyes in such a way that I imagine his body working against me, kneading my flesh, pressing with each breath that I must draw because of what he is doing to me, entry and the speeding of my blood.

When he looks off, away from me, I sense his release and step back with a limb-twitching shiver.

Glancing at the base of the curtain, Enan whispers a few words to himself. The curtain rises. A technician in the wings has pushed the button. Enan smirks. "Performance," he says. Beyond the footlights, the room is now empty, the house lights on. His eyes sweep across the floor. There are no seats, only the small steel plates remain. The seats have been unbolted. Standing room only. The production is billed as a play, but, as can be easily imagined in these timid days, some have claimed that the actions are questionable. The dialogue is too graphic, too vivid; the action, brutally honest.

Enan has said indignantly, "This choreographed violence is already staked out inside each of us. It's in there. In here. Actual. Real. Why do people object so strongly? Why do people behave so extravagantly, denying this blood-thirsty part of their selves?" His questions are usually rhetorical. They are more statements than anything else, as if he has been overly aware of the answers for far too long.

"Performance," he shouts into the empty theatre, listening to his voice carrying. He then whispers, "Extension of the self." Staring at me as if the joke is obvious, he laughs with his lips closed. Soon, he lets us know that the time has come for a change. "We need a larger venue. We need designers. Props. A crew. The money is there." His head jerks as if the unexpected impulse of a thought has charged him. "Terror is in," he insists, seeming slightly awestruck by his own words. "A slogan for the billboards."

"Broadway," Num growls, reclaiming his conqueror's stage voice. "Broadway is next." Reaching down, he raises my severed finger from the floor. It is a prop. Before the play, I bend my actual finger forward and hold it in tight to my palm, then I glue the fake one on. It is part of the script. The finger comes off. It is filled with blood, much like what travels through us, but not wanting out.

Num offers the finger to me and I allow him to place it in my opened palm. Smiling caringly, like the perfect father that I know he will be, he then circles and stomps around the stage in a pompous arc, imitating the march of a Roman guard, playing the part, entertaining us, pretending we are his new children. He speaks deeply as if announcing the entrance of an emperor, "Broadway, Broadway, Broadway..."

"Unquestionably," says Enan, his face brimming with severity; the harrowing expression that makes him what he is. "Time is all. Controversy. Censure. Publicity. Art."

My answering machine is filled with messages; requests from journalists, television hosts, and charities. Ludicrous suggestions from crazies of numerous sorts. All counting on my cooperation. Enan has told me to contract an agent to sort out these cumbersome aspects of my new career. The agent will deal with the debris. I have no aspirations to appear on television or in motion pictures. I enjoy what I am doing. A live audience waiting for a view of what will soon be cheating them, these people somehow cheating their maker by catching sight of another's final moments, or pretending that they are the ones powerful enough to withdraw the gift that is my life. Each of them imagining that they are Num.

People throughout the city are talking, people are wondering if what takes place on stage is genuine. The national media is paying attention. Women are worried for my life, as if they have no lives of their own and must therefore concern themselves with me instead. They seem to take offence at the meaty sounds of blows that shake me on stage. They believe that I am being battered. They wonder, can the sound effects be so realistic? And I ask myself, what difference does it make if the blows are staged or actual? The intention is to amplify reality, so therefore they are — at the very least — real.

I listen to the messages, bits and pieces; propositions entailing large sums of money, pleas for romance or mutilation, guarantees of fame, glorified pronouncements — my need for salvation. I slip off my shoes and step toward the bathroom.

Pausing, I unhasp my jeans and push them down along my thighs. I stand outside the bathroom door and stare at my distant reflection in the mirror above the sink. My panties are pink and tight, revealing a hint of the crack that men kick from and long to crawl back into. The sight arouses me and I want to open up so desperately. I feel exhausted, but in a very sexual, filthy way. There is a bruise along my hip. Another bruise along my jawline is a deep speckled purple framed by a sickly yellow. I brush my amber hair back away from my face and skip ahead, struggling to pull my jeans clear of my legs. In the bathroom, I dip a facecloth in warm, soothing water and lift it to my jawline. Wince when it finds its mark. But then I smile, fooling even myself. The bruise disappears when I rub a little harder. I feel my heart beating faster, like a teenager in love. The make-up easily washing away, having served its superficial purpose.

II

When the scandal first hit the newspapers, officials from the Catholic Church suggested that I accept a publicity agent to handle the "extreme unpleasantness of this matter," as they put it. It would be at their expense. They employed trained personnel to deal with such affairs. I told the monsignor who visited me that I would consider their offer. He seemed pleased and smiled graciously. I had no doubt of his sincerity, but I did not have the courage to contact him again. I could not fall back into the arms of the practise that had played such a large part in doing this to me. I drew further into myself, into the hurt, staying away from my friends. They seemed so helpless and awkward all of a sudden, not knowing how to console me.

I found a little café on Slattery West, drinking coffee there and losing myself in books. I do not know how Enan found me. When he first introduced himself, he appeared so familiar, as if I had seen him before. I thought perhaps I recognized his face. There had been a man who seemed to be following me for days after the scandal, but I payed no attention to this, casting it off as one of the paranoic effects of trauma. Enan seemed to come to me from nowhere and I could not resist him. He was like all of the friends I had lost, only *he* understood me even more now because of what had happened to me, of what had been taken away. He knew all the words to fill the emptiness, treating me with delicateness, reassurance, and always the perfect explanations that made things seem more complete and understandable.

"You wear a cross every day, every minute," he professed, laying out the appropriate course of behaviour. "A big cross around your neck. You see, like this one. Do you like this one? Take it. Go ahead. Put it on. Yes. It's very nice. It looks impressive. Very impressive." He smiled as I stared down and touched the pewter design where it lay against my chest.

"You wear that cross and you tell the press that you were, no, are a religious woman. You still go to church and pray, even after all of this with the priest. Religion is your life, no, was your life, until this happened and now you are struggling. Your life was very religious, yes. But now all of this has introduced you to another side of things. It has made you sexual. You have been tainted by something sacred, made sluttish. It's okay, only as an act. That's all. Don't be offended. If you want offensive, you tell them that now you like to get fucked in the worst possible ways. You're in need of salvation and this is how you go about filling the hole." Enan stopped to smile in a consoling way, as if he did not really care for the way he was speaking, but was merely doing so for my own good. He sipped his tea and used the side of his hand to brush a few crumbs from the café tabletop onto the floor. All the while, his searching eyes never left me. "You're wounded in the holiest of places, the place where creation squeezes through. Sex and religion. They know their place from way back when. The Bible and all the nasty little bits. This way, if you follow what I'm saying, you incite the religious and you arouse the sexual at the same time. You blanket everyone. The sacred-minded are thrown for a loop. They have to decide whether to save you or condemn you for your wickedness, while those others, the sexual ones, long to have you. They fantasize elaborate schemes involving your blessed body."

Enan's eyes left my eyes as he glanced down at my blouse. When he looked at my face again, his expression fell a little. "No, I'm sorry, you're blushing. I was just noticing how voluptuous your body is. You have a strong body. Fair skin and your hair is like nothing I've seen before. The colour's real. I can tell. It's beautiful. If you listen to me, just listen, I promise you that you'll gain a voice. A huge audience will listen when you talk about this injustice that has been perpetrated against you. The crowds will want you in one way or another. Believe me. *Their* voices will be your medium. The people are a medium in themselves. Word of mouth, the most successful broadcast tool there is and ever has been. Gossip is the original long-distance mode of communication. People are their own entertainment institution for themselves, by themselves. Their own spiritual government of one. Nothing can stop them from seeing and believing inside their own heads. Believing what they *want* to believe, not what others want them to. They are not electronic, but they are the base." Enan firmly pressed his fingers against his chest. "They are physical."

All the while he was speaking, I had not moved an inch in my seat. I realized that I was breathing through my opened lips. I glanced down at the café tabletop. There was a touch of whiteness lingering against the blackness of my coffee. I thought of cream, but the thought was heavy, seeming impossible to carry off. It meant nothing. There was no way to counter what Enan claimed. He was so right and spontaneous in his words that I was mesmerized.

Enan went on, "So this priest had himself in you."

I wanted to tell him what had happened, every detail because I knew that I would feel better, but I could not find the courage. Even though I felt I had known him for a very long time, he was still a stranger and something inside of me said, *be careful.* I tilted my head to speak, but instead found tears rising to my eyes so that I could only nod quietly.

"Yes," he said. "I think I see it. That lingering glow. His cock through your halo. You were a virgin before all of this. But now you see through wide open eyes."

His words made me cry. They did not offend me. They were horribly accurate and they were what I truly needed. I bowed my head and wept.

The scandal with Father James took place approximately three months before the opening day of Enan's play. Shortly after the news of Father James' arrest appeared in the newspapers, I had thought of seeing a counsellor, but it was a frightening thought that left me feeling even weaker than I

believed myself to be at that time. To visit a professional was
to admit that something serious was wrong. Enan pledged as-
sistance, telling me he had read about the colourful details in
the papers. He claimed to be a therapist of sorts, insisting he
specialized in Retaliation Therapy. It was a joke, and it offered
practical relief.

"So you told a friend," Enan continued, "and the friend told
the newspapers for a few dollars. News story of the week. A
real friend. And the priest is carted off, first exiled from his
parish. A slap on the wrist. But now arrested, like any man
who commits a crime. The law still has a problem with arrest-
ing God's workers. How can priests possibly be guilty when
hooked up so closely with the Creator, capital C? They get
lighter sentences every time. But the priest did this to you. He
did this in the name of The One. Not only sex, but an inhuman
act. Bruises." He pointed at my face. "What was he trying to
prove with that? Was he punching the demons out of you? A
carnal exorcism of sorts?"

I remember laughing bitterly, my anguish only tightening.
A moment later I told him that I was scared, then broke down
and cried openly and freely for the very first time. Tears wet
my placemat and fell into my coffee cup. The café went blurry
as I glanced around to see who was watching us. Several faces
stared back at me, but they were nondescript through the
tears, and, subsequently, I knew they did not matter.

Enan leaned forward, gently wiping away the tear trails
with his fingertips. He said, "What are you scared of?"

I sobbed, "God. Why did he let this happen?"

Enan said, "Why God? Why are you scared of God? Why not
the air, or the fields, or the water? We breathe, we eat, we
drink. If you want to be scared, then rip yourself open to see
what's powering your body. There you have what's guilty. Your
body is the only thing smitten by this so-called sin. Flesh is
nothing. It's worthless. It comes and goes. But your mind can
free itself. Look at the asylums. The people in there are already
partially free, the mind wanting out because of what the body
has done, bits of it tearing away. Don't be fooled. What happened inside the priest's body is what did this to you. And it's
the air and the fields and the water that keep the body alive.
Fear that. Fear the elements as one wicked life-sustaining

force, if the trembling inside you needs to fear something that
adds up to one."

After several meetings and much discussion at the café and at
my apartment, I began to feel the weight lift. I began to see in
other directions. I could no longer find the devotion in me to
pray. It seemed as if I slept more soundly without praying before bedtime. I dreamt less often and I had more energy when
I awoke in the morning. I thought of Enan and became more
aware of my body.

Enan spoke often of his one-act plays that had been pro-
duced. The reviews were not overwhelming, but some of them
were encouraging. He hinted that he was working on a major
piece of theatre that would draw much attention his way. After suggesting — for many weeks — that I would like to hear
about his new project, he finally asked if I wanted to read the
script he had been, in his own words, "wrestling with forever."
I felt enthusiastic that he would want to finally share his work
with me; something I considered to be one of the most private
things imaginable. When he appeared in my doorway with the
script in his hands, he would not come in. The moment he
handed over the thick yellow envelope, he told me he had to
leave. He seemed embarrassed, which was so unlike him.

I remember kissing him and saying, "Thank you." He
walked away, looking slightly worried. Closing the door, I was
anxious to see what the pages contained. I hurried to my
kitchen table, pulling the manuscript from the envelope as I
sat and turned over the top page with enthusiasm and perhaps
with a touch of personal excitement as well, hoping there
would be some reference to me in the words. At first, I was
somewhat shocked by the rawness of the images, but I soon
began to sympathize with his point of view. It was a brash
statement. The details excited me in a very physical manner.
I was forced to step away from the script several times and relieve myself right there against the cool linoleum flooring,
lying on my stomach with one hand down my pants, slipping
my finger in and out and along the narrow gleaming hump of
flesh that led me toward climax. My cheeks burned with pleasure. I was beginning to fear Enan, but I found myself playing
out this fear in my mind as I struggled to satisfy myself. It was

intriguing. He had become my new priest, my sexual confessor, and I told and showed him everything. There was no shame. He had wiped it out.

Several days later, Enan telephoned to let me know he had secured financing for the play. He did not ask what I thought of the script. He avoided the topic, speaking briskly and making a date for later in the afternoon.

At our usual café, he sipped his tea and patiently explained each intricate aspect of the plot to me: "The first part of the play is symbolic of the crucifixion. Act One. When the woman is on the cross and she is naked and screaming as they cut her, she is the Mother of God who has lost her son. It is *she* who has suffered most. It is *she* who was crucified when they nailed up the Saviour. It is *she* who was left to endure the pain for years and years. She was alive. Jesus was dead, otherwise excused."

"But what about Act Two," I had to ask, "where the man beats the woman and accuses her of past crimes against him, tortures her and cuts off her finger and fires the gun into her face?" I felt myself seeping wet between my thighs and I crossed my legs to trap and absorb the new swell of fluid.

Enan raised a hand of protest. He closed his eyes, as if everything was so simple and I did not understand. Calmly he shook his head, then opened his eyes once more.

"Another crucifixion," he insisted, "twentieth-century style. But now the flesh. The sins against the flesh leading to the forced freeing of the mind, or fleeing of the mind. The carnage and its result. The original sin is ours." He swept his longish bangs out of his eyes and leaned closer. "Women made it, and now the flesh must keep coming forever. It keeps squeezing out of the stink hole. You like that? Yes. Stink hole made that way by what enters it. How we are destined to always torture each other, to enter each other, to occupy, to assault. The flesh keeps coming, excuse the pun. Not funny, hey? Well, the Garden of Eden set the stage. We live for The One. We die for The One, and we live here hurting each other because we are distinctly guilty. The only guilty living things on this planet."

I sipped a glass of water that the waitress had delivered, trying to soothe the burning that seemed to have ignited in my lungs. I touched my cheek with the back of my fingers and blew up, smiling in an apologetic way before asking, "But who's The One? You know, which end of things? God or the Devil? Who makes us do these things?"

Enan smiled carefully, his fingers reaching to gently trace the outline of my lips, across once and then twice so that it tickled.

He said, "The true question."

After licking the itchiness from my lips, I asked, "And?"

Straightening in his seat, he would not take his eyes from mine. They flicked slightly from corner to corner, needing to connect with what he was offering me. He wanted for me to understand, and I realized that he was somewhat disappointed that I did not grasp the idea. Perhaps it was the entire point of what he was attempting to do with the play. I was about to confess my lack of interpretive skills (often, in the past, having trouble with certain sequences of the Bible) when he said, "It's a matter of social translation. Who is The One?" Enan took hold of my fingers and carefully meshed them with his, "The One is who the people want most."

III

It seemed like years ago, but it was only five weeks since I had agreed to do the play. Enan convinces. He comes from all angles, from every extreme, yet he lives there in the grey area; beyond categorization, beyond right or wrong. If I kneel in the darkness of my bedroom, weakened by the impossibility of the prayers that I knew so intimately before meeting him, I know that he will interrupt me, his image whispering newer, reasonable words for me. If I touch myself in the thrill of morning, the cool sheets against me, I know it will be his fingers slipping in so easily and completely.

Enan pulls off his black turtleneck, then steps out of his equally black denims. I notice the shine of his dark shoes when he sets them — side by side — flush to the wall, the tips facing in. With my eyes closed, I see all of this. With my eyes opened, I see nothing except the still bedroom of my apartment. I do my deed; the one that others are quick to label — filthy. I pleasure myself, for myself and by myself. I think, if this is dirty or filthy, then all of us are dirty and filthy, for this is the feeling that we come from. If the stiff penis and the wet expectant vagina are filthy, then we are filthy. If semen is disgusting and untouchable, then we are disgusting and untouchable. We are naked at birth, yet we are made nervous, even offended, by this nakedness. Here lies the essence of our hypocrisy. The confusion that torments generations of our disgustingly conceived children.

IV

Enan telephones to tell me we are moving to a larger location. The critics are enthused. The majority of reviewers and freedom of expression spokespeople have jumped onto the bandwagon. Others are furious, rampant with rage and peddling morality like so much middle-American lemonade. "They're all just word-bashing each other. It goes on and on. Nothing changes," Enan explains. "A man believes what he believes. Play with that." Then he stops and I wait as he braces the necessary silence that will empower his coming words.

His voice through the wire:

"Values and ideals are crumbling. People are a might defensive right about now. The world developing so many cracks. We fit in there. Only a matter of time before it opens wide for us."

Later, in a vacant ornate-ceilinged theater, I ask him what I have waited to ask since his telephone call:

"How? How is the world opening?" I have come to need his replies in ways I could never possibly explain.

He steps down the wide, deep stairway, his footsteps silent against the scarlet carpeting. Glancing at the walls, he says, "The people are."

"For what?"

He says, "Everything they've always wanted."

Regarding the rich sculpted circles in the ceiling, he touches his cheek with a delicateness that thrills me. His eyes trace down, along the Roman plaster faces on the walls. He flicks his head to the side, tossing his bangs out of his eyes. The walls are a deep red. The Roman faces are cream-coloured.

Enan smiles secretly. "The Romans are everywhere," he says, nodding to himself. "People never forget what happened.

Conquerors. The Romans. The British Empire. The Nazis. Now, the Americans."

I cannot suppress my enthusiasm. I have to say, "Very classy place."

Enan stares at me and his eyes take in my body with a look of slow certainty. Then he questions my needs. He asks me if I was thinking of him this morning. Did I hear him whispering for me last night when he was half way across the city, writing me so indelibly into his thoughts? He asks me this each day we are apart and he has made it real. He makes everything real. His larger-than-life personality will not leave abstractions to their flimsy selves. Action. He is a shaper of thin air, gouging out his cerebral intentions, uncovering their hidden agenda, instating substance and dimension to what he believes.

I stare into his eyes and they are the same. They are identical, with identical centers of identical concern. Staring, we sense the smiling magic that holds us silently. The symmetry of his eyes dip down to the symmetry of my breasts, my legs trembling so that I must tighten up my lower muscles, stop myself from forcing my body on him, right here beneath the steady faces of the Roman guards and emperors.

V

It ends in fire, of course. Four weeks into production at the new location, the theater is set ablaze. Groups with powerful, almost vicious, wills have been picketing the site since the first performance at the larger venue.

From the play's inception, Enan has been adamant about securing insurance coverage. He files to collect the payment.

"I expected this," he tells me over lunch at our new meeting place — Bistro Amour. He lifts a forkful of spinach quiche and chews. "It's all part of the play." He flips through the script that rests beside his plate. The script seems to be thickening each day. Page 6,567. Right there." Stabbing the page with his finger, he confirms by reading, "Fanatics burn down complex. Production moves to larger facility — Radio City Music Hall. Exterior. Wide shot." He laughs, "I've incorporated movie lingo. Keeping up my hopes." Then he tears out the page, crumples it into a ball, and tosses it over his shoulder into the empty booth behind him. "Destroy the evidence. Of hope, I mean."

I shake my head, amused, happy that he is capable of always retaining his sense of humour, against all odds.

"Everything is out of union," he says, scanning the floor.

I do not really want to, but I must inform him of the death threats I have been receiving. First on the telephone, then — after changing my number — notes posted to my door. It is something that needs telling, sharing. Comfort. Quickly flipping the pages to an earlier scene, he briskly rips out another page, then rather indignantly proclaims, "I wouldn't know anything about that."

I sigh and rub my face. "Not funny. I'm going to have to move."

"So sue me," he says, but when he sees that my spirits are low, he adopts a more caring tone. "Get some rest. The production is suspended for a month."

"Radio City Music Hall," I say, forcing a smile. "Next stop. Who'd have ever thought?"

Enan smiles with closed lips, his jaw working as he chews, swallows, then takes a big gulp of milk. It leaves a moustache and I wipe it away, then slowly lick my fingers for him.

"The top," he says. "Rising to the top. You see?" He pokes his fork against the air between us. "Everything starts in the gutter, washes out, calms down, holds its force, but dilutes itself a teeny bit at a time to accommodate a wider audience. We'll be a trifle more artsy at Radio City Music Hall. We'll be coy and double-entendre. We'll get the same message across, but it will be sublimated. People won't know what hit them, until they wake in the middle of the night, boldly facing their instincts. Their sexual hunger will seem unbearable, and they'll tangle with each other until they have untangled the disorder that is the pure energy of sex, until the momentum becomes monotony and they expect every movement, languidly face their boredom. Then comes the affairs with an adequate sampling of men or women. Finally — when these possibilities have been exhausted — they'll seduce their children in their cozy beds because this is the ultimate offense. The blow against creation. Supreme taboo. The big no-no that keeps popping up on television or in the papers so we can become completely familiar with it. The more sacrilegious the violence, the more exciting, because not only are we excited by the act, but by the idea that we are railing against the very inkling of creation that is allowing us to perform such atrocities."

Enan pauses to cut through the remaining crust of his quiche. I know that he is thinking about the cheque that he is to pick up in the afternoon from the insurance company. He has received the call this morning. Swallowing the remainder of his milk, he bends across the table and kisses me with his wet, cold lips.

"But let's be artsy and double-entendre," he says, wiping his mouth with his white cloth napkin. "Let's be coy. Maybe we'll even be cute, as long as we split the definitive." He holds up two fingers. "Two meanings," he says, "we'll touch everyone."

VI

I am constantly pursued. Crowds follow me along the streets. They offer slogans that promise to set the world right, to seal its many moral gaps. Words — neatly arranged but theoretically ridiculous. Opposing viewpoints that suit no one. Scuffles break out — not only between the leftists and bullying conservatives but also between the various factions of each extreme. People shout in my ears, even though I ignore them completely. I will not be changed. It is the responsibility of no one to give in to such soul-crashing force. One side accuses another. People drop like flies behind me. A stab wound here, gunfire there. The police are obliged to grant me an escort: Two officers who are successful in evading the crowd, briskly leading me away, and then raping me without mercy in an alleyway.

"You asked for it," they tell me. "Who do you think you are?" one of them says as he tucks in the tail of his blue shirt after elaborately emptying his bladder against my violated body. The other one fixes the knot of his navy blue tie. He says, in a sing-song tone, "I've seen your show, missy."

Weeping and clutching at my clothes, I shout through the dampness and stench, "I'm an actress."

"You're just a disgusting cunt who gets off on it. It's no act."

They both laugh. They straighten their hats the way that

only policemen can. Their power is the supreme power of what
is common. They hold the choice of liberty or persecution in
their hands. They are able to send you on to the higher powers,
to have you judged by the system that will not rest until it
finds change in you. Policemen are the Limbo men. They are
outside of the law, yet they are the law themselves.

"We're actors too," they say, laughing at the idea. "Isn't
everyone?" They toss me a folded square of paper and stroll off
toward the dimly lighted movement at the opening of the
black alleyway. I wonder momentarily about that light. Perhaps it comes from an opened backstage door. I look up and see
the thin edges of the buildings, the tiny lights like stars above
me. The vague impression of a black metal catwalk. With a
shudder of recognition, I sit up and feel the semen running out
of me. Unfolding the paper, I discover it is a rental form from
a costume bank. Enan's signature is scrawled across the bottom. I recognize the flow of letters from my pay cheques. I read
the words on the order as if I have practiced this moment for
my entire life: "2 times Item number 12 — Policemen outfits.
Complete."

The lights begin to fade out. The crowd is on its feet, cheer-
ing, impelled by the energy of opposing beliefs. Blatant
falsehoods and obvious truths. They brace these undertows,
unwilling to admit to the confusion charging out of them, as
they wrestle with a sense of what the play is concerned with.
The force of their applause — to punctuate or drive off the
ambiguity, hands reddening in reply. Snapping their palms
against each other, their minds flash with inane speculation,
Must I cast out this uncertainty or struggle to understand it?
Yes, I do. I almost do. And if not, then to pretend. And the
rush swells greater, the audience craving mortally to sit pretty
with The One. To understand anything at all that would justify
the price of the ticket, stamped 'life' with a small L.

From between my body, a murky fluid dribbles down onto
the asphalt. I cannot see a thing as I stand on the large black
stage. The lights will not rise. There is only sound; applause —
hollow and sharply snapping against my eardrums. The audience is noticeably pleased that I am left sightless, they too
finding familiarity, comfort in the dark.

The warm fluid chills and thins, slipping faster down my

legs. But enough has emptied within me to splice the continuum. I am a woman. I am open, vulnerable. I wonder: *This semen, is it real or just a liquid substitute pumped into me for the performance?*

Enan has told me, The One is what stirs beyond the connecting point when a woman is entered by a man and they both shudder divinely, sensing something — beyond their own skins — warmly embracing them. It is that special, non-physical place connecting heart to gut. It directs compassion and brutality. It kisses and it kills.

Roses drift through the darkness and tumble at my feet. I can smell their scent. I step on them, aware of both the silky petals and the harsh pin-pointed thorns. Hypocrisy has always commanded passionate replies. I am human and when I turn both ways at once, energy conflicts, clashes and multiplies itself by two. No solitary form of belief is ever mutually acceptable. Enan has told me so. And I believe in him. And I believe in myself. Duality being the only thorough and solely uncontestable truth.

Rabbit's Pa

I
LORNA

The cat jumped down the trailer vent with a spring rabbit in its jaws. I heard its paws hit the chipped countertop then strike the linoleum with a clunky sound. The rabbit was soft and furry and bulged around the edges. It was ginger-coloured and the cat would not drop it. Instead, the cat stood next to its kittens and stared at them. The kittens sniffed nervously.

I did not care what the cat brought in anymore. There was no stopping it. Jordan would look after the disposal. Things of this nature I leave to him.

He is outside in the misty darkness. I hear him whispering and then I hear him stop and curse angrily, shouting in a strange, overly dramatic voice, "SLOWLY, LIPS OPENING, HE SMILES LIKE THE SLICING OF A KNIFE." He figures himself to be a poet, but he's more dangerous than anything else. His voice carries and I think of the neighbours running parallel to us in their motor homes. Ours is the worst of them all. Ours is a wreck with cracked beige fiberglass and bald tires, parked like forever in this mud hole surrounded by black trees.

I roll over in bed and stare at the white panelling. I tap it with my fingernail, sensing the hollow impression inside of me. The feeling brings other things to mind, makes me wet with certain thoughts. Gently, I touch my breast. I trace the nipple and wait for Jordan's screaming to stop.

"GASOLINE," Jordan shouts. I can picture his thin neck tightening up with the fury of what clutches him. That's all I can see when I hear him shouting in the distance like that. His skin pulling close around the words. "GIMME SOME GASOLINE AND I'LL GET THE HELL OUT OF HERE."

I swallow and begin to hum a song I remember from my grandmother. She hummed it while she rocked me as a child in her chair. It is a religious song but I can't remember the name, or the words. I hum it sweetly, savouring the lull. Then I feel the cat's weight landing on the edge of the bed behind me. I feel its paws stepping and then something dropping. Something falling from its mouth.

Jordan: "HEY! WHAT? YEAH, WELL SHUT UP YOURSELF." His voice comes closer, "YOU JUST TRY IT FOR A CHANGE."

The cat meows once to get my attention, then purrs, rubbing its warm head against my back, against the cotton of my nightdress. I cannot turn. I will not. I wait until the trailer door swings open and I hear Jordan stepping in, mumbling and stomping mud from his boots.

"Hey!" he says instantly. "What's that dead there?"

I turn my head and see Jordan standing inside the narrow door, watching the cat move against me. He watches and I roll over, the nightdress pulling at my legs. I tug it free, seeing him in the soft shadows cast from the battery-operated light on the table. The glow making him look so warm and quiet.

"What're you doing?" I ask.

"I don't know," he says. He stands exactly six feet tall and his blonde hair is a dirty brown from the mist. His face is taut; shallow cheeks and a heavy jawline. His eyes pull me in. His eyes are not watching me but they pull me in just the same until I have to look at what he is watching.

I see the white cat lift the rabbit in its jaws. It turns and plunks down from the bed, moves along the short corridor to a place beneath the sink where the three kittens lay curled together in a box. The cat jumps in and lets the rabbit drop from her jaws.

I think of my belly. Jordan looks at me and I look at him. I have this urge to touch my stomach. I want to show him what I've been keeping a secret, but the image of the rabbit dropping from the cat's jaws has startled me.

I sit up and slip my legs over the edge of the bed. The linoleum is cool. I take my feet back and tug at the night dress, pulling at the hem where it has slid up around my thighs.

Jordan watches, the soft battery light in his eyes and on his cheek. He stares at my legs, then covers his face with one palm, tilts back his head and breathes heavily into his hand. I hear the sound like breath through a mask. A man struggling behind the screen of an oxygen tent. I picture him dying. He'd like that. He's tragic. Always making a performance out of pain. Right now he has this terrible toothache. Had it for days, maybe weeks. But there is nothing to do. We have no money for pills. We have no money for the dentist. We are in the midst of the woods, in this trailer park with no gasoline. I imagine myself pulling the tooth from his jaws. I imagine myself bending and popping the jagged bottom from its roots, tearing out the cavity. Then I think of my belly, and cringe, going weak in the knees.

Jordan moans a little, gingerly pushing at his cheek with his fingers. He watches my legs while he does this, his eyes tracing up, and I know the battery-light is revealing what's underneath my nightdress. I can tell by the way his eyes stop when they find my breasts.

One night, a while ago, while he was pleasing himself with the sight of my body like this and touching his cheek, I remember him saying, "Can't you feel the life pull of death?" He's said this before. He's said it after sitting in silence for hours, staring at the cat with her kittens sucking and pushing with their paws. "Look," he said, pointing at how they were feeding. "It's what they're draining." Then he tapped his cheek and winced, finding the tender points on my body with his eyes. "It's the same sort of throbbing in here."

Jordan holds the rabbit in his hands. He stares down at the loose way it moves when he shifts his fingers. Then he turns for the door and crashes out. I hear him running off, his boots sucking mud, then the off-rhythm splashing as he hits an occasional puddle. Then silence. But I know he is breathing. I can almost hear the sound inside of me. Or is it Jordan's breath that tickles and sometimes makes me shiver?

A smile comes. For some reason I remember the first time Jordan told me he loved me. He was eating cherry jello from a plastic cup and he slowly raised a spoonful of the shaky substance, held it level with my lips. I saw the light sheening in contorted geometrical shapes.

"Have some," he said, nodding his head once.

I opened my mouth and he slid the spoon in. It was then, as I felt the rubbery coolness slip around the insides of my mouth, smoothly dissolve and melt — sweet and warm with the taste of cherries — that I heard him say it. He was watching me with a look of amusement and total devotion.

"It comes apart and melts cool then warm in your mouth, like love," he said. "I love you," he said, two years ago, but there was something in the way he said it; the way he truly meant it that sent tingling shards of fear through my body, like a delicate, glass sculpture splintering within.

II
JORDAN

"My wife is burdened with a great measure of misunderstanding." I tell this to the rabbit. Even though the rabbit cannot hear, it is consoling to tell him. He understands what I'm feeling and how it needs to be said. He's dead and so there's no mistaking the scope of what he knows, and how it's more than any of us presently hold in our heads.

My breath is awkward and stumbling, as are my legs. My tooth and gums are pulsing around the cavity. The cavity has a pulse all to itself; decay possessing its own slow heartbeat and set of intentions. I pause at the edge of the shadowed trees and turn, look back at the rows of trailers gleaming dirty-white beneath the blue-black sky. I need to take a breath because everything is so still it scares me into realizing just where I am; the position of my feet and the eyes I'm seeing out through, but can't see back into my head with.

"What do you think," I hear myself saying. I hold up the rabbit so it can see. "There's something in that, hey? The way they look. Glowing; almost sacred. The meek shall inherit... well, you know the rest. Us being the meek." I laugh at that one and move to toss the rabbit into the trees with the rest of the dead things I've disposed of. But I stop myself, my stomach speaking up for what I was blind to see.

"What am I doing?" I say. I say this to the rabbit as I touch its paws, stroke them and feel the natural strands; the smooth growth of fur.

"Whom I affectionately refer to as Stew. You're my rabbit and I'm your pa. I'm a rabbit's pa." I smile at that one, stare off into the trees because they're so black and unmoving. "I'm lucky 'cause I'm a rabbit's pa." I laugh, the force coming up like lava. I laugh until I cough, choking. "You hear that Stew," I gasp, lifting the rabbit's lifeless head from its slump. Using my fingers, I make it nod. It agrees with me, absolutely. But, suddenly, the fun is gone. The fun is gone. I look toward the trailer and realize, the fun is gone.

"You hear that," I say to the rabbit, staring at its glassy, hollow eyes. "But what would you know about fun, anyway? Just look at you."

III
LORNA

My fingers move to the place. The silence and the misty air from the opened trailer window fill me with a wild sensuality. Woods and darkness reminding me of the patch between my legs. Slow entry, followed by a dank welcome. The thought of the child inside me makes it even worse. I lift my hips and use both hands to tug the nightdress up until it is away from my legs. Lifting my bum from the cool sheets, I rise, then settle, ease my thighs apart with one finger working, curling at the place beneath my warm belly. Slipping in, easily and purely and wet coming out; the tip of one, then two. Drawing in, I rise with the thrill, lift and settle, a rush of pleasure forcing my groin higher.

Breathing, I smell the sweetness of rain releasing and wish I was outside in the grass with the water coming down against my warm skin, now warmer. Dreams of watching my own naked body, facing the sky and the clean pure rain, clean rain coming, transparent and washing clean, gently striking, stroking, dribbling as it courses cool then warm, beading and releasing. Rain all over me as I move with the wild fragrant grass fresh and alive beneath me, around me. Surrounded and

sucked by moistness. Hips up, not touching. The muddy
ground wanting to smear its kiss against my bum. Hips lifting,
staying up, quivering as the rain releases, hissing like hot shivers, as I release the rain and taste it so sweetly afterwards, taste
it on my lips and smile with my eyes closed, such sleepy satisfaction that I do not first realize that I am covered in mud, the
hardening of it against the curves of my skin, the trailer I have
crawled from, the door open, and my nakedness beneath the
brown mask that has been fitted to my skin. Looking up at the
trailer's opened door, I see Jordan standing next to it, staring, staring down, his lips moving silently, certain words still in his head.

"It was wonderful," I say and, unexpectedly, he smiles and
holds the rabbit toward me with both hands. And it's alive. I
think it's alive. Trembling and easily convinced, I see it move,
but its just him moving the rabbit's head with his fingers behind its neck. It's just him.

The kittens race, half sideways, half bouncing, chasing each
other. One of the small white ones clings to its mother's leg. It
bites and clings as the mother walks. Jordan laughs, points
with the wooden spoon he's just pulled from the stew. Liquid
spots the linoleum. I rush and wipe it up with the towel I'm
drying my hair with. I have washed myself from top to bottom
in the stand-up shower stall next to the bed. The pressure is
slow and the water dribbles. With the hand-held nozzle in
hand, I guide the trickling against each section of skin. It takes
half an hour to complete the job. It takes that long to get clean.

The white mother cat stares up at the stove. I wonder about
the father of her kittens. I wonder about seeing him. Always a
mother with her kittens, but where is the father? Where is the
father? I want to scream at this realization. I want to rush outside and tear up the grass, slash down all the trees, strike a
blow at nature as punishment for the rules it has set for us.
The father is roaming. The father is always roaming. The
mother alone with her kittens. I look at Jordan and hold back
the tears. My bones are aching and I feel so useless.

The mother cat watches the stew. It licks its pink nose with
a tiny pink tongue, and waits. I see the almost transparent pink
inside its ears. The red sheen of light striking blood in its eyes.
It stands and does not move. The three kittens are behind her,
jumping on her back, slapping at her tail, biting her legs.

IV
JORDAN

I think, if I had some gasoline we could go somewhere. A drive would be nice. I could handle the desert. Arizona. Indian art. Big pottery. Masks, maybe. Magic. Any change would be welcomed after four months of woods; flies, rain, bog, mud, and sharp-tangled bush. Like my thoughts, now, sharp-tangled and wanting to prick me.

"Ow!" A kitten has its needle claws in my leg, climbing. I quickly bend from where I'm sitting to look under the table, shake the kitten loose, then look up to see I've spilled my coffee. Lorna sits across from me. She's reading an old magazine. Something about sex. My eyes scan the headline: "Sex in your seventies."

"What're you reading?" I ask.

Lorna shakes her head without looking up. Her eyes are busy. A few seconds later, she says, "Nothing."

"Oh," I say, flicking my fingers in the spilled coffee, flicking it her way so that she looks straight up at me and smiles with a slicing "ha-ha" of sarcasm.

V
LORNA

The cat scratches at the door. I've closed the vent since the rain started. The kittens are everywhere; climbing up on the counter and knocking things over, racing up the bed sheets as if in competition, down across the floor, pouncing all of them. I stand and let the cat in.

"Watch it," says Jordan. "Don't push your luck."

I don't say anything to him. I ignore him after having to do what I do to myself. He won't touch me lately. He won't touch me, but I know he's doing it to himself in the bathroom. I listen and I hear the pages turn in there. He's got magazines in there and I hear the pages rustling, then stop. The side of his half-closed fist soft but fast, striking home.

I don't look at him. We're separate. We do it to ourselves. We sleep and sleep close with comfort, snuggling, but everything else we do alone.

Opening the door, I see the cat has something in its mouth;

a grey clump of fur with thin stem-like legs, twitching. It's too small to be a mouse, but it looks like one. A shrew.

"Get out," I say, jerking and kicking forward. The cat hunches down, tries to squeeze by. I kick and its eyes are mean, steady, vicious. It hunches lower and backs out. I close the door and turn to Jordan. I glare at him. He's reading the article I was just reading. A few seconds of absolute silence, before he looks up at me.

"What?" he says. "Lorna, what's your problem now?"

"We've got to get away from these woods."

Jordan laughs and looks back at the magazine. He flicks a page.

VI
JORDAN

Today alone: first a shrew, then a bird, four more shrews, followed by a rabbit. Lorna tells me this. Lifting her hands from the table, she looks over my shoulder, fixes her vacant stare on the curtain that's pulled across the driver's cab. She counts the dead things on her fingers; one shrew, a dead bird, four shrews, a rabbit.

I look to my right, out the Plexiglas window that's set above our table.

"Listen," says Lorna. "Please."

I face her, "What?"

"What're you watching?"

"The rain's stopped." My eyelids ease shut. "I'm tired," I say. My lips feel numb. I think of my speech. It's slow and sticky. I speak without looking, letting my words slip out into darkness.

"Tomorrow. I'll get some gasoline, tomorrow and — "

"Where? Where?"

"And then we'll go for a ride. A slow one, looking — "

"Where?"

I open my eyes and watch her. Her long, dark hair is wet from the shower. It hangs to her bare shoulders. She's sitting there with the towel still wrapped around herself. I stare at the shadowed crevice between her breasts; the curving rise of perfect balance above the edge of the towel line. A fragrance breezes to me. It is sweet and gentle; a perfumed soapy smell that calms me, like a memory of childhood. Lorna is smiling

with a tiny fraction of her bottom lip caught behind a tooth.
She looks cute, the way the tooth catches her lip like that. It
makes her seem younger, unknowing, almost adolescent. She
seems to be changing. I just notice this now. The features of
her face have softened in the past few weeks. Not only that —
a few extra pounds have filled out certain areas of her body.

"Gasoline," I say, emphasizing the syllables — good and
slow — so the word sounds dangerous. "Gas–o–line."

Lorna shakes her head, but the action is slight and she is
unsure of it. Her eyes widen, asking for more; detecting the
promise of rough sexuality. Denying but accepting it, wanting.
With both hands she grips the edge of the towel where it's
tucked in, waiting to unfurl the material.

"GAS — O — LINE," I implore, eyes skimming down the
fabric.

Lorna's fingers freeze against the top line of the towel. She
hears the cat scratching at the door. The cat is not meowing. It
has something in its mouth. Lorna has something in her
mouth too, but she won't say it. She won't let it drop.

I reach into my pants pocket and shift in my seat, pull out
the rabbit's paw and lay it on the table. I let her see it, then lift
it by the bloody end, pull one of the tendons that's dangling
loose. The digits spread away from themselves. I pull and release, watch the digits pulse.

"It's alive," I whisper.

Lorna touches her stomach and gasps. She turns white as a
ghost.

"What's the matter?" I ask her. "Something you ate?"

VII
LORNA

"Nothing," I say. But I feel the rabbit's paw opening in my
stomach. I feel the stirring. Jordan only pretends to support life
by pulling that paw. I support real life inside of me. But this life
is real and will not stop after the strings are let go. I stand and
hold the towel against me, afraid of revealing myself to Jordan.
I want to move away, but I cannot. I have to watch the short
furry fingers spread and close. I have to feel them inside of me.

"I'm the rabbit's pa," Jordan says in an electric fit of exhaustion, laughing and laughing through a dry throat.

With the sounds of the cat scratching at the door foremost in my mind, I nod and step closer to him. I lift the bottom edge of the towel with both hands and let him walk the rabbit's paw up across my thighs.

"The wilderness," he says, nervously catching a glimpse of my eyes, and nibbling on his bottom lip. "It has to go back, to home."

"Yes," I say. And he walks the rabbit in, uses his thumb and index finger to show it the way. The claws smooth and blunted. The fur so soft, slipping quickly in. Jordan pulls the tendons and I feel the sweet pulsing inside of me.

I slap his hands away and grasp between my legs, gently tug the tendons myself. Everything inside of me. Me, I think, closing my eyes to imagine my profile in the mirror, my naked stomach round and throbbing, like something kicking slowly inside. Muddled sounds of wet squeaking. Rabbits dropping out of me.

VIII
JORDAN

Six a.m. with a flashlight I don't need because it's almost light, I crouch on the dirt road and feed a thin plastic tube into the gas tank of this big pick-up truck. No one seems to be alive in the backwoods at this time of morning, and I don't want to see anyone. In this light they'd seem way too sharp and real. Sight of someone like a dream punch; limbs twitching as I wake.

Just borrowing a little. Anyone with this much gasoline can afford to lose a little. If I can fill the red plastic container three or four times, it'll be enough to get us halfway out of the woods, somewhere in between; pastures or prairies, a middle point that separates woods from desert.

Anyone who leaves a pick-up alone on a backroad like this deserves to have their gasoline stolen. I lick my lips, then suck on the yellow-tinted tube to get the flow going. I suck real hard, feel the stinging, I spit and push the tube into the red container. A spattering of dribbles, then the flow. I spit again. Wipe good and hard at my lips.

"This'll do it," I say, only noticing the words a few seconds after saying them, so I finish it, "This is a start. This is a good start. Out of here."

A rip-buzzing comes to life in the distance. I flinch and the tube slips out of the container. Gasoline spills around my feet, the thin stream hitting my tattered sneakers, soaking into the holes along the edges, wetting my socks and toes in an extra-cold way. I wrestle with the tube to fit it back in. Someone is chainsawing wood. Someone is using this pick-up to haul it. A man's hands on a chainsaw — far off in the woods — and it's buzzing like crazy.

"HEY!"

I suck breath and my head jolts up. A neck muscle flinches and cramps, pulling down on the left side of my face, but I have to ignore it.

"Didn't figger dere was two of us," the man sneers. "Huh?" He's smoking a cigarette. He takes a deep draw, then looks at the long-sharp-red-hot tip. "What ya want dat gasleen for? You're not go'n nowhere."

I shake my head, shrug my shoulders, stand, slip my hands into my back pockets, shake my head again.

"Git away from dere," he says, his words almost hissing.

I look at the container and inch away from it. I look at the container as if it's a meal and I'm starving. It's like that. No difference. My body hungry for wanting out of here.

"Move," says the man. He's a big man, wearing a red and black lumberjacket. He's wearing loose worn jeans and work boots. His hair is short, thick and white with a yellow tinge along the bang even though he can't be more than forty.

"You fuh'k wit my gasleen," he says. "You know who I'm?"

I shake my head, glancing at the container. I can see the shadow of the fluid inside. It's rising slow, getting full, and I think of making a grab for it. I could grab it and make a run. I could do that. It'd only take a second. Just to grab and turn and forget about what's coming behind me.

"Don't try't," says the man.

The chainsaw rips and screeches like a mechanical horse, rearing.

"Blackstrap Hawco," says the man. "You 'member my name, ya piece a shit?" He goes for me with the cigarette

clamped between his teeth. He swings but misses. I get him in
a headlock and squeeze. I squeeze and squeeze until I hear him
choking and he's punching at my stomach, but my stomach
can take it. It's tight from hunger, and the muscles don't let
nothing through.

The chainsaw buzzes and rears, gallops through the confusion, tearing down the land.

I squeeze until the punches come slower and my feet feel
warm. My feet feel strangely hot until they're unbearably hot
and my legs are burning, then scorching like the static of my
steady scream. I release and the man drops to the ground, rolling away from me and clawing at his throat. He's trying to
breathe and I remember the cigarette that was in his mouth
and the gasoline that my sneakers soaked up. I remember for
an instant as I look at my legs. There are flames on me like
trickery, rising and hazy, orange, visible then gone, but still
there, creeping up through the smoke that's filling my nostrils
with the smell of myself cooking. And I'm down too, rolling
and kicking, gasping because my chest is cold despite the heat.
Through the haze of my flesh, I see a mirage; the vastness of a
desert, the dry wind roaring toward my face, coming like a wall
of invisible water, waiting to strike and kill me with thirst. My
hair shrivelling. That smell of skin tightening against a dry
wind that keeps getting hotter, until the skin splits and the lips
crack, streaming some mystery fluid.

And through the wavering flames, I see the man on his
knees struggling to throw dirt on me until the fire's out, the
man stumbling to his feet, slamming the pick-up door — a
boom through the crackling — and racing off. Screaming, I
hear the screech of the chainsaw climbing for the sky to slash
a hole for me — until my screams and that ripping sound find
their place inside each other, and are one and the same. Unan-
swerable and complete.

IX
LORNA

The kittens race and roll each other to the ground. I watch
them play. They are not thinking of their mother at all. Their
mother is no longer scratching and they are oblivious to her.

They couldn't care less. They are heartless. Tiny tongues and mouths, stupid and laughing through that soft fur. I gather them up; one by one, open the door and toss them out. I am crying. I am crying as I do this. Wiping at my nose, I slam the door. There's a silence that frightens me. No tiny meows or paws softly clumping across the linoleum. I throw myself onto the bed and cry. I cry the most I've done in years and suddenly — for some silent reason — I think of Jordan. I sit up and wipe at my eyes with the butts of both hands. I sit cross-legged on the bed, tugging at my nightdress, arranging it beneath me like I'm expecting someone; a visitor, a special guest.

The cat is meowing outside. Inside, I lay back and touch myself. Inside, I think of Jordan and his height and his nakedness; his big hand holding the severed paw. Whispering: "It's good luck." I think of Jordan as a father and it makes me smile. I can't concentrate. A feeling is making me restless, because I don't know what it is. I've got to sit up again. I see Jordan holding a baby in his arms, looking down, startled and wondering what to do. It seems funny and I blurt out a laugh, then another and soon I'm laughing steadily, until the feeling moves off so that I don't understand it anymore and I'm crying instead for the humour having pulled away from me the way it did; realizing it was really sadness all along, disguised and buried beneath my dumb giggling. "Stupid," I whisper through teeth set tight against each other, "Stupid, stupid..." I'm holding myself around the belly with my arms, rocking back and forth on the covered foam mattress. My back keeps whacking the panelling behind me, so I stop and let my feet hang over the edge of the bed. Bare toes tilt down to test the cool linoleum. The chill makes me smile to myself and I stand and walk across the tiles. I see the rabbit's paw is resting on the white-topped table. Jordan had been playing with it and slipped his big gold wedding band on one of the digits. It's still there and I pick it up and it's stiff and the digits don't spread anymore when I tug on the pieces that're hanging out. A thin string of tendon snaps off between my fingers and it breaks something open inside of me, too, because I suddenly can't stop shivering. A sweat-like fever rises from the realization that there's no way now of hiding from the plain truth; this understanding of what I'm actually holding in my hand.

The Hole That Must Be Filled

I

ABSOLUTE VACANCY

The roof is open above us and grey doves float from wall to wall, gliding against the blue, like ashes held by a water's languid current. On still wings, they drift before settling atop the building's high walls, its desolate concrete shores running vertical and intruding upon the sky.

At my bare feet, pigeons bob along the floor, stepping closer and pecking for my toes. They do not bother Vee. Standing in the shadows of the cement stairwell, she seems as abandoned as the expansiveness of this warehouse. Only half of her face is discernible, her skin splotched shades of mangled green and brown. A single bloodshot eye observes me, twitching as it blinks. She has been curious like this for months, appearing each morning and remaining until the light wanes and stretches across the cool cement floor. It is then that she gradually recedes, as if the progression of dusk's shadows has skillfully pried her loose.

Darkness breeds a sense of dislocation, further inciting the grief-stricken of Slattery West. Frantic bellowing and the disgruntled stomping of feet compels them toward action.

Below the broken windows that gape like mouths stunned by a blow, footsteps slap the pavement. Crazed sounds carry up to me as if through a tunnel. People continuously running, alone or in clustered groups. They are wordless and fleeing; one solid clot of fear wresting their bodies out of shape.

Vee does not return at night. Although sometimes, when I am forced to swallow a handful of Corium to sleep — deep and dreamless — I have felt a body climbing into bed beside me, holding me closely around my shoulders and crying. Hiccuping. Giggling hesitantly.

My mattress is pushed off into a corner of the building. A minor section of roof remains in the space above me. It covers approximately eleven feet square. I am protected, but the risk of collapse remains a concern. When it rains, I can sit with my legs pulled up close to my chest and watch the water strike the smooth grey concrete, collect in shallow glassy puddles. The rain rarely blows in on me. There is little wind. Although, occasionally, I sense a few stray drops coolly dabbing my skin, cruelly hinting at the haphazard possibilities of spiritual refreshment.

My wife does not know where I am. I telephone once a week to blankly inform her that I am healthy and alive. She seeks comfort elsewhere. Our bond has been afflicted by the most tyrannical despoiler of contentment. Her mother, a retired loans officer, has moved into our house, and they console each other over the death of Vee.

I do not require consoling. I have discovered this place, and its stark surroundings mirror the absolute vacancy of these feelings that have overtaken me. It is as if I have propped this structure up around me from the sighs and regrets that have become my preoccupation.

Standing from my mattress, I move toward the window nearest me. The steel grid — once set with small square panes — is bent and rusted. Tiny points of glass protrude from the edges. Each window casing is rectangular and all are set in rows along the extended walls. Pushing my face flush to the grid, I glance eastward, brace the great distance where Slattery Street runs into the city, night leading toward faint light, which purposefully connects to neon colours, punching the darkness. To the west, Slattery dips into pitch blackness, the rutty asphalt only vaguely lit by firelight before vanishing. I have walked in that direction, ebbing as far as despair will allow before the rubble blocked my path. Filthy chunks of cement, and oily swamps, sandflies buzzing, ghost-like and spirited in their invisibility. Black hearts strewn everywhere, faintly pumping, stogged by their new drug-like lag of anguish. For weeks after the death, I lived in the numbed self-absorption of that wayward region, slowly working my way up Slattery, toward this vacant building, to find my niche in the ruins of a more comfortable desolation.

II
DREAM VACATION

One knows where one belongs; the massiveness of this abandoned warehouse pins me to the smallness that I accept as mine. I am insignificant in its hollow and remain here for as long as possible before I must walk toward the city for medication. Sleep in the form of tiny capsules, green and smooth in my hand, almost metallic in the way they roll against each other. Additional supplies are required. Tins of corned beef, Irish stew, green peas, corn, bottled water. I secure a bundle of outdated newspapers for the nightly fires. Rotten beams of wood are torn loose from the collapsed walls. Rubble is despair's fuel. It is unattached, dislocated and belonging no where. Only the raging brashness of fire can alter its form, the blossoming of flames. The body breathes, the brittle frame of skin and memory is granted warmth.

In the city, the doctor asks me how I am. I tell him I cannot sleep. What else is there to say? Awake, always. A constant, insubstantial companion to myself.

"You take these," he says, writing a script for the proper medication. "They won't hurt you as long as you don't take more than the prescribed amount. One every eight hours."

"Certainly," I tell him. "Of course," I insist, my fingers extended for the white paper that will surely purify, alleviate the heaviness that has formed like an insidiously slow-cracking black stone in my soul.

In the pharmacy below his office, I charge the script to my wife's health plan. I charge my supplies to her grocery account. We owe each other nothing, but everything as well, and the vacuum inspired by such extremes hugs and shoves at our distant bodies, disparity evoking our retarded slur of love.

At dusk, walking back toward the abandoned buildings, I listen to the bleak harmony of moans emitting from the three-storey hollows. Their pleas are brutally suggestive, as if night is a mere underling to the truer pessimism they desire.

I lean out my window. Fiery shadows pulse beyond the black windows across from me. Orange and red shadows flicker among the many melancholic shades of bruised hearts, spitting out what ails them; the crackle and snapping of wood. Smoke rising languidly. The sedentary moaning. I lie flat on my mattress and tilt back my head, allowing a clear passageway for the release. Self-condemnation prods like a slanderer into my sores, and I moan in unison with the others, the voices seeming so different, yet absolute and identical in their intentions of loss.

Vee watches me eat my lunch; a tin of cold mushroom stems. I drink the juice. It is murky and rich with salt.

Vee rolls a cola bottle toward me. It clinks along the concrete floor and slows beside where I am sitting. Inside, there is a rolled up note with adolescent hearts drawn along the paper. I pick up the bottle, grip it around its neck, and briskly toss it for the window, where it twirls through the hole and descends in a slow arc. Moments later, I hear the faint flat explosion.

Vee gasps, her single bloodshot eye jerking with fright.

"It's not working," I angrily explain, holding firm, attempting to reason with myself. Vee points a rotting finger my way, her arm slipping from the shadows, lifting into unforgiving light.

"Sweetie." I force the words through hard-edged teeth. "You're dead, baby. Dead."

The air cools off at night. I take a breath and my teeth sting. The air is shrill against my cavities. It jabs into the tender roots like needles. One tooth came out last night in my sleep. Something jagged against the back of my throat woke me and a coughing fit traumatically ensued as I struggled to sit up. My heart punching the sweat through my skin.

There is also an infection in my right hand. A week ago, I scraped it against a piece of rusty steel sticking from the wall. I kept it in my pocket while in the doctor's office, wanting the infection to take its proper course. It has a purpose, a dubious life all its own that wishes to mirror mine. Now, the wound is green around the edges and smells like nothing that has ever struck me. Ingrown toenails swell pink as they inflame the skin, fluid leaking away from me. But I am deserving. My body has sketched the blueprint for my downfall. It aims to turn me out, wanting to break clear of me. I am a traitor, limping through this heart-wrenched limbo. There is a hacksaw beside my bed should anything need to come off. I comfort and nurse the thought: There is no way, ever, of leaving here whole.

Physical realizations slowly displace the debris that is my flimsy inner self. The ignorant and assuming portions of my soul dim, and only the sturdy truth of biological heritage remains to soundly outline the complex.

Newspapers blow around me. They circle in slow intriguing whirlwinds. A broadsheet catches against my feet. I read a headline from the travel section: DREAM VACATION. Smugly, I wonder about these words, knowing how they mean so much to me, and an anonymous laugh nervously escapes my chest. It comes unexpectedly, the sound rolling and booming as it fills the warehouse, crackling off into the corners, then bouncing back, as it rushes up to face the sadness of my suddenly sorry expression.

Tonight is a night for sleep. Absolution from heart-racing dread and cold sweats. Five Corium and, in time, my eyelids sink, drag me briskly under. I descend and rise toward a pleasant thoughtless suspension. The dark is warm, deadening my lips. Vee kneels into the mattress and kisses me. I am certain of her position, her chilly hands carefully placed onto my chest. She is everywhere, her breath like fingertips, tingling. Eyes blind but searching, her frigid tongue pries into me. Her hand down my trousers, nipping at my sex with her sexless touch. A mockery made of all, as her tongue throbs and swells against my lame tongue, numbly taunting my lost virility.

Good morning, I think, awaking in a blank state of mind. One thought, *Good morning*. I do not remember sleep. Instead, I recall a lack of sensation, a friendly, yet vaguely perilous void.

The space next to me holds the indentation of a thin body. A fossil set into the mattress, soft and continuing to form. I slip my palm into the crevice. Somewhere, Vee closes her eyes and purrs, longingly.

"Alive," she whispers like a girl with two wet lungs, sunken cheeks, swollen eyes, struggling for air, gurgling, a thickly fluid inquisitive tone glazing each bubbled breath, rounding out, slowly popping, huge transparent membranes snapping open, but offering nothing to claim as reasonable, nothing inside to claim as mine, merely the energy-succeeding systematic release of air. Christ! The marvels of life.

III
INFECTION

A man in a forest-green raglan and a beige scarf tucked inside his lapels walks along the warehouse flooring. His hands are in his pockets, his hair freshly clipped and stylish, trimmed short along his neck.

Tipping back his head, he studiously analyzes the open hole above us, the sky as one huge blue ditch. He does not see me in the far corner, on my mattress, carelessly watching him. Stooping, he picks up a stone and tosses it toward the grey doves.

"Yaahh," he shouts. "Move it." The doves flutter up, swim against the sky, then settle on their shores again. They do not worry about a man so far below, a man so uselessly small. He strolls forward, stares down at the floor, where a wide bar of bird droppings has collected. The man steps back and curses. As if in gesture of retaliation, he whips a short cylinder from his pocket, uncaps it and coaxes out the roll of brittle paper. His hands unfurl the parchment and he holds it up, glancing from wall to wall, whispering to himself. Counting steps, one foot after the other, he walks, the sound of his smooth soles sweeping the concrete.

I stand slowly. Still, he does not see me. Bending forward, I pick up the hacksaw and confidently hold the handle. It fits smoothly into the crevices of my palm. The man's sense of purpose disturbs me to no end. *Off with his head.* This is what Vee would say. Even in adolescence, she quoted from her favourite fairy tale books, announcing these ideas as if to playfully salute the stubbornness of childhood simplicity.

And this is what she whispers now. Behind me, in her place in the derelict stairwell, she whispers, *off with his head*. The easiest solution. I turn to regard her and she is nodding; face half in, half out of the shadows, bloodshot eye burned a deep glossy red by sea water. A tangle of greenish-brown kelp majestically draped around her lovely pale throat. She spits up water and a tiny red fish slips out, flapping speculatively like an untried tongue as it strikes the concrete, inches from the greenish pallor of her toes. Vee's t-shirt is shredded across the front, torn by edges of the most elaborate coral, one cadaverous nipple extending from the fabric. With her steady fingernail, she slices the material. Mangled patches of flesh split open, marring the idolized teenage fullness of her breast. Two words set across the t-shirt: DREAM VACATION, the letters slowly running in a blur.

The man's footsteps fade. I look down at my hand and the gangrene is spreading. The gangrene is the colour of the man's green raglan. Perhaps he has stepped from my wound and now plans to take this structure down; the man, like my hand, threatening to displace me. He will destroy my comfortable desolation. I lift the hacksaw with a start, having momentarily forgotten its presence. Drawing it low and close, I press the wide, razor teeth against my wrist and tug back. The steel points tear into my skin, catch and briskly pop open the surface, until the entire area is raised and red, swelling as I work through the white sweat and the sizzling in my ears. Hacking unsteadily, I find sloppy disappointment in what I am telling myself, how the strokes must be deliberate and forceful, but I find it impossible to accomplish even this measly chore. I am halfway there, dissolving into unconsciousness. The bones splinter, bend and dangle. I see my skeleton somewhere else, an instructor with a pointer, tapping, far away, this hand the only thing covered by skin, this hand connected by a flimsy section of discoloured tendon. My flesh appears white and empty; the greater unmuddied body of another who has built me. The instructor cracking the pointer across one knee. Cracking it. Cracking.

I hear the hacksaw strike the floor, reach with a weightless hand to seize hold of the twitching fingers I am dismantling. I tug them until the hand snaps free, something clicking, the sound distantly buried in me. I swallow. Thick disconnected fingers jerking against the living fingers that hold them. Blood spurts from my arm. Rushing as it does, the red fluid fills the pool of sparkling whiteness that presses in on me, eating up my eyes, then blaring into my ears with a ferocious sound/ buzzing and ringing at once as the building tips sideways, slowly, nicely. One final home-run crack into unconsciousness.

IV
PROVIDENCE

I wake in a hospital bed, my stump wrapped in a bandage. For weeks, I will not say a word, finding no comfort in the packaged sterility of institutionalized answers. They settle nothing. But then I ask the doctor, "When can I leave?" He tells me I can leave whenever I choose, but he does not recommend an early departure. He suggests a course of physiotherapy, just two floors down. He tells me I should telephone someone close to me. He is happy to see that I have spoken. My words have made his day. He explains the availability of professional help. Guidance. Counselling. Nutrition. Exercise. He is calm and patient as he talks about the mind, so that I smile at the importance he entrusts in his shaman beliefs. I understand more than he could ever dream of systematically storing on his clinical chart. My thoughts reel with the undefinability that lurks forever out of reach. No pencil tip. No paper. No synoptic connection. Simply the spirit excreting another chewful of waste.

"Hands-on experience," I want to say to him, but the irony of the thought is much too bitter to expel.

I regain my strength walking the corridors. Three days later, I change into my street clothes, and leave via the stairwell at the end of the hallway. They did not tell me who was responsible for notifying the hospital. They simply said they found me lying in the street toward the end of Slattery. I prompt my own scenarios, imagine the hospital receiving several anxious, yet anonymous, phone calls. Bland voices impressing the need for my well-being, so I could rejoin the stricken of Slattery West and further torture myself. I imagine the muddled calls of those who reside in the buildings surrounding me, those who have felt the death of another, my partners in the tragedy of flesh voiding its soul.

Or, perhaps, it was the man in the forest-green raglan who notified the hospital, wanting to integrate me into his plan, to salvage what little remains of me and claim my innards as a work of industrial resurrection. There was a certain brash clumsiness about the man with his cylinder of blue-veined plans. I call him Providence for his caring mechanical guidance, his struggle to efficiently re-shape the world through the physical and chemical workings of man's ever-wobbly ingenuity.

The man in the forest-green raglan carefully arranges the marker pins on his map. My face is drawn on the head of one such pin. He has stuck me here, and I realize that his heartbeat is rampant and pounding from the concentration of his task, the jerking as a surge of manipulative power, or to the beat of a heartfelt, pitying rhythm. I try to concentrate within myself, to discern the truth, but the images are infinite and evasive. I must admit to myself: Thoughts have no focus. They are merely brief insubstantial shards to which we wrongly, pretentiously, apply depth.

In the concrete building, on first sight of the man, I noticed the furious pulsing behind his raglan in the space above his heart. His plan was not to save the building, but to rescue me from my own neglected body. By condemning and wrecking the structure of my comfortable desolation, he would cast me out into the street, and quickly construct another building to house a variety of stabler lives. Day by day, this man called Providence is wishfully revealing his architectural plans for a new spirituality — clean, livable space that is certain to (and so simply so) absolve and re-shelter the morally bankrupt such as I.

One thought. Fleeting. I stomp it with my foot.

Someone has swept the floor clean in the building while I was away. Someone has straightened my things; my hollow shell of a radio, my tins of food neatly stacked in a pyramid against the wall. My bed has been covered with fresh sheets — the straightest white and pale blue stripes running down the length.

I glance behind me and see the concrete floor, my footprints wet in the faint dust that has settled. It is raining outside, but it is dry in here. Dark with only a vague wash of light through the windows. I look up and see that someone has constructed a makeshift roof of wooden planks. Someone wants to rebuild my life, and I sadly assume it is Vee.

My left hand opens and closes. The fingers stir. They startle me like this; without the presence of their symmetrical twins. My pinky presses awkwardly against the finger beside it. It irritates me to the point of nervous stutter. I wonder where my right hand is at this moment. Being forced to use my left one, it seems as if my sense of focus has been magnetically redirected. I bend the fingers of my left hand and my right-sided thoughts wander elaborately.

Someone is making an appeasing home of this place for me. Or they are attempting to drive me out. My new home beautiful has come to resemble a theatrical stage; a play of utter confusion where I cannot locate a single gritty prop.

All of these things done for me; for or against me. Death of another inflating my sense of identity. My ego threatened by this trauma. Me. It is not the death of Vee that I am mourning. Rather, it is the brilliant light that her demise has cast upon my certain mortality. Snatched from the air as she was, Vee's body has left a gaping hole into which — I realize, one day — I must step.

Kneeling onto the fresh sheets, I rub my palm along the fabric and stare into the concrete corner. I lie down and notice a rat standing on its hind legs; still and watching me with pink infinite eyes. I am tired, my body heavy from the long walk back.

"If I could just get inside of you," I mutter from the woolly clutches of sleep. "Be you."

My eyes are closed. They want to open, but new left-handed dreams tempt me. I see the rat in my head as it chatters humorously, and turns, casually sweeping its thick ribbed tail.

"To be hated so," I sleepily plead, the weight of my exhaustion pleasantly confounding me. "To be despised."

The rat curls its soft, grey body and scampers toward the

safety of the crumbling wall. It sniffs there for a moment, then stops, nervously regarding me.

"To be touched by such ugliness," I quietly cry into my clean pillow slip. And so goes my dream. Lovely seclusion as my lame ego draws in. The startled penis as all of me.

I understand that the sadness I feel is pity for myself, for why should I feel sorrow for Vee? Quite simply, she is dead. She is nothing. Gone. No sadness. No happiness. I am not sorry for her. I am sorry for myself. I am pounding *my* own heart and drowning in *my* own pain. I am so afraid of her hollow sacred breaths that pursue each of mine. I dream belief. I dream a warm hand on my cold shoulder. And I awake with a start to see the closeness of the ceiling. The unbearable beauty of two bugs mating there. One black dot atop the other. My blunt eyes through which I cannot cry.

That night, I hear them moaning and stomping on my roof. Planks are shoved away to tumble down, heavily crash and clatter against the floor. The roof opens up to uncover their disfigured outlines staring down; some of them without hands, arms or legs. Hobbling, awkwardly shuffling, limping slightly forward and back.

They whisper stale phrases to each other; words of standard issue, pronounced flatly in guilt-ridden drones.

"No, no way," whispers one of my neighbours, "he tries, thinking now to rebuild his life. Dumb... misdirected."

Whispers another: "Forget it..."

An eight-foot plank crashes down. Dust languidly rises. I can smell and taste its blandness, or is it the siftings of decay, mingling in my blood? Vee's ashen powder losing its fragrance, settling on my lips.

Whispers: "Could he have saved her? Could he have..."

Long, thick planks of wood collapse inside and beyond me. The black sky opens up, its oppressive weight further encouraging my sense of apathy.

Whispers: "She was young, beautiful girl, growing. And she resembled him, much resembled. Not growing now. No one growing."

Quick laughter.

Dust floating in the air. Brown shovelfuls of dirt settling in my veins. Vee through the haze. Swollen and naked. Round along her belly and thighs. Her throat, her wrists, bloated by death's pregnancy, the splitting of all skin, wider, when black labour hits.

Serious spastic whispers: "Yes, guilt. Smother, dismiss, no concern. Guilt. Life... a single point, one focus, loss of, only of, itself." The solemn voice fades, rushed by a pack of gleeful shrieks, slowly deepening, husky and volatile, saddening against the flimsy thought of hands that now touch nothing. A monotone of dull idiot sobs.

Hands over her crack, Vee pisses through her fingers. Black Juice.

"Daddy," she says, coquettishly biting her lower lip. Arms slowly, mockingly swimming through thin air, she teases. "Rescue," she says, whimpering, tittering, showing me her perfect teeth.

Laughter high above me. My crippled neighbours expelling their amusement. A rumble of mongoloid disjointed stutters, overlapping and feverishly bucking out of synch, "Wuh-wuh-wee nuh-nnknow."

V
MOVING BACK

Rain streams down on me. It patters against the concrete flooring like childish laughter. Children playfully circle me and my wife. We stare out at the ocean where Vee had been swimming. The children hold hands and skip around us, their shrill carefree sing-song deprived of the dense calamity of mature knowledge. Their tone makes them hurtfully one as their words grow more and more insistent. Sweet ocean accompaniment guides their lyrics. Waves. They are singing for our compliance, wanting to bury us up to our necks in sand.

Moving back. The beginning of our vacation. A time of rest from the culmination of stress and work. Outside our hotel room, along the hallway of the fourth floor, I can look down, through the huge pane of the glass compound, to see Vee silently swimming in the pool on the second floor. She glides, expanding and retracting under water, as if each stroke is a breath, drawing her forward.

I watch her resurface at the end of the pool and pause, buoyantly holding onto the edge as she runs a hand over her sleek hair. Seconds later, she gracefully turns to dip back under. She is strengthening her stroke for the rush of the sea. She will swim in it tomorrow. To test the current, she tells me. Enough pretending. Do or die. Sink or swim.

The treason of womanhood prompts her, the extending of her body beyond its self.

"What's your point?" I remember asking her.

"I just have to, Dad."

The ever popular — something to prove. How often have I fallen victim to such social pressures? But Vee was not prepared for the fleeing from all that can and will go wrong.

It is a trick for us to live beyond what we have proven. Sometimes displaced by death, other times reprieved. It is only the spineless character named Providence who carelessly covers his eyes, thus leaving chaos unattended to manically divide the lot.

I stand on the beach with the warm sand between my toes and the full sun blazing onto my forehead, my cheeks and arms. The heat is delicious and giving to every inch of my skin. My wife stands beside me, holding my hand. We watch Vee swim out into the rising white foam. She bobs in the grey tumultuous waves, turns and lurches toward us, awkwardly signalling as her mouth opens and closes, spitting out what wants to enter her.

"Look," she calls, "look how far I can go." She shouts, swallowing a mouthful of white frizzling sea water. Coughing, she appears stuck, wanting to pull free, to know the openness of alive now. The liquid mass surges and settles, holds her as she gasps, her words so small, but seeming free and smooth for an instant: "What do you think? Look at me. Look what I can do. I love you. Do you love me more?" The undercurrent tugs her body down, only her fingertips above the crests. Moments later, she reappears, panicky, water gushing from her stiffening throat. Waving her arms frantically, "I'm...fine," she attempts, shouting. "I'm okay." Coughing and sputtering, she is clutched by a force far beneath her. Yanked under again, her eyes still open. Salt water stings and fills each hole, one vast spilling pool of tears rolling over her.

We watch with the sand between our toes, the sun beating on our faces. My teeth are clenched and my wife's fingernails cut into my soft palm.

Vee has made it on her own. She has legitimized our fears, and we will never see her again. We are speechless with disbelief; unwilling to understand that only through this bleak, doubtless separation is it possible for a child to brace absolute and unconditional liberty.

"Why" is the word of the moment. It is scripted elaborately on the calling card of grief.

"Look at what I'm doing," Vee calls down.

I stare up at the sky to see her standing on the lip of the concrete wall. She lifts her hands and grey doves flutter, attached to her fingers by guide wires.

"What are you proving?" she implores, walking, as if on a tightrope.

I shrug and pull my legs close to my chest, hold them for fear of how hers are stepping so close to disaster.

"I'm dead," she says and shrugs as well, equally unresolved in her passion. "I wanted to prove something."

"What? What is there to prove?"

"Who knows?" Vee laughs light-heartedly and watches her fingers move. Spinning on one heel, she carelessly shouts, "There's no point in anything when you're dead."

Geography of despair. Dank and dark furrows. Black dirt gives way behind each progressive footstep. Depressions that I sink into, sink deeper with each step until the ditch's lip can close above me, but refuses to do so, always allowing the slightest murkiest glimpse of light. The geography of despair is a vast, intangible sense of climate. The weather never changes. It is heaviness with a hole cut through the center, only the hole is much denser than what it has been cut from, and you fit into it so perfectly.

The man in the forest-green raglan struggles to overcome

this geography. He is concerned with reshaping emotions out of steel, bulldozing all crumbling structures of faithlessness well beyond human sight. Providence prays for cross-beams and foundations to become my nature. Once the land is cleansed, the spirit harbours the immaculate. It is simple mechanics. Reductive spirituality.

But Providence does not realize that the geography of despair is undefinable, without longitude or latitude. Its plottings become the form that is the soul's disgruntled outline — a theological product of man's ever-changing morality — struggling to fit beneath my skin.

VI
RESURRECTION

Dusk drives Vee farther back into the shadows. Receding, she says, "I'm rotting. I'm no one. Remember me alive and with light in my eyes. That's all."

"I miss you," I tell her, knees against the stone-cold flooring as I cry the warmest, fullest tears of my life. "I want you back. If only I could...if only you were...if only I was..." I tempt myself with such crippling questions. They occupy me; shadows cast from greedy selfish abstractions. I strain for discovery of answers to a dilemma I secretively realize is hopeless and futile.

"You're silly," says Vee. "Just watch." In the final soulful light before darkness, she bends her tongue with her fingers, tears it loose in demonstration, and playfully tosses it. "Catch," snaps her tongue in mid-air, slowly curling down, tumbling toward my open mouth to lodge there and tangle with mine, so I cannot even speak. I cannot even say to her, *You leave me so lovingly haunted and choking*.

I lift a thin piece of splintered wood from the rubble swept into a corner of the building, crack it across my knee until I have four pieces. Before searching for a top, I make certain each strip of wood is the exact length. Then, I stand and nudge through the chunks of cement and broken beams along the edges of the warehouse. A section of glass catches my eye. A reflection of the fire I have lit behind me pulses in the glass, flickering to pass on its reassuring, conspiratory warmth.

I grip and lift the sharp edge to see it is a perfect square; one of the small panes from a window that had tumbled out and landed on a tear of cardboard box, unshattered. Returning to my place beside the fire, I kneel and awkwardly attempt to stand all four wood pieces on their ends while carefully placing the section of glass atop the short posts. The structure remains in place when I nervously guide my hands away.

Rising to my feet, I toss another piece of wood onto the fire. Sparks scatter for an instant and the flames lurch and hang. With uncertain interest, I wander around the model of the tiny house that I have erected, questioning the ease with which the task was performed, the flames from the fire longing so desperately to lull me toward revival.

But it is not until the fire ebbs that I hear Vee's words. The recognition of her voice is painful, for there is no other who will ever speak as she: "I have that piece of you to keep me warm," she says. "That place inside of you that feels so empty; it is the part I have taken away from you. I'll sleep with it forever." She would cry if she could, but the release of tears requires a body to enviously mimic the elements, "Your love is keeping me warm."

VII
FORGIVENESS

The man with the green raglan pays another visit. This time he walks straight for me, briskly and with purpose. Pulling open his raglan, he displays the tiny man fixed to his chest. The miniature crown of thorns on a festering head. The squirming puny body like a worm puppet.

"Get the point," the man says sharply, forcefully drawing closed the flaps of his raglan. "What could you possibly know about pain?"

"Nothing," I admit.

He snaps open his raglan again and stomps forward with one foot as if to startle me with the sight. The tiny figure — secured to the place above his heart — weakly opens and closes his tortured bug-sized eyes.

"The equipment is coming," croaks the tiny man, his head

resting on a weak angle. "To take this place down. Your will is in jeopardy."

"How can I understand?"

"Religion," squeaks the voice, twisted dry lips scraping painfully over each other, "is the fiercest of bulldozers, ripping through human uncertainty. What are you harbouring?" he pleads, weeping. "I forgive you. I forgive Vee." Gasping in agony, he tautly dangles from his cross and stares skyward. Wailing: "I forgive each and every one of you, again and again. How much must I endure? How much forgiveness? Centuries. Centuries. I am filled with the cancer of excuses. Forgive those who murder, the grim illness of men who rape thy neighbour's wife, thy neighbour's children. To pardon the sloth-like progression of foolish thoughts, of petty sins. And above all else..." He hesitates, seemingly fearing the paramount wisdom of his own words. "I unconditionally absolve myself for kindly permitting the continuance of this massive, over-budgetted string of funerals."

Providence pulls closed his raglan. I see the blue crosses tattooed onto the backs of his hands.

"You're just another grey dove," he says, pointing upwards, "moving without bearings. A rat with clipped wings, huddled here.

"Find direction," he insists, "that will close your opened body." His knowing eyes stare down at the house that I have built, the glass roof covered with soot from the extinguished fire alongside of it.

"Clean it up," he says. "So you can see through your roof again, down and into your true workings."

I smile at him.

"Hey!" he snaps, slapping at my arm. "That blasphemous smile!"

"See through my roof again?" I say, amused.

"See down into your life," Providence commands, "instead of this remorseful slum that confines you, glorifying your own anguish, your own fraudulent self-importance. What do you feel? Guilt. Self-pity. Regret. This powerlessness you sense is your uncommitted love of God."

"This is my home," I offer.

Providence stops himself from slapping me again. He holds his raised hand in the air for a moment, then steps away. "Tomorrow, the workmen come. The walls will be beaten loose. The space cleared. You will see everything come apart. All the pain exposed. The circuits of nervework beneath the shell of this dwelling. Mere flesh. Like malformed teeth of the soul being pulled, you will feel new skin and sense the clearing."

VIII
TRANSLATING DESPAIR

With hesitation, I step from the building (the deciphering of an urge prompting my departure). Fearing the demolition may result in my literal collapse, I nervously edge away from its impending and consumptive certainty.

Turning one way, there is light, the other way, darkness. I can move toward sight, toward the company of others, or to the west, into the darkness that is my mono-self.

People are standing on the rooftops watching me. Limbless, blind and crippled, their souls gashed open and glossily dangling below their knees. I unwind the bandage that covers the stub of my right arm to discover the stump is healed over. The fingers that lifted Vee from crib to childhood, gone. A huge scab covers the wound. I begin to peel its edge loose and it comes away freely; the new skin suddenly fresh, alive, pink and breathing.

I turn for the lights that flicker tentatively, almost foolishly, against dusk. The city draws me with the promise of sight, however shallow. I am seduced eastward, despite moans of objections, despite the barrage of limbs that are tossed at me. Hands, feet, fingers, impotent cocks.

"It was your fault," drone the voices. "Or it was our fault." They moan louder and viciously beat themselves until their bodies are one throbbing, purplish-black tattoo.

My right hand, the hand I used for many simple things, has been severed. I regard the blunt limb and think of Vee, her bloodshot eye closing. My missing fingers guiding shut the lids. Left-handed fingertips sensing textures with new-found perception. I must switch the sides of my brain. Simple grey understanding and acceptance of the wound. My fingers trace the scar tissue like braille, translating despair into sensual invigoration. A series of rising bumps that will guide me back toward sensation, toward the touch of my wife, the fusing. Wedded bliss.

I stand amidst this slum and pray to Providence. I snap his hand away from his careless eyes. But he simply laughs and lifts his other hand, making himself blind while he prods the figure beneath his raglan with his free hand. I attempt to mimic his carefree smile. But he does not see me anymore. His eyes are covered as he steps backward into the ominous west.

And I must wonder if I am cursed again.

My sense of direction is imbalanced. I stare down at the carnage of severed limbs that tremble around my feet. I lift a hand from the road, hold it to my stump and twist it one way, then the other. It will not fit. It is a woman's feminine hand. I let it drop, watch the fingers bend against the pavement, cushioning its fall, but the fingers do not straighten. A partial rigor mortis has set in. A stiffness to be worked against. And I can only guess at the years that must be endured before my thoughts begin to loosen.

My fingers sense momentum as I reluctantly step away, but they are ignorant and out of sync, knowing little of what they must touch to be forgiven.

The Throat

for Timothy Findley and
William Whitehead

Walt Coombs lumbers down the path from the bootlegger's house, arms hugging three cases of beer close to the belly of his green overalls. Unlaced boots scuff behind the van as he turns and bends by the side door to set the cases on top of three others. The stack tilts on an angle, leaning to fall, but Walt quickly braces his knee against the cartons and yanks back the sliding door. Dull afternoon light spills into the hollow, revealing an oldtimer named Wenzell, who squints from his seat — a wooden box pushed flush against the metal-ribbed shell. His lips are dry, and he mumbles, "Uhhhh?" as if someone has questioned him and he must strain to provide an answer. He squeezes his hands together, unaware that the sudden light and noise is what has troubled him.

The beer cases are quickly tossed around Wenzell's feet, boxing him in, and the door slides on its runners. Booms shut. He stares down at the cartons and thoughtfully scratches his head. A woman's name tempts him. He begins to say the name, but uncertainty smothers it, coming down like a woollen mitten muffling his lips. Wenzell is doubtful if words have escaped his mouth. He wonders whether he has already spoken and simply forgotten the doing. Thoughts moving backwards and into the future at once. Wenzell regards his memories as incidents yet to happen. He worries about his memories as if they must be untangled and played out, resolved in the coming days.

Up ahead, two doors open and shut. The oldtimer turns for the windshield to see Walt nodding at Wenzell's son, Leo — the nervous stick of a man in the passenger seat.

Walt winks, twisting the ignition key. "Done," he says, his shaggy, rust-brown beard bobbing as he laughs with an easy-natured heartiness. The engine turns over, but Walt shows no interest in prompting the accelerator. With both arms, he leans on the steering wheel and stares ahead, listening to the low wheezing of the motor.

Leo glances back, his eyes first inspecting Wenzell's face, then his body, seemingly in search of a clue that will confirm Leo's familial obligation to scold his aged father. Finding no sign of misdeed, he faces the bootlegger's house, discouraged and bitterly unsatisfied. His slow, shallow eyes stare through the windshield, blankly observing the still scene before him. The green-black clot of trees and the house resting on a grassy incline to the left of the grove.

"Way't fur 'er t'war'm up," says Walt. "Or she be kick'n' t'da 'eye 'evens." He sets his eyes on the rearview and then turns, playfully waving at the beer cases as if they are children or tiny animals. With gleeful anticipation, he spits into his hands and rubs them together.

Wenzell mumbles a curse. Dull eyes wet with cynicism, he raises his white-haired hand to tug on the beak of his cap. The cap is filthy and decades old; the John Deere logo is faded and unlike the one currently in use. Staring at the floor, he fiercely pulls at the cap and stomps his feet, drumming the floor and grumbling a threat as if in blind confrontation with a foe.

"Outta me way," he gripes, scowling as he kicks the cases. The bottles jingle a reply, a glassy sound of voices that Wenzell — with tilted head and steady eyes narrowing severely — suspiciously attempts to decipher.

"Punch drunk," says Leo, thin hands tucked between his knees, pushing down to bury them deeper. He is shameful of

his fingers; long and like a woman's. When he watches them
bend and grip, the sight softens a place inside of him that he
feels certain should be hard and impenetrable. He agrees with
himself on this thought, his gaunt head twitching with the
aborted intentions of a nod. The idea angers him, but his eyes
remain sheepish as they glance at Walt.

Easy laughter spills from Walt. His arms lift from the steering wheel and he turns in his seat, regarding the compartment
of the van.

" 'Ey?" he calls to Wenzell, eyes widening in mock observation. He laughs until he coughs, then hawks vigorously, rolls
down his window, and spits into the clay ditch beside the bootlegger's house. The house is a long rectangular box painted
bubble-gum pink with black trim along the windows and
eaves. Hubcaps are nailed to the front clapboarding and are
gleamless beneath the overcast sky. The sun is trapped low and
set behind the horizon's expansive line of somber trees. At the
rear of the house, long, tall rails of wood rest on their ends,
leaned against the front of a shed. A naked child catches and
holds Walt's attention. It stands in the brown driveway, merrily crouching in the dim light, its head dipped downward
spying the stream of urine that pours from between its legs.

Walt grins at the child, flashing his two remaining teeth;
sharp and set apart with nothing but glossy pink gums separating them. The child finishes passing water, then clumsily tests
the fluid with its toes, making mud prints along the dry dirt.

Walt twists back to a view of Wenzell reaching down to tear
open a case. He groans as the cardboard flap rips in two, the
thwarted effort forcing him to sway on his wooden box. Even
though the van is not moving, he struggles with balance, and
stares down, curiously observing the bottle caps.

"Muriel," he says, reaching into the carton. His hand hesitates for a moment before snatching hold. Drawing the bottle
loose, Wenzell freezes, his doughy face startled by the uncovered hole; the narrow blank filled with shadows left by the
beer's extraction.

" 'And 's one 'a doze," Leo says, glancing at Walt for encouragement. "Reet on. Reet, Walt?" A quick tongue darts out to
lick his lips. His pale skittish fingers reach back, the finger-

nails dark and bitten down. He will not look at them.

"'Ey, Pops?" Leo calls, hand groping the air. "'And 's one 'a dem."

The oldtimer rolls his eyes toward the voice. Wide lines deepen on his face as concern furrows in. Struggling with reason, he slaps at his sloppy lips with the thought of wiping them. He opens and closes his mouth as if testing the words Leo has just spoken. Two fluidy eyes catch sight of his hand holding a bottle; the fingers pressed tightly against the brown glass. Wondering, he stares at the contents as if it's something new to him; a worthy item that tempts a smile.

"Geev 's dat," says Walt, pushing forth his thick-fingered hand, steady and demanding alongside Leo's slight arm. He loudly snaps and wiggles his fingers, emphatically stating his case.

The oldtimer leans ahead, ignoring his son, and hands the bottle to Walt. He hears Walt first above the low utterings of his son's voice. His son's lame character forcing Wenzell to understand that anyone could plan against Leo in the worst possible way without Leo realizing the difference.

"Wenzell's punch drunk," says Walt, twisting off the cap and rubbing his palm across the small circular opening. He pokes one finger into the hole and flicks it forward, making a popping sound. Chuckling at Leo, Walt catches sight of the hungry, dejected eyes watching the opened bottle, how its tip rests so close to Walt's lips.

"T'irsty?" Walt says, relinquishing the bottle to Leo. The hand loses its uncertainty, moving swiftly for the beer. Leo sweeps it up and — tilting back his head — allows the fluid to gush into him. He swallows rhythmically until the beer is drained, then thrusts his head forward as if rushing up from under water. The cool liquid cleanses away his sweat, bathing his throat and stomach, refreshing his parched will. He makes a noise of supreme satisfaction and then belches. Quickly refocusing on his father, he gently elbows Walt and winks. "Wenzell's reet dopey look'n', reet? Ain't 'e?"

Walt ponders the notion. He scratches his red beard before giving a quick nod, humorously — but distantly — in agreement. His eyes stare easily, attempting to unfocus. He has been distracted by other things and must work to pull himself away from his thoughts. Wheezing a laugh, he guides down the gear shift, nudges the gas peddle with the tip of his steel-toed boot and is pleased by the muffler's husky rumble. He thinks of his gravelly voice and growls to himself, mimicking the sound.

The tires roll along the dirt fronting that narrows toward a rising road. Walt cuts the wheels sharply to the left and circles away from the house, the steering wheel slipping through his fingers, straightening before they amble up the incline, turn onto the main dirt road to wind above the black spruce groves and scattered meadows of tall blonde grass. Walt falls silent, thinking ahead to the highway, thinking back to his earlier thoughts. Their destination; the smokey hall in Cutland Junction where Gordie Hynes is guaranteed to get a beating. He hears the music and sees Gordie Hynes with his heels clicking and spinning, twisting the woman in his arms. Gordie Hynes, who is deserving of a smack to the head. Long overdue. Walt's fingers grab for the headlight switch. They grip the silver knob and pull, but the headlight beams are barely visible against the oncoming dusk and so he resets the switch.

A red light glares on the dashboard panel. A leak in his oil pan. Its glow is distracting, as if the light is taunting him, bringing to mind the glaring face of Gordie Hynes. His thoughts tighten around one image. Another beer would ease things nicely. The mere thought of another beer is quick to offer stirrings of relief. He recalls pouring in a quart of oil this morning and knows that he will have to add another when they make it to the Hall.

Walt eyes the rearview, sees the distant bootlegger's house sitting lonely in its gravel ditch down in the valley. He thinks he can see the bootlegger, Blackstrap Hawco, standing behind the big window, his grey yellow-tinged hair thick and combed away from his purposeful eyes, his hands in the back pockets of his work denims.

A short black dog swaggers out from behind the house and rolls in the dirt. The naked child toddles toward the mongrel, foolishly holding what looks like a large, broken shovel unsteadily above its head. Walt shifts his eyes from the road to the rearview as the bootlegger's house disappears; an angle of evergreens overtaking and hiding it from sight before the scene plays itself out.

The oldtimer coughs and coughs, his fingers weakening from the labour and he curses, an unopened beer bottle dropping from his hand, rolling with momentum along the aspinite flooring. Walt quickly glances back and — reaching down — effortlessly scoops up the beer.

"T'anks Wenzell," says Walt, the length of his beard swaying against his chest. Gums sheening, he pops the cap and winks to no one in particular. "Finest kind," he muses before swallowing.

Leo peers back and winks, too, mimicking Walt's sense of assurance, but a tinge of mockery is also evident. The oldtimer sneers and clenches his teeth. His skin seems made of water and flour and fine grey dust sprinkled here and there. His jowls tighten. His jaw shifts forward, eyes suspiciously peering at Leo as his blue-veined hand dangles, reaching down for another beer.

" 'Old on 'ta dis 'n," Leo bravely announces. He clutches a beer in his hand, stares into the bottle and shakes the brew barely covering the bottom's brown glass. Disappointment slackens his features. The oldtimer is guarding the cases and Leo must ask for another, at the mercy of his father. The beer bought from Wenzell's pension check.

Walt concentrates on the dirt road. He takes a long serious drink. Droplets stick to the hairs of his moustache and he licks them away. Cackling, his pink gums glisten with light. He raises his beer in salutation to the wilderness that surrounds them, tilting the bottle to one side and then to the other.

"Gardy Eye'ns," Walt shouts. "Da fuh'ker."

"Go fur d'Junction," says Leo, pointing at the road with his index finger, holding the bottle and pointing, then gleefully slapping the dashboard with his free palm. "Punch da fuh'k outta 'im."

Walt winks at Leo. "Race driver. Mad Dog Walt, reet?" The bottle is shoved between his legs and he seizes the steering wheel with both hands. His expression tightens with faked concentration, his throat harshly purring, "Rrrrn, rrn, rrrrrrn."

They both laugh and pound the dashboard.

Wenzell stares and awkwardly jabs at the air, as if fending off their merriment.

"I'm nar fool," he spits. "I n'ose wha' ya'r up to."

The van slows for a stop sign ahead in the distance, the dirt road gradually running out, ending at the grey highway. Walt checks both ways for traffic, then cuts the wheels, jams the gas pedal to the floor. A slow rumble guides them down the deserted pavement. To either side of the highway, barrens run inland for half a mile, the dull rust-coloured landscape tinged with traces of muted green, dry red bushes, patchy bogs and huge grey boulders. The barrens stretch inland before colliding with a dense line of black forest, the bland sullen sky pressing down.

No one speaks. They are thinking of the dance at the Junction. Leo has hopes of finding himself a lively and easy woman. His hopes are built the same as always and — as usual — lack fulfillment. His mind is set on dancing, but he will not have the courage to rise from his seat, drinking and shouting and watching instead, until his head defies him, striking the littered table top.

Walt is hoping he won't find his wife. He hasn't seen her in three months; not since she abandoned him, taking his hundred and forty dollars from a haul of birch, and his wedding ring, swearing he'd never wear it again because she was going to hammer it to pieces, and she is just as welcome to stay away from him, live in the trailer out on Blind Island with Gordie Hynes.

Walt hates his wife. He says it to himself, over and over and with a passion that must mask the truth of how he loves her more than anything, believing he can do without her company, believing any lie that succeeds in mending his pride. But Gordie Hynes will be taken care of just the same. Wife or no wife, Gordie Hynes is due for the worst possible kind of beating.

"Gardy Eye'ns," Walt curses, spitting out the name that has strengthened his weakening thoughts for the past three months. Three months worth of nights alone in his big bed with the pink bedspread and without a wife, thinking of what Gordie Hynes was doing with her, thinking of the possibilities; every imaginable filthy and disgusting episode that the pain could present to him. Repeating Gordie Hynes' name and feeling the anger power him, the anger snatch sleep from his eyes and make them burn.

"Gardy Eye'ns," he says again, this time loud enough for Leo to take notice. A bloody racket, Walt assures himself, and then a woman to tell him how many punches he'd got in and what kind of damage — the more permanent the better — he'd done to the face that took the pounding of his fists. A woman to explain the details because his memory would be washed away by beer and rye and the only vague remembrance would be the fury of sound and solid punches delivered and received; the whirl of violent scuttling and bodies slamming. Drunk, he will crack open Gordie Hynes' skull with the sledgehammer in the back of the van, in the wooden box of tools he'd built behind the rear wheel well. Then find a new woman. Maggie Fippard, or Lil Hobbs. They're easy enough with a few beers in their sagging bellies. Get them in the washroom with their slacks down around their ankles and their fat cool arses in both his hands. Savouring the notion, he barks to himself: 'Fresh, wide-open k'nt.'

There is no mistaking Walt's and Leo's thoughts. Their expressions are squat and expectant. Images are held in their minds like fingers pressed into flesh. They cradle pictures of well-shaped women; ones who have been longed for all of their lives, but never discovered. The women appear completely different in each man's minds (age, and hair colour, shape of face, legs — slim or thick), but are identical in certain sexual characteristics.

Walt and Leo silently drink their beers. They believe in the brand of woman whose vulgar sexuality will make them king above all men. Their longings compel an alcoholic thirst, their groins growing hungrier for wickedness — a desire that weakens them with as much command as the boozy lull of beer.

Wenzell takes a long drag on the bottle, waits, and then belches. The sound resonates, ringing through the empty space of the van. He likes the taste. Belching again, he traps the gas behind his lips and slowly lets it out, tasting.

"I 'member," he gruffly insists. Coughing with a vengeance, he spits onto the floor, wiping the white stubble along his chin, swiping at his lips. The buttons of his grey and blue plaid shirt are unfastened, revealing a patch of bleached-white hair against a chest as brown as tree bark.

"Wha?" Leo looks back, waiting for word from his father, but his father is speechless.

"Say some'n'," Leo threatens, screwing up his face. "G'w on. One w'rd outta ya. J'st fuh'kin' try't."

Wenzell stares. He slowly smacks his lips together and watches his son face the road as the van slows and curves off the darkening highway, past the narrow green sign for Cutland Junction, and over the dividing bump, onto a dirt road.

Walt checks the rearview.

"Git dat radio fex't," says Leo, stabbing the buttons. "I means it. Git it fex't."

Walt glances at Leo, "A few in ya now. Re'dy fur da racket."

Leo opens his hand and stares at it, smiling now, certain of how special his fingers are. He snaps them above his head and drinks from his bottle, then loudly sings an old song, stomping his feet on the metal floor.

"I 'MEMBER!" shouts the oldtimer, banging his fist against the side of the van.

"Jay'sus!" Walt mutters, his foot darting for the brake, but hovering there, hesitating before coming down, realizing it was only the oldtimer who had struck the van.

"Wha?" asks Leo, shoving his steady arm over the back of his seat and holding it high, leaning, waiting to take a smack at his father.

"I w's gunna tel'ya."

"Wha?" Leo gasps with anger, pointing with one certain finger. "L'uh, shut yer face."

Wenzell insists: "Some'n' I learnt in da slaudder'ouse."

Leo's lips whiten, the blood draining and drawn inward toward the rage that pumps like an infected heart. Shaking his head, he turns and tilts back the bottle in dismissal. A triumphant smile widens with each swallow as his eyes turn softer. Amusement now plentiful.

"At it a'gin," says Walt, waiting for Leo to finish chugging.

"N'ver lits up." Thirty feet ahead, a ginger-coloured rabbit hops onto the road, pauses for an instant, flashing its gleaming eyes, then hops across, down the opposite incline.

"Lo'd'd, 'e is," Leo says, grinning and pushing his thin chin forward. "Pops is fuh'kin' lo'd'd."

The oldtimer thinks of the number forty-four. It reels into his head without warning and he is startled by its unsummoned presence; the number like the face of a person to which he cannot put a name.

"Farty-far y'rs in da slaudder'ouse," he announces, exhaling with sudden relief, remembering. He stares at the bottle. "'Member?" he whispers.

"N'ver says wha'," complains Leo. "Nuts. Whack'd outta 'is skull. Crazy ol' fart. I kno's wha's 'e's trub'l. Been wit' 'im. Nod da likes 'a you wou'dn't know 'bout 'im. Me is what kno's."

Walt watches the road. The headlights have brightened into whitish-yellow cones; funnels that move them through the almost whole and complete darkness. The dirt road is brown fading toward red, smooth and well-travelled before suddenly connecting to asphalt, the tires striking the bump, speckled greyness revealed and moving before them, but the surrounding trees black and still.

"Ask 'im," says Walt, feeling anger churn inside. Thinking of Gordie Hynes, his grip tightens on the steering wheel and he calls, "Wha's 'e on a'bout?"

"Ain't 'n'couragin' 'im." Leo tips back his beer. Finding it empty, he leans over his seat, rises up and reaches, dropping the bottle into its slot and snatching hold of another. He flashes a quick, threatening look at his father.

"Watch it," Leo snaps, "or I'll flatten ya."

"I cut 'em, 'n t'was like some'n' dat..." Wenzell's eyes blink away the tears. His mouth grimaces attempting to contain the anguish, but his lips tremble defiantly. He bites them hard, shivering. "I 'member'd it. Da slit wh'n da skin op'n'd easy like...Like some'n..."

The scope of Walt's headlights stretch far. They sweep along the road and race ahead, revealing a washed-out metallic glimmer in the distance, the glimmer becoming a car as the van rolls closer. Walt recognizes the make; '85 Oldsmobile. Pale blue. Dark blue hardtop. Its rear lights are flashing in sync and the paint sheens against the dark forest, the car growing bigger and brighter until Walt can see a man kneeling by the front wheel. A tire jack is set in place and the driver's side of the car is higher, the left front wheel off its bolts. Two tires lay in front of the car along with a road map, pinned flat to the asphalt with a rock at each corner. A man kneels beside the car, his hands joined and level with his chest. He lifts his head and mournfully stares at the van as it passes.

"Buddy's pray'n." Walt laughs and punches the horn twice. " 'E got da gear," he says, watching the man in the rearview.

Leo quickly rolls down his window, sticking out his head to shout amusing words, but nothing comes and so he angrily tosses an empty beer bottle into the trees where it spins and whistles faintly then slides through a progression of hidden branches before clinking onto the tangled ground.

" 'E got da gear fur fex'n dat." Walt shows Leo his two teeth.

"Fuh'k 'em fur stop'n 'n me woods. Townie faggit in me own woods." Leo winds up his window, his arm and shoulder vigorously working.

" 'Ard stuff, you. Reet tuff now."

Leo leans back in his seat, brooding for a moment before his frivolous look is suddenly reinstated and he slyly peeks at Walt through the corners of his eyes.

"Ya t'ink Connie's gunna be d'ere?" he asks.

"Da k'nt'll get wha' she's after then." Walt shakes the steering wheel, lashing and strangling it. He imagines his wife and what she has done. Which men have been inside her crack, who has emptied himself and made filth of her. Shaking his head with reeking disbelief, he stares at the road, his shoulders hunched and knotted with tension.

Leo laughs and slaps Walt's knee. "Geev it ta da peddle." His eyes watch the speedometer needle climbing over the height of the circle and down the other side. "Da lousy k'nt she be wantin' fur ya ta straighten 'er."

Walt's eyes fill with a warning, but he will not look at Leo. He feels the speed and curses the road as if punishing it.

Faster.

"One leg up 'n da chain 'n da udder keckin'. Da pig swing'in' 'til I tuk ahold 'a da front leg 'n did da job." The

oldtimer smacks his damp lips together. "Dat slit op'n'd up. I
w'nt'd ta tell ya. Slaudder. Da slaudder like some'n' else. Wit'
da slit op'n'in'. 'Mind'd me 'a some'n'. Fodder ta son. A talk I
had'a tell ya. Some'n' 'bout womb'n; wha' dem do and den
what dem c'n do ta ya. Like dat." His tongue moves around in
his mouth, savouring the emptiness that threatens to turn
sour. He spits and spits, scraping his tongue with his teeth. "I
don't wan' dem doin' what dem did ta me, ta me son. Weak
like ya'r. Not da cuttin' like dat. Dem eyes tel'in' ya some'n'
else. Tellin' 'bout w'at dem're rightly seein' in ya." A tight dry
sob, an anguished cough, bursts from his lips and his words are
cramped and weaker. "Dey cut ya up sl'o. Dat's w'a t'was. Not
fast like da slaudder'ouse. Not ov'r da t'roat 'n fast, but sl'o
in…in da 'art."

He slams his chest and coughs another sob, clutching the
bottle with both hands, pleading:

"I nev'r w'nt nar womb'n cuttin' ya da way dem did me."

"Wha's 'e on about?" spits Leo, turning to face his father.
He anxiously shifts in his seat and shouts, "Wha's ya ravin'
'bout, ol' man? Keep 'er quiet. Shut yer trap, ya 'ear me, or I'll
murd'r ya reet on da spot."

Wenzell looks up from the bottle and squints as if searching
through a fog, attempting to clarify a distant object. He rocks
on his crate, and then stares at the side door, the woods moving beyond like one continuous wet black smear.

"Leo," he pleads. "Is too painful, me son. Go fast. Don' let
'er 'appen."

"Mumblin'," Leo shouts. "Wha' da 'ell 'r ya mumblin' 'bout?"

Walt glances away from the blur of road, fixing his sights
on the rearview. The oldtimer's worried eyes staring back, face
pale and frightened in the half-shadows of the hollow.

"LARD T'UNDERIN' JAY'SUS!" bawls Wenzell between
gulps of beer. Eyes wide and watching through the side window, he sucks from the bottle as if drawing his last breath.

The black bulk of the moose rises from the recessed brush,
up the bank to the stretch of road, its long limbs striding like
a man on stilts. Walt stomps the brakes and cuts the wheels
ahead of the animal's pace.

Two wide strides and the moose is paused, facing the van, its ears twitching with wonder as the vehicle screeches, stops dead, fiercely bucking for an instant before settling back on its rear wheels.

The moose, like a shadow masked by harder darkness, drops out of sight.

A solid object has pounded the rear of Walt's seat, bounced, then slammed onto the floor. In a colliding instant, beer cartons have slid, and bottles crashed inside their cases. Sounds of heavy and light objects shifting in a manic instant where movement and stillness come together to clash and rebound, sending bodies reeling blindly against their useless wills.

In the sparkling stillness following the explosion of glass, Walt touches his forehead, lowers his fingers and stares at them. They only slightly resemble the digits of his hand. They seem full and larger, covered with a dark oily fluid; black but mingled with a secretive creeping tinge of the deepest red; warm and smelling like copper. He thinks he should do something. He has a feeling, but he cannot remember what it is that tempts him toward the completion of the thought he has now forgotten. His chest trembles with a laugh. Regarding his green coveralls, he struggles to make sense of how things have slipped out of connection. He realizes: I am in a van, and it has stopped, and it stinks of beer. Twisting the ignition key, he listens to the silence he had not expected. The dead engine makes him feel as if he is deaf and mute. He squints at the vague pavement. Mouth baffled. Eyes perplexed. Slowly glancing back — as if held in buoyant suspension — he sights the dome light outlining the image of an oldtimer on the floor, the crushed cardboard cases frothing beer suds, the tools from his box are scattered across the wet glass-sprinkled aspinite. He regards the empty seat beside him, eyes shifting toward the hole where the windshield once was.

A cool breeze rises, fingering his skin in a peculiarly intimate manner. His eyes shift within themselves, extending their range of focus, staring further off, thirty feet up the road, along the course of weakening headlights, before the beams meld with a wall of blackness, to see a man's illuminated body with its face against the asphalt. The right cheek is flattened along its red, fleshy edge. One glossy eye sheens in the light as

it twitches and widens. The desperate expansion. The singular
and compulsive need to see.

Walt steps down and pauses, standing still beside the van. He
stares ahead, hesitant before wandering into the scene, stepping over the legs of the moose. Somewhere behind him — as
if from down a tunnel — there is the sound of the van's side
door rolling open. The oldtimer moans and curses as he jumps
out without looking at Walt. He staggers toward the gravel incline by the side of the road and, grumbling, tugs down his
zipper. The ends of his plaid shirt hang past his waist, the
faded, baggy jeans loose around his hips. His bladder empties
with a steady, forceful rush and he sighs, pacified by the black-
green expanse of forest before him. He can almost see above
the trees, the height of their imposing peaks threatening him
in a personal way. Set as they are, they appear only inches
above his head. They are taller than him and he finds need to
challenge their sense of confidence. Their superiority. Rising
on his tip-toes — in an attempt to tower above the flat forest —
he stretches and leans toward the dark sight, shouting accusa-
tions and waving one fist. The stream slows to a dribble and he
shakes himself dry, calling and shaking himself toward the
trees, jeering and teetering forward. At first he does not recognize the sensation of his boots sliding beneath him, the edge of
the clay embankment crumbling. Then, with an abrupt shout,
he slips — one leg going first, snapping — before clumsily tumbling sideways, down the incline — a scramble of movement,
of impossible struggling, and spitting as dirt rushes into his
mouth.

The highway runs black in both directions. The red tail lights
glow around themselves, but go nowhere, offering little reassurance, only a menacing blur. The headlight beams leads so
far, but — like the power of a flashlight — simply reveal the
immediate; extending to Leo's body and dissolving into a grey
haze, which eventually merges with the blackness of a wilderness night.

Walt stands above Leo and watches his friend's fingers stirring speculatively like the antennae of a crushed bug. These
fingers of the left hand are scraped and bloody, sand and tiny

pebbles imbedded into the cuts. The right hand is tucked beneath the body, arm twisted upward with the elbow down, demonstrating an otherwise physically impossible angle.

Crouching beside the body, Walt places his palm flat to the back of Leo's blue shirt. The fabric is warm and damp and the flesh beneath it trembles, like the purring of a cat.

"Hey?" Walt enquires, pressing, and hearing his voice as if a stranger has spoken near by. He glances around, but sees no one.

Sticky sounds rise from the pavement. They are liquid-slow and forced. Indiscernible.

Walt bends nearer, carefully lowering his ear as close as possible without touching, listening to hear. This new clarity. Pure and delicate sounds sputtering from between two pulpy lips.

A moment later, Walt finds himself looking away. Control is out of his hands. Other forces direct him now. Simple things. Sounds from beyond the darkness, vague but distinctive; leaves stirring against each other, tempting, tiny clear-green insects snapping loose from the sacks on their mother's bellies, instantly eating, hot streams of breath from the nostrils of animals. A smell of clear, vast quantities of air. He regards the van and the dense shadow of the moose; crippled and on its side. He hears its low groan like a deep-throated lamentation rising above all things. He feels the guttural sound in the asphalt, where his knees are pressed flat and taking the weight of his body. He must rise from his knees. He is much too close. When he stands, he feels as if he has been lifted by the elbows. Breath so empty and strained, but seemingly effortless.

He stares down at Leo; body stopped, fingers creeping, but going nowhere. Gurgling words; jellied and rising. Bubbling up.

The oldtimer climbs the bank. He is crouched low, painfully dragging a snapped leg. Half way up, he curses, seized by a grimace. The pain halts him, but he will not obey. He lifts his fist and punches the edge of the broken bone. It cuts into his hand, scraping and digging. The jagged points have pierced the skin of his left leg — the bone snapped clear, the dark marrow visible — and he is at war with it.

"LARD SUFF'RIN' FUH'K!" he shouts. "Christ All Mi'dee!" He spits a clump of wet dirt, violently hawks to clear his throat. The grains of clay grind between his teeth. He coughs until his eyes stream water and then he stops, taking time to scrape his tongue clean with his teeth.

The sound draws Walt's attention. He detects the presence of the oldtimer; the tiny distant man who shivers with movement and makes noise. Walt squints and wets his lips with a thick tongue. Mouth slightly open, his gums catch the brazen assault of the headlight beams.

The oldtimer follows the gravel shoulder, cautiously keeping his distance, as if it is a line he must follow. Occasionally, he totters onto the pavement, winces, then steps back to the soft merciful clay, limping to cushion his stride. The shoulder of his plaid shirt has been torn open and tiny trails of blood zigzag into his skin, catching and beading along the white hairs on his back. When his eyes settle on the cow moose, he staggers to a stop.

"Dead," he whispers with restraint, spitting lightly, "She dead. Me Gawd, fine'ly." Hopeful eyes straining to catch a glimpse of the other body on the asphalt, he leans and moves sideways to secure a better look, his right foot sliding along the edge of the gravel bank, the heel attempting to dig in, to no avail. He tilts weightlessly. Vision of the greyish-purple sky, eyes almost making out stars, he quickly drops, sideways and then backward, over. Dirt and gravel rushing up sleeves and pant legs. The tangle of low brush stinging his skin, scraping with its brittle fingers, merciless entanglement holding on, but rolling with him.

Again, Walt flicks the ignition. He feels no sense of panic. He is not frightened. Only his thumbs tremble in an unfamiliar way. Out of habit, he tugs on his beard, nervously flashes his gums. The smile is troublesome and refuses to free itself. The sky is low and brooding, settling in his agitated blood. Eyes narrowed with wonder, a laugh bursts from him, then he is confused again, his forehead etched with deep creases.

The door opens easily enough. He steps down and moves to the front of the van. The moose's hooves are extended in his path. He trips, regains his footing, but refuses to view the kill. Popping open the rectangular hood, he reaches in, twisting the black battery wires, examining the distributor cap. He spins off the wing nut of the air filter casing, lifts off the dish, examines the filter, sticks his finger into the choke, opens and closes the flap against its spring, then replaces the pan and spins the wing nut back into place.

The hood slams. He moves back to the door, climbs up, clicks the ignition. Nothing. Not a word. Not a sound inside of him. He pushes a round knob on a stem and the headlights disappear. He leaves them off and watches the faint scene gradually come to life with a muted light all its own.

The moon is masked, but visible, its glow revealing the fluid progression of bruised clouds. Walt perceives the strange moonlight against Leo's body. The same soft hue lies upon the body of the cow moose.

The animal groans a nightmare sound. It is in pain. Its stone-like head oppressively scrapes the asphalt, but its body does not stir.

The oldtimer's eyes rise above the embankment. He struggles up, without pausing, and urgently limps — cursing, limping, cursing — toward Leo's body. He sees the moose with its weighted head shifting, back legs unexpectedly jerking inches at a time, like the spring of a timepiece torn from its casing, fitfully uncoiling. Front legs motionless.

A car'll come, a truck, thinks Walt. But not until the dance is over. Three, four hours. No one moves from the dance at the Junction Hall. He remembers, That's where we're going, We'll go there, soon. My wife, he thinks, is waiting. No one is late (we're late) for the Hall dance and no one leaves early. It is a regular event, Walt assures himself. All bodies drink until the booze is gone. Maybe four, five hours. Yes, thinks Walt. A long walk to the Junction Hall. Who's walking? Someone's dancing. Heals clicking and spinning. His wife with her legs drawn up, ankles touching her ears. Everything open. Walt amuses himself. He tugs on his brownish-red beard and laughs, as if to relieve himself. "Oo's walk'n?" he mutters.

"I'll walk," says a voice, but it is his own voice. He pulls on the headlights to lead the way. The asphalt reveals itself. Dismal pools of fluid beside a pale body in the distance. Limbs twisted and pointing up. The oldtimer bent over the body, his

grey-haired head darting up to stare back, face washed out like
a startled ghost caught in the act.

Walt dabs at his forehead to check for blood. The wound feels
pasty but has sealed itself. He probes and then studies his fingers as he hurries into the darkness, out of the headlight's
range.

"Da moose. Is 'a she," calls the oldtimer from where he
now stands, dipping his head behind the animal, and shouting,
"A' she. I'll show ya. Gimme some'n'. Cum on. Some'n' ta do 'er."

"Da t'roat," Walt calls, his voice low and seemingly from
someone else's mouth as he rushes through the blind wall of
country air that he has disappeared through.

An object tumbles from the darkness. It hits the asphalt —
a soft metallic scraping as it slides — and the oldtimer limps
toward it, bends and curses, raising the folded hunting knife.
He opens the blade and stares with astonished memories, running his hard thumb along the keen edge.

He shuffles toward the moose, crouches and bites the pain.
The strength he demands must be summoned. Silence for a
breathing minute before he pierces her hide with the tip, cutting and pulling the skin up and away from the pinkish-white
flesh, the moose groaning and dragging her head along the
abrasive pavement.

"Wenzell!" Walt shouts from out of view. Panting and gasping
for words, he rushes back into the subdued light. "Der's
a'nudder moose up 'a 'ead on da road." His throat contracts and
he pauses to swallow the clot of dry fear. His arm rises, pointing toward the darkness. "Spread 'a ant'lrs like dis. 'N da black,
stan'in' dere. Jay'sus! Huge and stan'in' dere." His voice falters,
losing its insistence, his vague manner suddenly reinstated,
intrigued by Wenzell's actions. The oldtimer, smiling and staring up as if to share the secret, slices further into the thick
hide, and pulls it away where it drops and collects in heavy
folds against the asphalt.

"Da t'roat," says Walt, drawing his finger across his own
throat in demonstration. "Da t'roat, first. Skin 'er lay'dr."

The oldtimer stares up in confusion. He sees Walt hurry
toward the van and climb in. Where is he attempting to go?

There is no point. Everything has been taken apart. Disassembled. It is what the oldtimer has been waiting for; the laying out of past and present. All elements displayed and scattered around his feet.

Walt pointlessly turns the ignition key. He flicks off the lights so as not to attract the male moose. It may charge. It may just charge them. Moose have been known to do it. Walt has seen it happen. He has seen it and tried to punch his way into them. Them or a man. Memory cleverly tricks him. Every nerve twitches as if he is stumbling into sleep and waking. Someone or something coming at him. He opens his eyes. He is sleepy, or he is dreaming. He smiles and knows that this is real. He can feel his smile. The true and reassuring stretch of it.

The headlights now gone, Wenzell gloats at the sudden darkness. Welcoming it, he stands, tucks in his shirt tail and limps toward Leo's body. The pain is to be cherished. Worshipped. His son's fingers jitter only slightly. The gurgling ebbs. The oldtimer watches one helpless eye revolve his way. Kneeling, he recognizes with certainty the pain widening in that glistening swollen eye.

"No," a whispering hiss, "She warn't do it t' ya." Shocked and staring around the scene, he lifts his son's head by the hair and nods. "She warn't. Nar one'll make ya out ta be d' fool." The knife breezes across Leo's throat, like a quick gasp drawing into itself, and the thick sputtering turns to silence, only the gentle steaming trickle of blood against the hard road.

Walt scratches his shaggy beard. His eyes search the dashboard. He cannot see what is the matter. The headlights remain off. Why off, he wonders. His fingers flick them on. The greenish arc of numbers magically glows from the speedometer. Walt stares above the strokes and digits, through the wide rectangular hole where the windshield once was. Splinters of glass protrude around the rim like the teeth of an underwater relic. The night air is cool on his face. He sees the oldtimer bent over Leo's body.

A body, Walt thinks. He listens for a sound, but his attentiveness goes unrewarded.

"I 'member," mutters Wenzell's far-off voice. He stands

with his hands shoved into his loose pockets, the jagged edge of a bone torn through his pants. He watches the dark blood around his boots. The seeping of the fluid like a languid stream of recollections; depthless and expanding at once, and in the midst of this flow he recalls how he'd wanted to tell his son something about the slaughterhouse, but now he'd shown him. Now, his son understood what it was he was trying to say.

"Like 'dat," he hesitantly offers. "On'y 'a womb'n open'n' up like dat 'n cuttin' ya at da same toy'm." Wenzell nods with determination — a job well done — and smiles sympathetically, in a paternal and utterly necessary manner.

Walt searches for words. Through his thoughts, he rummages for descriptions of what his eyes see, of where he is, of what he has become, of the disjointed cast of events that holds him at arms length, as if away from himself. But he fails to discover the switch that will spark connection; observations clumsily spliced onto understandings. He hears the half-skinned moose groan, watches it imploringly roll the unbearable weight of its head. There is no answer. No quick response. No rally of witty cracks. He cannot think of one. Instead, he senses the moose's groan as if trapped in his own throat, forming from his meaty soul. Rising from his lungs like the thickest, blackest part of disbelief wanting to swell up and fill his head with bleakness, with reasoning. He wants to cough, but he feels that whatever is rising — perhaps the fluid that has stained his heart — will catch in his throat, scalding the insides of his mouth, completely erasing his ability to almost think, as he is almost thinking now.

He coughs. The sound of the cough clears, then there is the sound of an approaching car. Walt turns to watch the vehicle. The pale-blue Oldsmobile slows and cautiously stops. The driver leans across the passenger seat. An expression of friendly caution. He rolls down the window that keeps him safe.

"I guess I don't know where I am," the driver calls in a wary voice that cracks and turns so suddenly frightened it appears repentant — words spoken through the wall of a confessional. "I'm lost." A meek smile troubles the man's face. His head is round and his grey hair thin along the forehead. Two tiny eyes are quick and nervous behind wire-rimmed spectacles. He licks his lips and sniffs.

Walt stares at the cow moose. He sees the oldtimer bent there, skinning her as she moans. The hide is almost clear now, only to be cut away from the legs and the bulk's steaming pinkish-white flesh. The reasonable heart still pumping; lifting and settling. Walt thinks, The throat, but says nothing.

The driver climbs from his car, leaving the door open and holding onto it. The insides of the vehicle glow; the red upholstery plush and spotless. The man edges away, drawn closer to the sight, another step, squinting. His suit is navy blue and a red tie hangs over the front of his buttoned jacket.

The oldtimer pants, mumbling as he vigorously skins the moose. He shifts and wipes a torn sleeve across his forehead. The edge of the material is darkly wet and dangles loose, but he pays it no bother.

The man does not believe what is happening. Intrigue draws and repulses him. About to pass uncertain comment, he checks the impulse, eyes darting away to an object that has slipped into his field of vision. A man's body in the distance.

"My God!" says the man, one hand springing up to grip his face, fingers pressing in. "Oh, Jesus!" Another hand clutches the frames of his glasses, he stares at the oldtimer, then darts a look back, searching for his car, the opened door, the reassuring light.

Wenzell tilts up his face, smiling with unforgiving eyes.

"Gu'd meat," he says, winking with determination. "Da best eat'n', when ya eat 'er."

The moose snorts hot wasted breath, its huge eyes filling up with blood.

"Sweet Lord," the driver whispers, carefully stepping back until he stumbles against the door of his Oldsmobile.

"I'm going now," he announces, making a nervous, sensible decision. "Yes, I see what you're doing." He blindly grabs for the edge of his door and climbs into his car. Gripping the steering wheel, his fingers coldly fumble for the ring of keys set in the ignition. The engine turns over, revs, screeches, but goes nowhere.

"I can't help," he calls, his voice slightly threatening from the safety of the car. "I won't help you." With both hands, he

reaches for the door handle, weakly pulling it closed. Seconds
later, the Oldsmobile bucks and rolls away, the fading headlights stealing intensity from the scene, masking the obscure
threshold.

Walt watches the metallic outline grow tinier; its taillights
shrink until consumed. The unreasonable dislocation of his
body seems set in place behind his eyes. The receding car
seems to be his body, gliding off, tugging his vision away from
himself. He is weakened by the inferred thought that he has
just been witness to something he cannot entirely compre-
hend, something held together by another's sense of reason. He
collapses onto his knees as if falling through the ground, or his
legs cut out from under him. Straight down, but landing
steady. He forgets the movement and looks toward his knees
to see two hands like someone else's. Without sensation, he
wonders if he is waking from unconsciousness or slipping into
it. Then, as if from outside himself, thinking of nothing, but
then suddenly thinking of the male moose up ahead in the wilderness, he quietly says, "Hey?" But the words barely move
beyond his inert lips, barred by the knowledge of what he is
facing. The threat of another male's presence. Unavoidable and
always. His eyes swim with tears.

The large rack of antlers slips from the darkness into the
confined area of light. A snort of breath impels the oldtimer to
push himself to his feet. Straining and limping with a painful
shuffle, he stares into the stagnant gap between himself and
the male moose. Stomping his foot, he pivots for balance and
shouts, "YAHHH!", twisting toward a hop and waving the
knife, elaborately shredding the air. The moose stumbles back,
its hooves scraping the pavement as it swings its clumsy head
and turns, lumbering off. Its image withdraws further, shadowed vague, and then gone through the blackness that only it
can see into.

Wenzell smiles. His grey face washes white as he stares into
the headlights, his challenging eyes wide open.

"Mine," he shouts, squinting against the glare. With a stern
nod, he crouches down, the grainy asphalt pushing into his
knee, the broken leg bent only slightly, straight as possible and
angled away. "Muriel," he whispers, "Lees'n ta me." He
thrusts his knife into the pinkish-white flesh and blood sprin-

kles across his face. "Way'k up," he insists, licking the warm flecks from his chafed lips, and stabbing, deliberately and forcefully, into the carcass. "Way'k up. Way'k up. Muriel? Way'k up, me luv."

The oldtimer pauses. His face is hot with the narrow streams of fluid that creep along his cheeks, droplets hanging from his stubbled jawline. He stares with a deep liquid mask changing across his face. Sniffing, he listens. Sound gurgling from the swollen throat.

The moose is whispering to him. Words of death-do-us-part. Sweet utterings that forever calm him. It rolls its sorry eyes, expectantly watching Wenzell, jaws mechanically opening to affectionately display a set of flat yellow teeth. Its thick tongue loosely slips out, smearing the oldtimer's boot. An offering. A meal forever, if he could bite into it. He thinks of cutting out the fleshy fob. Soup, he instructs himself, as steam curls from the hollow of the moose's mouth.

Buffer Zones

for David Monroe Bowring

It's been six years since I stole Stan's girlfriend, Kirsten. Stan's my brother, but I couldn't help it; the way things turned out. Back in my days of independence — when it was absolutely necessary — I used to visit Stan's apartment. My mother would contact me on the telephone, insisting that I deliver snippets of urgent news. No matter how adamant my refusal, my mother would continue with her telephone harassment until I agreed to her terms. The contents of the news was usually ridiculous; useless gossip about people from the street. Such and such about so and so. I knew what she was really up to: all she wanted was for me to check up on Stan, make sure he was okay. Always a temperamental little boy, my mother used to say of him. A boy in need of extra attention.

Stan didn't own a telephone, didn't believe in them, called them deceitful, and cursed at every pay phone he passed on the street.

"The voice," he used to say, "is different."

Kirsten would usually be at Stan's apartment on Freshwater Road, continuously painting the walls and trim a vivid colour, rearranging the L-shaped couch and television stand, or just wandering around in half of her underwear. I say "half" because she would never be wearing just her bra and panties. It was a combination of underwear and summer attire: a bra and a pair of shorts, or a t-shirt and her panties. It was this sort of thing; always half and half, like she couldn't go one way, all the way.

I was attracted to Kirsten's carefree style of sensuality, and we quickly became friends. Whenever visiting, I would always mention outrageous figures from Harper's Index and she was certain to be pleasantly amused. Stan, on the other hand, was not pleasantly amused, not even moderately amused — which would be more his style. He did not appreciate Kirsten's behaviour in front of his own brother, and instructed her — quite explicitly, so there would be absolutely no confusion — as to the appropriate code of dress.

Stan never forgave me for stealing Kirsten, and forgave me even less when I married her three years ago. After the wedding, he disowned me. Called me up and said he never wanted to see me again, ever, although I've seen him since creeping around outside the house. Once, I thought I saw him dressed in green army fatigues, crouching and running with a rifle clutched to his chest. Or maybe it was just one of the neighbourhood kids playing a game. You see things in the corner of your eyes sometimes and it could be anything.

Either way, I think Stan's a little loose in the head. Those times at night when the telephone rings and no one's there; I believe it's Spooky Stan, listening for a clue, finding solace in the instrument of deceit that has suddenly become so attractive to him.

"It's that nothing again," says my wife, Kirsten, holding up the receiver as if it's a piece of laundry and she's passively awaiting a verdict — clean or dirty.

"Hang up," I say.

Kirsten shakes her head and laughs with her lips shut. She gently sets the receiver back on its cradle. Then she turns toward me and rubs her top and bottom lips together as if she's just put on lipstick, only she hasn't. It's merely a habit she picked up from when she was a teenager, making sure her lip gloss was evenly spread.

"I don't understand," she says.

I glance up from the magazine I'm reading, "Understand what, Kirsten?"

"How it could be Stan?" She pulls the elastic out of her ponytail and shakes loose her strawberry-blonde hair. "You said you thought it was Stan. But, like, isn't he in the army or something?"

I rest the magazine flat against my lap. It would be useless to continue reading. Things had to be explained or Kirsten would not leave me in peace. Sighing, I let my head drop back. To further demonstrate my dismay, I rub my eyes, slowly, but good and hard.

"I told you," I say. "My mother called two weeks ago and said Stan was out. Remember?" I straighten my head and look at her, opening my eyes wider so she gets the point.

"Remember that? When I told you."

"Oh, right. Stan's out." Kirsten laughs, standing beside the blank television with her hands on her hips, her eyes fixed on the beige carpet. She silently mouths the words, Stan's out. Then she shrugs her shoulders and laughs again.

"Mom said Stan's been out for months."

"Stan," says Kirsten as if she can see him; his face winking up at her from the carpet. She's wearing that expression, like she just punched him in the arm. An old pal. Buddy, buddy.

"Good memories?"

"No," Kirsten corrects me as she steps toward the sofa. I ease my head backwards again and close my eyes. The cushions sink a little with Kirsten's weight when she sits beside me, her thumbs delicately touching my closed eyelids.

"Stan's crazy," she whispers. And I sense the tiny puffs of her breath tickling my ear as she leans closer. "Crazy with a capital C."

For the past few months, a short time after Stan's release from the army, a dozen white roses have been delivered every other week. They appear on the doorstep like twelve beautiful little ghosts. They're white roses because this girl, Dorothy — who I used to go out with — loved white roses. And both of us — Stan and I — know exactly what happened to Dorothy. Stan's just rubbing it in.

I used to receive scenic cards in the mail, too. They were from Cyprus, and the same thing was written on all of them: 'Dorothy would have loved this view.' The cards were never signed, but I knew who they were from. Stan was stationed over there. It was easy as hell to figure out. He was trying to spook me. All his life, he was trying to spook me. The way he locked me in the kitchen closet when we were kids; the broom and mop handles stiffly attempting to trip me backward into a greater, more chaotic darkness. The way he flicked off the light in the bathroom when I was vulnerable, and left it off until I was screaming and smacking the walls with my fist. And once when we had a fight over the loose change I found between the cushions, and he was trying to get even, he told me that Mom and Dad had been killed in a car crash when he knew very well they had only gone out to dinner. He knew it, but I didn't and I remember him standing there and smiling, saying, "Mom's dead. Dad's dead. You're nothing but a lonely little kid. I'm the one who owns you now."

Kirsten stands by the big living room window. She carefully parts the white sheers and stares out. The way she holds herself still, I know she's listening for something. Her jeaned legs shift slightly and then she shoves up the sleeves of her denim shirt, rolled up to her elbows.

"What's so interesting?"

Kirsten mumbles, um-hmm, which means "yes" to whatever it was I said to her. It doesn't matter. She's not listening.

"Something interesting?"

She turns and looks at me.

"What?" she says, scratching her nose. "What're you saying, Bill?"

"I just asked, what is so interesting out there? That's all. Just a question."

"What'd you mean?"

"Nothing, forget it." Frowning, I stare down at my magazine.

"Nothing's interesting, Bill."

"Oh."

"Relax, take a pill, it's just the street."

The doorbell rings and I find a dozen white roses on the front step. They're arranged in a green glass vase, standing upright on the concrete. I kick the delivery into the shrubs under the big window and shift the door mat with my foot to cover a few rose petals that fell loose. All I need now is for Kirsten to find out about the roses and Dorothy. I can't hide anything from her and if she asked she'd see it in my eyes and keep coaxing until I told her everything. She wouldn't be impressed. Touchy the way that she is, she'd have a nervous thing or two to say about what happened.

"Who is it?" Kirsten calls from the kitchen.

"No one," I call back. I glance around the yard. My eyes stop on the hedge and I examine it. It needs clipping. Beyond the hedge, a car speeds by — a whoosh of sound — and then everything is silent and exactly the same again.

"Well then," Kirsten says, now standing right behind me, "why are you standing here with the door open? And why are the hairs on the back of your neck pointing at me?"

"Cold," I say, sticking my head further out the doorway to scan the ends of the house.

"Shut the door," she says. She touches her hands against the skin under my shirt and I jump a foot or two, lose my balance, and tip on the doorstep, one foot out onto the concrete landing, the other foot in the house. I turn around in this position and stare at Kirsten. She smiles at me, drying her hands with the red and white striped cuptowel. Her brow is webbed and she's studying me with curiosity. When she's done, she flips the towel over her shoulder so that it rests against her denim shirt. Then she yanks up the waist of her jeans.

"What's your problem, schizo?"

"Nothing." I step into the house and Kirsten reverses, takes one solid step back so that she's still facing me.

"I need a belt. One with a big Navaho buckle. You know the kind," she says. "I think I'm losing weight."

"Your hands are freezing," I say, holding my palms up to her. My eyes confirm the warning. "Just stay away from me."

"How's the sandwich?" asks Kirsten. She's sitting at the dining room table putting together a jigsaw; a huge picture of four trees with blazing, autumn leaves. There are too many orange pieces for my liking. I tried to help her once but the futility of the task set me in a severe depression. Everything suddenly seemed senseless. I had to go to bed. I was exhausted.

"Perfect," I say, licking mustard and mayonnaise from my thumb. She looks out at me through the rounded archway that connects the living room and dining room.

"Good," she says, punching a mismatched jigsaw piece into place. Then she says, "I'm hearing strange noises outside the window in here."

"What kind of noises?" I try to swallow, but the bread is suddenly made of sawdust.

"Noises, you know, like snappings and rustlings. Someone tripping up." She stands from the table and creeps toward the window, hands held limply in front of her like a cartoon character. She leans forward a little as if she's sneaking up on whatever it is that's causing the sound.

I sit up on the sofa, straighten my back so I'm alert against the threat of attack.

"Have a look," I say. "The window."

"Right, Bill," she says, glancing back at me with a look of disgust. "Yeah, I think I can figure that much out."

"Fine. Have a look."

"Shut up, Bill," she says.

The doorbell rings again and Kirsten flinches, straightens, and sighs as if the sound has ruined everything.

Kirsten says, "Answer it."

"Not interested," I say. I lean forward and pick up a newsmagazine from the coffeetable. I thumb through the first few pages and stop on a grainy photograph of a killer. The picture does not do him justice. He looks mean. He's not smiling. I wonder why?

Kirsten breezes by me and a second later I hear the door being flung open. Then I hear this:

"Stan!" Kirsten's surprised and pleased voice. I hear my brother's deep, low voice. I can't make out what he's saying, but his passionless monotone rushes memories straight at me.

"Yes, of course," Kirsten says in a cheery tone that's a touch shakey. Stepping backward, her words grow louder, "Come on in, Stan. Bill's just dying to see you."

Stan is wearing a green beret. He's wearing black leather gloves, black boots, green army pants, and a grey salt and pepper sweater. His skin is pink high in his cheeks and his hair is thinning along his forehead. But he's got a thick, black moustache to make up for it.

I lean forward and ceremoniously shake his hand.

"Stan," I say. "Good to see you." I notice there's a leather holster strapped to his belt. "Mom told me you were back."

"Yeah," he says, but that's all he offers.

"Come in," pipes Kirsten. She turns and leads the way to the living room. We all take a seat; Kirsten and I sit on the couch and Stan pulls up a footstool and sits there with his legs spread but firm to the ground, his spine perfectly straight. He joins his gloved hands and glances around, his eyes going everywhere, even up at the ceiling.

"Where were you stationed?" asks Kirsten. She elbows me for some reason, but I can't figure out why. I stare at her and see her lips are tight, her eyes fixed on Stan's face.

"Cyprus," he says, still checking out the ceiling. "You do that tongue and groove work yourself?" He looks at me, then glances back at the ceiling.

"Tongue and groove?" I ask.

"The ceiling," he says, pointing up with a gloved finger. He squints at me suspiciously, like I'm a stupid soldier. "The ceiling, Billy. The pine stripping. Tongue and groove."

"Oh," I say. Kirsten elbows me again and I edge a little away from her, trying to hold in a wince. "No, that was there when we bought it."

"A lot of pine in here," he says.

Kirsten stands up and waits, as if she's forgotten what it was she was going to say or where it was she was going. Stan looks at her. I look at her. She blushes and rubs her lips together.

"How about a drink?" she asks.

"Don't drink, thanks."

"A sandwich?"

"Don't eat," he says.

I laugh and Kirsten laughs, but Stan's as serious as anything. He glances from Kirsten to me, then back at Kirsten. Only now I notice that Kirsten's staring at his holster.

"Why don't you just sit down," he says.

"I've got to pee," she says, almost pleads, her knees shivering slightly. "Is that okay, Stan?"

"Why ask me?"

She shrugs. "I'll just be a second, okay? Alright?"

Stan stares at her and a sense of restrained fierceness constricts in his face. He looks her up and down.

Kirsten backs away, bumps into an antique side table by the stairway and hurries up the stairs, turning and laughing nervously on her way up.

Stan watches her, then sets his steady eyes on me.

"So, what's happening in Cyprus?"

"Babysitting the Greeks and the Turks, that's what."

"Oh."

"Listen, Billy," he says. "I finally learned what I needed to know. Now I'm here for Kirsten."

I laugh and lean forward on the couch, joining my hands. I shake my head.

"Billy," he says, his expression unchanging. "Don't think I'm not serious."

"When I was in Cyprus we used to kick open the doors of the drug houses in the buffer zone along the border. The Greeks and the Turks used these abandoned buildings to peddle drugs to each other and to the soldiers. No one would ever be there after we came in like that — the noise, you know — but some of us would be hoping. I'd see the cigarette butts on the floor and I could tell how long the people had been there doing deals by the number of butts. I could tell who was there, too, by the brand of the cigarettes. I could pick up a butt and read the name on the filter and I'd know who it was. The Sand Monkeys — that's what we called the Turks — and the Guidos — the Greeks — really hated each other. They despised each other, religiously, but they were pals when it came to commerce. You get what I'm saying. You can hate somebody, but you can still do business with them. That's the world right there, in a nutshell. It's the same now. So let's talk commerce, Billy. Let's talk about Kirsten."

"Stan," I say to him. "I think maybe you should leave and get yourself some professional help."

Stan shakes his head and stares up at the ceiling, listening for Kirsten. I hear the window in the bathroom slide open and then a shuffling sound of quick movement.

"What's she doing up there?" asks Stan.

"What'd you think she's doing, Stan? What do women usually do in a bathroom?"

Stan gives me his nastiest look. He squints and points a gloved finger at my face, but he doesn't say anything.

Then he straightens his thumb and lowers it. He says, "Pow."

I stand up and move for the door.

"Come back here and sit down, Billy."

"Shut up, Stan." I hold the porch door open. "Come on, time's up. This isn't the old days, brother."

"I know what days they are, Billy. I used to use words a lot back then." He slowly rubs the back of his gloved hand under his nose, as if savouring the smell. "I used to talk and think more than I ever used my hands. The hands are what the army puts to use. You don't realize you have hands until you get into training. Your hands turn into steel. They can twist and they can shape things."

Stan swiftly rises to his feet and stands there watching the stairs. Then he walks for them. He takes the steps slowly with his hand sliding up the pine bannister. I follow him to the second floor, to the bathroom, where he gently taps on the door.

"It's open," Kirsten calls instantly.

Stan turns the knob and I see my wife leaning close to the big mirror, stroking on mascara. The window's open, but I know it's too small for her to squeeze through. I could have told her that. She's changed into a black dress with a low, low back and she's put on a dazzling combination of make-up.

She turns and holds out her arms. "Ta-da! What'd you think, guys?"

"Beautiful," Stan blankly states.

"Where are you going?" I ask her. "What's up?"

"The ballet, remember?" She stares at me, her eyes widening secretively. "The ballet's tonight. Sorry, Stan, we've got to rush."

"The ballet," he says like it's an operational password. I think he even winks at Kirsten, but I'm not certain.

"The ballet, Bill. Remember?" She nods encouragingly. A second later, she nods again. "You know, ballet."

"Ballet," Stan says, his narrow eyes taking a peek at me

before his elbow thrusts back and strikes me in the face. I see my arms flailing like the wings of a chicken attempting flight and then I hit the hallway wall, hearing a lot of solid booming noise. All kinds of loud sound, before I drop. But I don't remember landing.

I wake up with my face against the carpet, breathing the plush, dusty pile. One of my legs is buckled up under me and I slowly straighten it because it hurts. When I roll over, I see the light fixture up on the hallway ceiling. The light inside the smokey-glass globe is on, and so I know I'm alive.

"Kirthen," I say, but it's a numb sputtering whisper and I realize my lips are swollen. There's something small and hard-edged in my mouth. Splinters are pushing against the back of my throat. I cough and spit out a tooth.

"Jethuth, Kirthenn!" I brace a hand against the carpet and push up. I'm thinking about my tooth more than anything. I can't stop thinking about the gap. I open my mouth and search around in there. There's a space in the front and I don't know what's missing — one tooth or two. When I bring my fingers back I see there's blood on them.

The bathroom door is open beside me. I crawl for the wall and inch myself up. When I'm halfway to my feet, I smell perfume. It's lingering in the air. A sweet but sickly smell. My stomach muscles jerk as I guide myself into the bathroom. I lean on the counter, facing the mirror. With my thumb, I lift my swollen top lip until it touches the tip of my nose, and I see the gaping hole.

"KIRRRTHEN!" I shout. "THAAAN, YOU BATHARD."

The house is empty. I rush for the front door, but misinterpret the distance and bang face-first into the wall at the bottom of the stairs. It doesn't hurt. I just bounce back.

When I open the door, I see the street is empty. My car is in the drive, but I'm not going anywhere yet. I wonder if Stan was driving and, if so, what he was driving. I curse myself for not answering the door in the first place.

Back in the house, I pick up the telephone and call the police, but the policeman can't make out a word I'm saying so he hangs up after a few minutes of listening to me struggling to give my address. I'm shouting into the receiver, "THIXTHY-THIX ROETHDALE AFFENOO. HELFF."

I try calling my mother, but the line's busy. When I finally get through, she says, "Who is this?"

"ITH ME, MOETHER."

"You've got the wrong number," she says in a tone I've never heard before. "Go get sober," she huffs and hangs up.

I sit down on the sofa and hold my head. My tongue probes the gap where my front teeth once were, the ragged, pulpy flesh. Emotion rises from a quivering spot deep inside of me. It makes me feel like a helpless little kid and, pretty soon, I cry like one, too.

When I finally make it to the police station, the officer who I talk to keeps biting his lip to hold back a smile. I snatch the pen from him and write it all down on a sheet of paper: My name, my wife's name, my brother's name. I explain what my brother's wearing. I explain the situation. I tell them everything, even about me stealing Kirsten away from Stan — six years ago. Then I stab the pencil to the paper, putting the final period in place.

The officer reads the statement. He glances up at me every now and then. He nods, smiles, and swallows hard. Covering his mouth, he coughs and straightens his shoulders. I'm waiting and my eyes are wide, like white tire tubes with too much air.

"OOO THEE!?" I shout. "OOO THEE!?"

The policeman tells me to go home and rest. It's past one in the morning by the time we finish. I gave them my mother's phone number and they assured me they'd call her and get a make on the car my brother was driving. They assured me everything would be done within their means. When the officer first read that my brother was carrying a gun, he looked at me and said, "You're sure about the gun?"

"YETH."

He picked up the phone and called another officer, relaying the appropriate codes. Then he hung up and looked at me.

"You need a doctor?" he asked.

I shook my head.

"You lost a few teeth," he notified me, bending his head

low to get a better look into my mouth. With his hand aimed at my face, he wagged his pencil back and forth in the air. "Two front teeth gone." He leaned one way, then the other. His lips puckered to whistle, but when he glanced at my eyes he quickly straightened up and pressed his lips together.

I wanted to say, Not to mention a wife. I lost a wife and my two front teeth. But I wouldn't say a word. Couldn't. All the words turning truant and elusive, saucily refusing to come.

Needless to say I cannot sleep. I stay in the living room, sitting on the sofa with my head back, staring up at the tongue and groove, as Stan called it. My tongue can't help probing the space where my front teeth once were; the minced-meat section of gums.

I know Stan won't hurt Kirsten. I know that much. That isn't what he wants. I know she's safe as far as that is concerned, but I don't know what his plans are. What is the purpose?

And I wonder about another thing; whether or not Kirsten freely left with him. Did he take her by force, or did she just walk away and leave me out cold on the carpet? Maybe Stan had taken my pulse and checked my breathing. Maybe he'd assured Kirsten that I was okay and what he had to tell her couldn't wait. It was private information concerning me, and they needed to be alone. Stan could be very convincing. If anyone understood that, it was me. I am half-asleep, drifting off into elaborate thoughts of deception when I hear the front door close. My head pops up from where it's resting against the back of the sofa. My neck feels like a thick piece of rubber bent and set the wrong way.

I stand up and turn to see Kirsten strolling into the living room. She still has on the black dress, but her feet are bare. She's holding her black shoes in one hand, dangling from the straps as she stares at me.

"You look terrible," she says. But she doesn't make a move to comfort me. She simply stands in the same spot, with her shoes swinging slightly on her fingertips. She knows something.

"WWHAA HAFFEN?" I try to shout, but the sound comes more like a croak.

"What happened?" She laughs, spotting the gap in my

teeth. Her hand comes up to cover her shocked mouth, but her eyes still seem amused. In a moment she is serious again, remembering.

"YETH."

"Stan took me dancing down at The Colony." Kirsten gazes at the carpet and tries to look upset. "He wouldn't let me go. He told me some interesting things about you that I never heard before. He told me things." She whistles and meets my eyes with one of her sexiest cynical looks. "Oh-boy. He sure as hell knows you."

Kirsten tells me that Stan just dropped her off. She tells me that he told her things about Cyprus, things about the army and everything he did from the time he got up and took his shower to the time he went out on patrol in the buffer zone to what he did on his leave. He explained about the tourist girls on the beaches, sunbathing topless and how they just wanted a one-night stand with someone before moving on to another guy. It was meaningless, he told her. The girls were from Norway mostly and Holland. He told her about the Philippine whores in the bars looking for army men to buy expensive drinks for them. He told her about the heat and the snakes and how they'd roam in the buffer zone that separated the Turkish side from the Greek side. All the buildings in the buffer zone were abandoned and it was like moving through the ruins of hatred. This is what she said, what Stan called this place that he patrolled, this place he called his home. Kirsten told me he spoke the words proudly and with relish: The Ruins of Hatred.

Then she goes upstairs and packs her suitcase. I follow her into the bedroom and demand to know what she is doing. I don't think she understands what I'm saying because she answers me with: "I know what you mean. It's that time of night."

When she's finished packing, she drags the suitcase down over the stairs. She stands there and shakes her head at me, like she's finally seen me the way she was meant to all along.

"I don't understand you, Bill," she says. "Just to let that girl do what she did. Just left her for me. No word to her. You just walked away. Disappeared. So fucking cruel. So horrible the way she did it. This girl."

I stare at her. I try to lick my lips but my tongue hurts and it won't come out that far.

Kirsten's shoulders shudder. "I can't imagine how someone can do that to their wrists." She shudders again, making a sound with her lips like she's cold. "You know her name. Tell me."

I don't say a word. Nothing.

"Dorothy," she says.

I cringe at the sound.

"Right," she says. "Dorothy was her name. And you just let her do away with herself."

"I LEFFF ER FFFUR OOO."

A horn toots from outside. Kirsten opens the porch door then the front door and I see a taxi out there in the startling dawn. It's empty except for the driver and I wonder how it was summoned here. I don't remember Kirsten making a call.

"WHERE OOO GOING?"

"I don't want you leaving me," she says, "for someone else. There's no way I could handle that, either."

A policeman comes to see me in the morning. I'm trying to drink a glass of orange juice but the liquid escapes my numb lips and keeps running down the front of my white shirt.

The policeman looks at the trails of orange but doesn't mention it. I can talk a little better. The swelling has gone down, but the sharp pain kicks in every now and then, tightening up my muscles. I tell the policeman that my wife came back and then left again of her own free will.

"You're absolutely certain," he says, dipping his head slightly forward.

"Yesth," I say, softly.

"And what about this?" He nods toward my bruised lips.

I shake my head and he flips his pad shut. We're still standing in the porch. With a sigh, the officer turns away and pulls open the front door.

"That's all that can be done then," he says. He stops and stares at me. "I can't do a thing. You understand that?"

"Yesth," I say.

He shakes his head and closes the door. But I open it again to see what's going on outside. Not much. A car passes. A blonde Labrador retriever trots by, sniffing the sidewalk. The policeman glances back, about to stop, but I shake my head to let him know that it's over, so he dejectedly climbs into his patrol car and quietly backs out.

The roses in the shrubs under the big window are still fresh. I think of gathering them up. I think of bringing them to Dorothy's grave and laying them there. With little effort, I imagine the whole process. I know where she's buried. And I know the piece of me that's buried there with her. But I decide to leave them where they are. I hate the smell of roses. The overpowering odour makes me nauseous. It's too sweet. It's sickening. A semblance of Kirsten's perfume.

"Horrible," I shout at the roses, and slam the door.

I don't hear a word from anyone for over a week. I roam the silent house with thoughts that are not so silent. My home seems abandoned; foreign and untouched. I glance around the living room, where I stand with my arms limp at my sides. I stare up at the ceiling and listen, waiting for a wind to rise.

The telephone rings and it's my mother. She asks me about how I'm feeling and why I sound funny when I talk. I tell her I banged my lip on the cupboard door and she says I should be more careful. Then she asks about work. I tell her I was lucky enough to get a few days off — accumulated overtime — but the truth is I quit. I've had it with work. I don't ever want to churn out another press release.

Contrary to fabricated opinion, everything is not how it seems. Everything is not operating fine. We are not handling things — effectively or efficiently. Matters are more frightening than we could ever possibly imagine. I just want to reason with myself without the need to insert hopeful speculation. The time has come. The time is now. I just want to think and keep slipping my tongue over the smooth space where my teeth once were. There's something thrilling about the sensation, like my life has been granted a new beginning. I seriously expect to feel the jagged points of two fresh teeth — stronger and completely industrious — soon poking through.

Then my mother tells me that Stan has gone back to

Cyprus, but she doesn't mention Kirsten. She doesn't even ask me how my wife is.

"Stan told me to tell you that he enjoyed his visit."

"I guesth he did," I say.

"He did very much. He was gleeful when he came to see me, and he told me, Billy. I never saw him looking so good. He said that you two were getting along again. That everything was fixed up between you two. Things had been said that needed to be said and the air was cleared."

"We talked," I tell my mother, "about how thingth change. He told me 'bout Thyprsth and how they were justh waiting there for thumthing happen. Waiting for ah war."

"He told me they were only babysitting the Turks and the Greeks," says my mother. "Nothing exciting."

"No, you don't underthand, Mom." My voice is urgent and my mother tries to interrupt, but I won't let her defend Stan, not this time. "They were waiting for ah war," I insist, "juth itching to kill thumone."

Twelve days later, I receive a foreign envelope in the mail. A blue square envelope with colourful stamps. When I tear it open, there's a snapshot in there and nothing else. Nothing written on the back. Nothing more in the envelope. The picture has captured an image of a sign in the buffer zone.

I read it to myself: 'Attention. Beyond this checkpoint is an area of Cyprus still occupied by Turkish troops since their invasion in 1974. The invaders expelled 180,000 Cypriots of Greek origin from their ancestral homes and brought other colonists from mainland Turkey to replace them. Enjoy the sight of our looted heritage and homes from inhabitants of these areas who are forbidden to return.'

I carry the photo to the kitchen and hold it against the refrigerator door. I slip a magnet shaped like a bunch of bananas over the picture to keep it in place. Then I step back and read the words again.

Six years ago, when I stole Stan's girlfriend, I displaced him and now Stan has displaced me. The sign could just as well have said: "Enjoy our losses, pigs. You have murdered us."

I am not expecting anything any more. Simple pleasures are gained by moving through this house, searching through closets and looking under beds, checking through cupboards to make sure that all things are in order. The grass in the backyard is growing tall and I walk through it in my bare feet and stand beneath the cool shade of the dogberry tree. I am not expecting anything. But two days later, on a quiet Friday afternoon, Kirsten strolls in the front door as if nothing has happened. With both hands, she drags her suitcase up the stairs like it's full of bricks. Above me, I hear her move down the upstairs hallway, then fall onto the bed, moaning.

"I went to Montreal for a break," she calls out, struggling with something. Maybe she's kicking off her shoes, or squirming out of her jeans. "You should see the stuff I bought. New things for you, too. Credit cards all gone the limit. So don't use them, okay. I was embarrassed a couple of times already."

"I quit," I whisper, loud enough so only I can hear the words, knowing how only I can truly understand them.

"I realized I love you, Billy," Kirsten shouts dramatically. "Come up. Come back to me, gorgeous." She laughs the laugh that tells me she is exhausted and out of control.

"I quit," I whisper again, "my job."

Kirsten is like that. Kirsten's a touch crazy, too. She's left the front door open and I watch it, expecting Stan to walk straight in any minute with a pistol raised and bang, bang, bang — a full chamber popped off into my face, the gun emphatically stating what he's been wanting to say for so long. Action, not words. But the door is just an opening and no one fills it. So I step forward and out onto the concrete landing. Slipping both hands into the loose pockets of my pants, I rock back and forth on my heels.

"Hey," Kirsten calls weakly, trying to restrain her laughter. "It's Friday, right? Why aren't you at work?"

I notice again that the hedge needs trimming all the way along, and in my driveway I see my car has two flat tires; one in the front and one in the back. Maybe the tires on the other side are down too, but I can't see them. I just notice this now. Someone has let the air out of my tires. It's the worst kind of tragedy — being stranded here like this — because I've got no intention of sticking around here. I slip my tongue over the fresh skin where my front teeth once were. The sensation is inspiring, and I swear I can feel the new jagged points.

"I've got playsith to go, too," I shout, turning back into the house. "Lot ah playsith."

I say them out loud and count them on my fingers.

A Nail Into Smoke

Adina lights a cigarette in the darkness of the Ford Galaxie 500, the hot orange rings of the lighter glowing as they rise toward her lips. Fire crackles on the inhale, then the cooling rings fade as she taps the lighter against the ashtray and slips it back into the metal hole.

It is raining heavily, splatters of blurry water obstruct visibility the instant the wipers sweep down. The road is like black enamel. The car, this one that I am doing my best to paint in detail, is not only like black enamel, it is like *wet* black enamel.

I have clicked on the two arm-lamps at either end of the painting and pointed them at the image of the car and the rain and the road. I have blended a reasonable measure of cobalt blue with black for the sky and an almost imperceptible tinge of blue for the road, as if the light reflects down from above, vaguely tinting the asphalt, but I have mixed no blue whatsoever with the steady black pigment that brushes the car to life. The scene is night and the canvas is seven feet wide by six feet high.

Adina and I are driving in the car and she is lighting a cigarette. She sits beside me with the small pointed flame blistering orange as she inhales, her face glowing warmly, sensually. The corners of her eyes lift with the sincerity of a smile and her smooth skin hugs her cheekbones. There is no blue in her hair, either. It is pure black, long, straight and combed back.

"What are you going to call it?" she asks me as she steps away from the fireplace in my studio and presses her naked body in behind mine, to fit snugly. I turn my head to admire her face, her chin resting on my shoulder, her painted lips pursed in observation.

"You see yourself in there?" I ask. "That little orange dot." I point with the brush. "Behind the misty window. You were smoking a cigarette, remember?"

"That rain," she says. "Mmmmm. I remember." She says, "That rain did things to me. The smell from the woods."

I nod and turn the steering wheel. The car veers off onto the muddy, gravel shoulder of the highway.

"What're you doing?" Adina asks.

"I don't know. I'm not finished yet." I step back from the canvas, my feet shifting speculatively, guiding me further into the center of the studio to gain a wider perspective.

"No, what're you doing, really?"

"This is the road, to the log cabin."

"Here?" exclaims Adina. "It's so damn black down there, all those trees. Are you sure you know where you're going?"

"Don't I always?"

"Sure." She looks at me with a sour expression. "Just what we need, to get lost again."

"It's a narrow road, it's the country. It's supposed to be that way." The car dips and gently rocks as the tires roll into the shallow, rain-filled potholes.

"It's cold," says Adina. "Do you feel it?"

I glance over my right shoulder toward the fireplace. Small stone sculptures rest along the mantlepiece, simulating shapes of sentimental collectables. The flames in the hearth are ebbing, although the hardwood floor beneath my bare feet retains a satisfactory warmth.

"It needs more logs," I blandly offer.

Positioned to the side of the painting, Adina stares at me, the image of the car level with her pale, upright breasts as if the intention of the road is to lead us there.

"Why don't you put on some clothes?" I suggest. "If the cold's bothering you."

"Why don't you roll up the window?" she says.

"Now, that's an idea," I say. "I was just letting out the smoke." I reach for the lever and wind in circles until the sounds of rain onto leaves and bushes scraping the sides of the black car are shut out like a lid coming down, sealing us in.

"Better?" I ask.

"Yes," she says, questionably observing my crouched figure beside the fire. I brush the particles of bark from my hands as she steps toward me with smiling intention, closer so that I hold her hips and kiss her warm belly. I lift the paintbrush from where I have laid it down on the hearth and paint a black hole four inches in diameter below the softest, youngest section of her belly. I paint it perfectly round and then push my fingers in.

"What'd you think?" I ask her. "You feel my fingers in there?"

"In where?" she asks, looking down at my hand slipping in and out of her flesh.

"The comfort hole."

"I know that hole," she says, tut-tutting.

"No, this is the one where longing finally gets a rest, real satisfaction."

Shifting her feet, opening her legs for me to reconsider, Adina says, "Here's the only hole men are really after."

"No, this hole." I nod at the one I have painted in the tender part of her flesh. "This is the space that men are always searching out in women. The hole that doesn't speak and doesn't see, smell or hear. Not for sex or squatting out the leftovers. This one's for comfort only."

"Sweet idea."

"That's what I paint for; to finger this...sanctuary, draw it wider in a woman."

"Bullshit. What do you really paint for?"

"Seriously?"

"Yes, seriously."

"To crawl into this hole in you that no one else can ever see or find." I move my hand around inside and sense the warm summer easiness of childhood; the lull of clean, sweet sleep.

With my other hand, I stretch the hole wider and reach in with all fingers. Leaning forward, I wait a moment, glancing up for the encouragement that is not there, before ducking in.

"You artists!" she says, laughing and shaking her head. "Always lying through your fucking teeth."

I climb up, but fall right through her, tumble to the floor. Landing gracefully, I roll and settle, clasping both hands around my knees and watching the fireplace, as if nothing has happened, being accustomed to such expulsions, her thoughtless lack of regard.

Adina speaks behind me, "Yes, but if I don't want you in there, then there's no way to hang on."

"A valid point," I whisper, again disappointed by her utter lack of enthusiasm. I want to tell her how my art can be such a frustrating task of translation and projection at once; a grappling to make tangible the disengaged contours of what we wish to define as the soul, to give substance. But she will not offer compassion, cannot offer what she does not hold as hers.

Instead, I receive kindless responses in the form of scorn and humiliation. It is implied that I must function as a master or not at all. My skill must be uncontested. Again, projection. So I vie for notoriety. Create an image of confidence and bravado. To be *seen* as a master, that is the trick. While all that I am wanting is compliance. Uncontested trust and lapdog conviction to complement the integrity of my work.

"If I don't want you in there," she says, "you'll just have to get off." Rain lashes against the car. We are parked with our headlights on beside the log cabin we have rented, and Adina pushes my face away from her breasts. She reaches for her ankles, clutching her underwear and raising her behind so she can pull them up. With delicate fingers, she guides her skirt down back into place and smoothes the cotton fabric along her legs.

"We'll wait until the rain lets up," I say, leaning on the steering wheel, a flush burning in my cheeks. Something inside of me needing desperately to spill out into her, wanting to race excitedly along with her thrill, nearing the climax that hints at enlightenment but then to lose sight of it as the spunk blasts loose. Art, so much like sex. The struggle to draw the unnameable urge toward pleasure and wholeness, but only to expel one's energy, to pale oneself in the doing.

"I'm sorry. I'm just not in the mood," says Adina.

I stand from the studio floor, speaking wearily, "You should always be in the mood."

Adina laughs, "For what?"

"Compassion, at least."

"You mean pity."

I turn for the painting, toward a more definite companion, the visual blending of cerebral and concrete that allows unquestionable gratification, the ego stroking itself. Ego as its own sustenance.

But the painting is of a memory, of one night. It is startling; the black car the way that it is, but is calming also because I have control. I have painted the scene of an actual memory, but only as I have wished it. I have fashioned its passing to settle perfectly in the place that its passing has left. And now it exists exactly as I desire. Inside and outside of me. A permanent still act of movement.

"Inside," she says, nodding toward the cabin. "We'll do it in there."

"Why not out here?"

"The woods are too creepy."

"Come off it. The truth."

"Okay, they excite me too. But I'm sort of frightened."

"What do you want?" I ask her. "Tell me." I glance away into the brooding trees, the dank scent of nature enticed into the air by rain.

"I want to be naked on the wet grass," she says for me.

"And feel the evergreen boughs against your beautiful ass."

"Yes," she agrees. "Exactly."

"You're always right," I say, forgetting what she has been talking about and concentrating on the painting.

"That was a long time ago," she says, gently, delicately placing her palms to her breasts, cradling the memory and smiling a hint of dark sexuality.

"No," I insist. "It's now."

"Are you listening?" she says.

I nod, "Of course I'm listening. Always." I brush a stroke of chrome onto the rear bumper, the paint moving so easily.

"I'm not in there now," says Adina. "Listen."

"Of course."

"What did I just say?" she demands, letting go of her breasts.

"Whatever I paint," I tell her, not needing to look to see. "That's what you say."

"You just believe what you want." Again, she steps in behind me, her hands touching my shoulders. Sensing her warmth, I close my eyes and listen to the rain.

"If I didn't believe in you, you wouldn't be here at all, in the flesh or otherwise."

"Oh, I'd be here." Her fingers carefully rubbing the shallow of my back.

"But you'd be someone else."

Her hands stop moving and immediately, before she has a chance to say a word, I feel changed.

"I'd be someone who doesn't want you," Adina admits, "like I don't want you inside of me anymore."

"It's you who's inside of me."

"Right." She laughs sarcastically. "The shit you get on with."

"Yes, but it's exquisite shit."

"You're just a lost man who fancies himself some kind of martyr. How fucking boring. You haven't any life to call your own, other than your stupid canvases and they're always ideas from the past. Always twiddling around with your little visions."

"Twiddle, twiddle." I smile. "What a great word. How accurate."

"And you drag me in there with you, splashing these magic colours from your fingertips, or so you like to think, screwing everything together, the past with the present, subconscious with conscious. What was it you called it? Trans...sectism."

"Transectionism."

"Yeah, that's what you call it. Isn't it? It's just too much. Why can't you get real for a change?"

"That is real. Everything swirled into a pot. What could be more real?"

"Be *here* for once, fully here, I mean. Sometimes I don't even know if I exist at all, or if I'm just in your head. I've had enough of walking the tightrope with you. You've got no sense of balance. I've had enough."

"That's what I'm getting at." I open my eyes to watch how

she moves. She thrusts a steady hand toward the lighted paint-ing, glowing in the otherwise dark studio. A dimly lighted sign that has already tempted us to enter.

Instantly, I strike out. I smash my fist through the wind-shield and the rain pours in on us. We have no protection. The oils begin to wash away and run, exposing the stark whiteness of the canvas; the void we know will overcome us if we refuse to internalize the colours, if we ignore sensitivity to face the senseless. Our one-way course that is the fate we struggle to outlive by relentlessly styling our thoughts into palpable objects.

Adina clutches my hand. We must run for the cabin. But the cabin is merely a prop; a cardboard cut-out that falls over when Adina pushes against the door.

"What have you gotten me into?" she shouts above the sounds of wind and lashing rain. She paws at her wet hair, flicking it away from her face like a tangle of lovely netting.

I stare at her and cannot find the words to explain how every subtle shade of colour makes her mine. I have drawn her here into the confusion of a scene whose depth only I have in-ternalized. Distorting the intention to maximize reality, I have gone too far and plunged completely into abstraction. I have created a glut, and am at odds to explain the excess to her.

Sadly, I must admit that I am lacking aesthetic restraint. But my ego refuses to accept truth as truth. Instead it pomp-ously assures me: Throughout history, those with inventive, prodigious visions have always failed to inspire, for who is there to ever understand such prophecy?

I have lost Adina in the way that I lose a glimpse of revela-tion in a dream as it teases me and then disappears when I awake. Struggling to remember what show of foresight my subconscious has disclosed, I sense the sadness of loss in what has evaded me.

"You're so full of shit," Adina says. "Pretentious asshole."

The good news is I can go on without pause, making her answer. A series of portraits called Speech.

The streets are black enamel. The car is *wet* black enamel. I cannot see where I am going. Alone in this dark car moving me, I sit beside myself, snubbing the drab premise that I am imperfect and parked.

The Muffled Drum

I

Wilfred's New Place was much like the place he opened first, only now it was a larger square room built onto the side of his house. The yellow clapboard dwelling with a cola sign above the second door was set down where the road slopes deeply and then rises before curving off into the woods toward the secluded penitentiary. Wilf bought a pool table at a government auction in St. Shotts and centered it atop a sheet of grey panelling that he laid in the middle of the new room. Men and women often slept on the green felt in the afternoon hours when they drank so much under-the-counter beer and black rum that they could no longer stand. Legs and arms hung over the grooved chrome edges, twisting off in all directions.

The bodies of a man and a woman rested there now while Wilfred blinked from behind the aspinite counter at the back of the room, his hand resting on the ledge while he nodded with his head on a permanent tilt close to his shoulder. The tail of his green and grey plaid shirt hung out around his waist as he nodded again and turned, dragging one leg, shuffling over to the big cooler at his right. Opening the long glass door, he popped the caps off two colas so the young boys could mix the black rum to make sure it would be sweet and not sting to such a wicked degree.

Hedley was sitting in his usual spot next to the pinball machine and, in keeping with his nature, was not saying a word, just staring ahead with his fingers firmly wrapped around a bottle of beer, his hair combed nicely and the top button of his shirt done up so as to appear presentable for the occasion.

Wilfred blinked at Gord and Clyde, who were pointing at Hedley and laughing and slapping the counter with their open palms. Gord was saying how Hedley never had it so good, how he looked better than ever.

" 'Elt'ier den I ever seen 'im," said Gord, smearing the laughing tears from his eyes with his pudgy oil-stained hand, while he sipped a drink from the beer bottle that some moonshine had been poured into. His face was small and his rounded cheeks burned red when he smiled to show two rows of badly chipped teeth from chewing the caps off bottletops. Whenever a bottle needed opening Gord was always quick to snatch it away, impatiently bend the cap off with his teeth while he watched the person who was waiting as if to say, "Dere's no trick ta dis. Ya jus' gotta 'ave balls." Breathing heavily, he moved his wide body to take a look around the room.

"D'at trip down ta see 'is sister in da sun done 'im da best." Clyde laid his long heavy arm down around Gord's rounded shoulders, fearing his knees would collapse from the laughter. Sensing the humour slipping off, he coughed and straightened up, weakly shaking his head and giving a merry sigh. Clyde turned to the counter again to face Wilfred's white oval head, which was tilted to the side and bent close to his shoulder. His greyish-brown beard brushed against the front of his shirt as he stiffly tossed a bag of Cheezies to a boy leaning against the pool table.

"R...r...rrright on," Wilfred stuttered, holding up a thumb and catching the coins — one at a time, and slapping each one onto the counter — as the boy spun them across the room. The boy, a slight sharp-featured adolescent named Gilbert, pulled open the bag of Cheezies and glanced at Gord and Clyde before giving serious consideration to Hedley. Strolling across the room, Gilbert pulled out a chair beside the opening that led into Wilfred's house. The curtain hanging there, separating the rooms, had fallen loose and Gilbert saw the small brown couch low to the floor, and the colourful crocheted quilt thrown over it, the woodstove in the center of the room with a black-bottomed kettle resting on top, and a small square of carpet under the wooden box that acted as a coffeetable. An orange and grey cat slowly leapt onto the box and curled up to sleep. Watching the cat, Gilbert sat down in the chair next to Hedley then glanced back at the men leaning close to the counter. The boy nodded with a smile, raising his eyebrows so that Gord and Clyde knew it was a joke as he casually offered Hedley a Cheezie. The room exploded with laughter, a grumble rising from the pool table as a man wearing a dark blue baseball cap twisted and tossed in his sleep, as if to fight off the commotion, before rolling dangerously close to the edge. Half of his body dangled for a moment, before all of him slipped over, dropping and crashing onto the floor. Bottles and windows rattled and the floor shook violently before the vibrations settled disagreeably, as if an explosion had been set off close to Wilfred's New Place. Two oldtimers sitting at a small round table by the door stared glumly at where the body had fallen. One of them looked at the other, their faces remaining unchanged. They each took a drink and glanced across the room to see who was making all the noise now. Gord was clapping wildly, roaring and shouting with a scratchy voice for an encore. He slammed a five dollar bill on the counter. "Five says Fran go'n ov'r nex'." Pushing his twisted fingers into his pocket, Wilfred pulled out a five dollar bill and matched the bet. "Nnnnno way Fffrrran go'n...I seen 'er 'ang on fff...fur' ev'r." The men started shouting and calling to Fran's unconscious body, until the uproar was muffled by the opening of the door and the sound and the feel of the winter wind pushing into the warmth that glowed from the space heater in the corner, slicing through the cigarette smoke and the dense stale lull of body heat. Aggie stomped in, with frost in her eyebrows and on her whiskers, and without pausing, turned and leaned against the door with both hands, shoving it closed before banging her boots clean on the blackened slats of hardwood floor. She did not bother taking off her red and white mittens or her pointy blue woollen cap.

"Da Skidoo's idl'n out dere," she announced with a toothless smile.

Wilfred blinked quickly. "Yy...yyy..."

"Come on Wilfred," Gord shouted, encouragingly, rubbing his chubby fingers together. "Come on, heave it outta ya."

"Yyyy...yyya g...got da sled?"

"Yeeeees, I got 'er. Yeees, I do in fact." Aggie rubbed her mittens over her rough deeply wrinkled face, and smiled with her eyes closed, her ravaged lips and white whiskers feeling the new warmth of the place.

" 'Edley," the boy called, leaning across the table and staring close at Hedley's steady unblinking eyes. "Down over Coombs Hill. Ya 'member Coombs Hill. Put da peekture in yer 'ead." He glanced back at the counter, at the smiles that stretched in unison, the chuckling, and something more; the slow rising and coming of wide open laughter.

"Cover'd in ice like glass," said the boy Gilbert. "Ya 'member wha' ya said 'bout it? One lass roy'd down da 'ill. G'wan, old Hed. 'Av a Cheezie firs' ta keep yer stren't up."

Three snowmobiles rose out of the valley, heading in parallel lines across the bald field of snow that climbed toward the powdered treeline densely clustered higher and higher up toward the summit of Coombs Hill. The sound of engines were distant, and a thin dark boy played the muffled drum while he watched from his place hidden in the evergreens, seeing the tiny moving specks that were the snowmobiles like insects on a huge white sheet far below his eyes. The round drum was stuffed with old rags and the dark boy struck it slowly, with purposeful momentum, the source of the lagging rhythm causing no misunderstanding. He had been told to do this. The face on the floor had told him in a dream and there was no denying that he should take heed of the words revealed to him, the words he believed he could see when the face on the floor opened its buckled mouth.

"Whitey's 'ere," Clyde called back to the others. He was the first to arrive closest to the treeline and had just shut down his snowmobile. Climbing off, he listened, hearing immediately the dull sound from in the woods. The snowmobile was like a toy beside his tall, solid body. He glanced down at the black seat, noticing a new split in the vinyl, then stared into the woods, hoping for a glimpse of Whitey, and finally sighting his partially concealed position. Clyde turned and shouted to the others, pointing up ahead and into the woods at the half image of the boy dressed in a black parka and black snow-crusted pants, striking the muffled drum with wide, slow swings of his arm.

"Look at 'im," Clyde shouted, spitting into the snow, then lowered his voice as Gord rolled closer, letting his engine sputter and die. "Crazy as da loon."

"What da fuh'k is dat," Gord rasped, leaning heavily to the side before slowly swinging his stout leg over the seat, and planting both feet firmly in the crusted snow. "Ya 'ear dat sound?"

"Is Whitey," Clyde insisted, dragging the sleeve of his light green woollen sweater across his nose. The sweater was tight and stained along the cuffs. "Whitey, in da woods wit da drum. Boom, boom. Lees'n so y'l 'ere, 'by." He pointed. "See 'im. Boom, boom, boom. Mak'n no sense t'all."

Gord growled at the thought of something he could not understand, and coughed, "Fuh'k'n idjiot." He turned and swayed back to where Aggie was helping Wilfred lean from the back of her snowmobile. One of Wilfred's arms was lame and set permanently against his belly. Aggie took hold of that arm, guiding him to his feet. Waiting close by, Gord stared at the wide wooden sled that was tied, with three-strand rope, to the back of the vehicle. Young Gilbert had been sitting comfortably behind Hedley on the sled, until Hedley had tipped back, pinning the boy.

Gilbert was laughing so hard he barely had the strength to slap at the body. He found it difficult to catch his breath, the weight crushing his lungs, until he was so weak that his ribs ached and it hurt his stomach and shoulders to laugh any more.

"Get 'im off me," Gilbert wheezed with hardly any air left in him.

Clyde briskly set one big leg to either side of the sled and bent down, taking Hedley under the armpits and easily yanking him up. Quickly scurrying to the side the boy freed himself, sitting up in the snow with his face against his knees, taking deep breaths. Shaking his head with giddy amazement, he straightened his woollen cap.

"Wha' ya star'n at," Clyde barked at Hedley. He held the body in front of his face and glared with mock accusation into Hedley's eyes, then glanced back, over his shoulder for reaction. Gord yelped a laugh and Aggie covered her face with her mitten and shivered wildly with her eyes closed, sucking in her bottom lip to bite down with shameful glee.

Sitting still and listening, the boy suddenly lost all sense of humour when he heard the flat sound of the drum rising out from the trees, the sound lingering high to come down and touch them, as if from inside their chests.

"Whitey," Gilbert whispered, concentrating on the sound and automatically rising to his feet. "Jaysus, Whitey. Fuh'k'n bas'ard, ruin'n t'ings."

" 'E's gut da right a'ever'n else." Aggie stared off into the trees, pushing her jaw to one side. "Dun't be at 'im." She whacked Gilbert on the shoulder, then shoved him so hard that he tumbled back into the snow. "Leev'm."

Hitting the ground with a quiet thud, Gilbert stared at her, feeling the pangs of pain in his behind. Aggie was not smiling. Nodding firmly with serious eyes, she swung back her laced-up boot, kicking snow at him.

Gilbert did not say a word, but simply stood, brushing the snow from the lap of his blue snowmobile suit, then turned away to look at how Clyde was working quickly, holding back the laughter that came up in his throat, as he tied Hedley to the thin posts up the rear of the sled. Gord stood there watching, with his arms resting by his sides, looking round and stuffed, as if he had been blown up with air.

"Hh...hhh...ow ya ggg...gonna sit 'im up?" Wilfred asked, dropping down onto the cracked vinyl seat of Gord's silver snowmobile, his bare hands turning pink where they were resting close to his lap. He sat there in his shirt-sleeves, breathing out the cool mist.

"Nar prob'em widt dat. He be li'l steef reet now. Sit 'im up's on'y da joke." Clyde kneeled beside Hedley and moved the body's arms back and forth, leaving them in certain comic positions while he glanced up at Wilfred to make sure the point was gotten. "Steef as ol' k'nt."

"Whitey done stapped," Aggie said, gasping. Quickly she turned and stared into the woods, but Whitey was nowhere to be seen. "Whitey's pees't off reet gud cause 'a dis. I'll 'ave ta go'n see'f 'e's do'n okay. Too late now ta falla af'ta 'im, see 'im t'mar'a n'sted." She nodded her head good and hard. "Yeees."

Gord and Clyde looked at each other and then down at Hedley, who had fallen sideways on the toboggan, his eyes staring off across the snow which ended along the rim of evergreens whose peaks were topped by a wintery blue sky that was so clear it seemed to glow.

Gilbert thought of Whitey and the drum that always made its presence known. As if to prove a point, to shove it all away, he rushed in behind the sled, stooping to push the back so that it slid along slowly at first, then faster until Gilbert's legs could not keep up, running bent awkwardly, and he fell onto his knees. He stayed right where he was, watching the toboggan race off, down the shiny crusted slope.

"Geev 'er a gud shuv." Clyde shouted with his thick gloves cupped around his mouth.

"L'uk 'a 'Edley fly'n," Aggie whispered, carefully licking at the brittleness of her whiskers. "Nut'n stop'n 'im now. Nut'n e'ver in 'is way'a tak'n off."

II

Whitey had dreams while he thought he was wide awake. Images and sequences of purification presented themselves. Struggling to understand, he dreamed about the face on the floor, and came to know that the face was who he should be listening to because it was always lying next to his bed when he awoke. The face and its body had been there for as long as Whitey remembered. He could not recall a time when he did not feed or clean the face, which had no definite features, and wash the body with its skin like wet cardboard that never dried.

The face was there, straining to lift its head slightly to snatch a stray look at Whitey coming in through the front of the cabin, kicking his boots against the door to drive the snow from them.

The face opened its lipless mouth to let out the horrible silence that it felt, then closed itself and opened again, this time a sound tearing loose, "Meeeeeeest!" The face shrieking, sliding and bucking inches at a time along the floor, until it was close to Whitey's feet. "Meeeest, meeeest..."

Whitey smiled at the face, then laid the drum on the table by the door. Pausing for a moment, he then glanced out the small window that overlooked the snow-laden banks of the stream running alongside their cabin. The water was still flowing, never stopping once, knowing that the slightest turn of hesitation would mean the setting in of something sharp and crystal, freezing solid, stealing its mobility.

Whitey bent to the face and touched its forehead. The face tried to smile but its intentions were all wrong and what happened looked nothing like a smile.

"Hedley Thistle's dead," Whitey informed the face, rising up to stand straight on his legs.

"Meeeeest!" said the face. "Meest, meeeeeest." Sloppily bending and twisting its blunt limbs, the face bucked across the floor, closer to the bed, then slid under, staying put.

Whitey lifted a cracker from a red box and popped it into his mouth, biting down and making the crumbs into mulch that stuck to his teeth the way he liked it.

"Hedley Thistle," Whitey whispered with his deep but youthful voice, which gave him a quality of agelessness. He stared blankly at the table top where he had laid the drum. A knot had fallen from the center and Whitey pushed his finger into the hole, admiring the fit. "He was a kind man, Face. I hate to see the end of him." Slowly glancing to the side, Whitey could see the face's huge lopsided eyes staring out from under the foot of the bed.

"Do you want to go in the tree?"

There was much shuffling and grunting as the face frantically made its way across the floor. Swirling around Whitey's boots, it coughed and squealed enthusiastically.

Outside in the yard, the thick rope was crusted with snow. Whitey tied one end around the middle of the bulk that rested beneath the face's head. The rope sank easily into the white flesh, seeming to dig in too deeply for comfort, the face's flesh almost swallowing the cord. Threading a pulley mechanism that Whitey had arranged many summers ago, he then slowly stepped backward, straining with the other end of the rope in his hands until the face rose from the snow and dangled higher, then higher, coming level with the wooden ledge set up in the huge maple tree that grew fifteen feet from the door of the cabin. Carefully Whitey tied the rope around a notched stump, leaving the face hanging there until the boy climbed quickly with his feet finding places between the limbs and his hands clutching around the smooth bark. Once on the platform, Whitey leaned out to first pull the face onto the landing, then in closer to the thick limb of the tree. He sat the face in a comfortable position, then climbed down to untie the knot. Once back in the tree, he drew the end of the rope up from the ground and wrapped it many times around the trunk and the face's chest. Tying a triple knot, he tugged with both hands to make certain it was secure.

"You can see good," said Whitey, standing on the flat wooden base high in the tree, sensing the strangeness in his legs at the feel of being up so high with such a clear view across the forest that led down into Cutland Junction on the west side. He could just barely see the grey tower of the penitentiary, and over toward the east he could see the dark blue water with the sun flashing white dots across its surface, and — not far from shore — the narrow piece of land they called Blind Island because everything had turned so bad out there after the iron ore mines closed down. "Remember to keep your tongue in your mouth," Whitey told the face.

The face stared, then shifted its enormous eyes toward the sky to follow the sound of a brown hawk gliding and dipping off.

"You hear me? Keep your tongue in your mouth or it'll be frozen."

The face shifted and jerked from side to side, coughing a long steady cough that went on for a seemingly impossible length of time before it settled. Whitey gently touched the face's soft cool skin, knowing this touch of understanding to be the only thing capable of quieting the face.

Climbing gradually down the tree, Whitey went into the cabin to find the small radio in its brown leather case. It was on the ledge behind the woodstove where he had left it. The face was making happy noises from its place high above the world when Whitey came back out adjusting the dials.

The calm even voice on the radio announced a cure for some long-standing devastating illness, and Whitey wondered what it could have been. As always, he repeated the information that he heard, thoughtfully pronouncing each word at least twice. Snow sprinkled onto his uncovered head and he gazed up at the sky to see that it was blue and clear, then looked at the face to see that it was squirming and making wet sticky sounds like laughter, its eyes staring down as the snow was kicked randomly from the splintery edge of the platform.

Whitey was always fond of Hedley Thistle. The man had treated Whitey with respect and charity, so he made the extra effort to get Hedley's body back from where it was still tied to the sled outside of Wilfred's New Place. Whitey heard the loud sounds coming from behind the walls: people shouting and bodies falling against the walls or dropping onto the floor, as he tied the steering rope from the sled around his own chest and, unhooking the latch from the snowmobile, leaned forward, dragging the sled along. Its runners left two clean and narrow dents in the snow, the weight of it breaking through the crusted surface. It took him most of the late afternoon to get the body back and he was sweating inside the warm hood of his parka, his hair plastered to his forehead despite the severe cold, which turned his breath to thick white clouds hanging in front of him that he walked into and through.

When the face saw the boy and the sled coming along the path through the woods, it shrieked and struggled to get free from where it was tied high in the tree. Whitey heard the frantic scuffling noise and let the loop of rope drop from around his chest, stopping to catch his breath before treading ahead to stare up at the face.

"What's the matter?" he called toward the sky, his arms hanging limply by his sides.

The face's mouth was moving many different ways and it was coughing and hiccupping in the manner that was its own particular method of informing the boy of what was troubling it.

"That's only Hedley Thistle," Whitey said, staring back and half-heartedly pointing at the sled. "It's only what's left of him."

Numerous reassurances from Whitey were offered before the face finally quieted. Its feet stopped thrashing around and the snow stopped coming down like handfuls of powder tossed from the platform.

"It's alright," said Whitey, staring back at the body that knew nothing but patience now, sitting in its place, waiting for whatever would be done to it. "Hedley's made it out, okay," he whispered so the face would hear. "I'm just going to sit him down over there, so he won't be tormented any longer."

III

There was a place in the middle of the woods where the stream ran out into Keels Lake and the ice was grey and weak, and there was open water where Whitey would wait at the edge of the woods, watching for lone snowmobiles. He could see them coming in the distance, breezing over the rises and slopes of the snow that appeared level because it was impossible to see the contours of the brilliant snow beneath the machines, riding straight and then striking the slant of an invisible bank that dumped the snowmobile on its side without any kind of warning. Whitey had seen several men ride close to the open water, then disappear quickly as if they had not been there at all. They were strangers on big heavy machines he had not seen before, men from up on the highway where they parked their city trucks and trailers and came down into the woods without any knowledge of where the open water was. Whitey had seen it happen three times, but only to people travelling alone. On each occasion, Whitey had waited until night and gone back to the highway to find the deserted car and trailer still there. He had then loaded up his sled and dragged the goods back to his cabin. The far corner of his cabin was stocked with many provisions: four red containers of gasoline, two boxes of food and assorted chocolate bars that the men had taken for lunches or suppers, and four magazines filled with pictures of dead animals and fish that smiling men kneeled beside, or held proudly in their hands. There had been other magazines as well with pictures of women without clothing, but the face had told him in a dream that the pictures belonged to the fire and so Whitey had used them in the woodstove, even though he could not forget the sleek images and how they sometimes displaced everything else that filled his head. Sometimes he would find a lone dog running wild that had belonged to the men that went into the open water. Whitey kept the dogs for a while, as long as he could feed them, and then they'd disappear into the woods, off to find a new master. He'd never see them again, or he'd find them frozen stiff the way he sometimes came across their carcasses, so that he'd take them home and set them up outside the cabin so he could look at them, standing there so hard and perfect. That way — at least — they'd have some use because there wasn't much you could do with a frozen carcass. It was impossible to bury in the steely hard ground and it was not a good thing to take them into the cabin because they would soon be warmed and just lying there stiff in a puddle of dark water along the floor. A smell would start finding its way out and things would begin growing in there, the dog's thawing insides soon taking on new wriggling life in front of the nurturing stove.

Besides the city men who were lost out here, there were other ones from around Cutland Junction who came out to the open water, riding dangerously close even though they knew it was there.

The boy Gilbert was one such person. Whitey watched the boy racing his snowmobile back and forth along the edges of grey ice that circled the open water. Sometimes, the boy would actually glide halfway across the open water, making a lot of crazy shouts, and he would not even fall through.

Whitey watched him attempt this trick five times before the boy drove off across the bright white stretch of covered lake, and did not return. Whitey waited, but there were no more sounds from other snowmobiles, only the scratchy hum of Gilbert's machine growing fainter. The city men were scarcer this winter. Every year there were fewer snowmobiles.

Moving back toward the cabin, following the stream through the woods, Whitey kept his eyes peeled for shades of darker white moving against the snow. Animals would sometimes be so close that he would step on the paws of the smaller ones or startle the bigger ones no more than three feet away from where he was walking, most things gone white and needing to dissolve into the landscape in order to survive, and that was how he felt then, wanting to become frozen like the body of Hedley Thistle, which seemed to watch Whitey from where he was leaned up against the birch tree alongside the cabin, Hedley's mouth open as if trying to say something and Whitey knowing that the mouth had not been open when he first set the body down. Stepping closer, he saw a furry clump of brown jerking out from the mouth. The fur did not move for a moment and then it came out further, showing itself to be a squirrel that hesitated, turning in the mouth before showing its head again. Coming out completely, it nervously jutted down Hedley's arm, pouncing off and across the snow, then clinging to the bark of a tree, staring up.

"That's what you wanted to say?" Whitey asked Hedley, leaning down and touching the frozen skin. "No question everyone's out to have a piece of you." He smiled sadly and turned for the cabin. Inside, the warmth was more than comforting, the heat from the banked woodstove still lingering forcefully. The face shuffled and kicked out from under the bed to stare at Whitey with its wide straying eyes, but it did not come closer. The face did not seem pleased with Whitey. It was not its usual self since the day that Whitey brought home the vacated body that had once belonged to the man named Hedley Thistle.

Whitey was eating a bowl of vegetable broth from one of the tins that the city cars had provided, when, suddenly, the door was shoved open and the boy Gilbert stood there in the doorway with a mean expression on his face. Whitey was surprised because he had never seen anyone come in through his door, nor had he heard the cranky sound of the snowmobile arriving, and he realized that Gilbert had parked his machine further back in the woods and walked so as to surprise Whitey. Whitey took this to mean something not very good, something out of the ordinary and shaped from deceit.

The boy Gilbert just stood there, his thin sharp-featured face glaring red as he pulled down the hood of his snowmobile suit. His dirty blonde hair was damp and trimmed straight across his forehead. Taking off his big leather mittens, he slapped them under his arm, tucking them away.

Whitey raised his spoon to point at the open door. Without comment, Gilbert spun around and shoved it closed, then looked at Whitey as if to say, "there, how'd you like that?" but, instead, he said, "Wha' ya do'n widt 'Edley?"

Whitey shook his head and ate the last few spoonfuls of vegetable broth. Licking his lips, he lifted the bowl from the table with both hands and set it on the iron top of the woodstove. When he returned to the table, Gilbert was sitting there with his hands gripping a hunting knife, lightly sticking the tip into the tabletop and yanking it out again.

The face made a noise from under the bed and Gilbert quickly looked to catch a glimpse of the eyes. He was surprised at first, but then he laughed at how the eyes moved without direction.

"Fuh'k'n weird mutt ya get dere."

Whitey looked toward the bed and smiled at the face. "Don't worry," he said quietly.

"I wants me body back."

"Hedley's not hurting anyone." Whitey stared at Gilbert's tightening mouth. The boy's nostrils flared wider, and Whitey could hear the breath coming out of them. "Just leave him alone and go back to your house."

"Wha'?" Gilbert made a sickening face. It was the first time he had heard words from Whitey, and he did not understand them.

"Wha're ya say'n, b'y?"

Whitey waited a moment, then replied, "Nothing."

"Da buy's look't fer 'Edley las' noy't'n dis marn'n'n dey nev'r even t'ot 'a look'n out 'ere. Was me." He pointed at his own chest, hooked his finger into the big zipper ring of his navy blue snowmobile suit and let it hang there.

"So I be take'n 'im or be cut'n ya widt dis." Raising the knife, Gilbert heard shuffling sounds coming from under the bed. Looking toward the sound, he did not see the eyes this time, but was vaguely aware of the presence of something sulking back in the low shadows.

"Hedley deserves the peace he's got out here."

Gilbert sneered and hawked, thickly moving the sputum around in his mouth, before spitting onto the floor. "Yer fuh'k'n screw'd, b'y." Leaning across the table, he sloppily pressed the knife against Whitey's cheek, making a shallow dent. "Got 'er?"

Whitey nodded and Gilbert stood back from the table and slid his knife into the sheath that was strapped around his leg, and pulled out his gloves from where they were tucked away in his deep pockets. With a wide cheating smile, he turned for the door.

"Just don't touch the body," said Whitey, remembering how Hedley had told him stories of a time when the trains came through Cutland Junction, not far from Hedley's house. Whitey had sat in Hedley's big, warm living room, and the boy had admired the smell of new carpet and the flashing of the television with the sound always turned down. Whitey liked to believe in the man's stories, but he had a feeling that things always were just the same as they were now. How could things be so very different? It made no sense. The man had given Whitey food and even offered for the boy to move in with him, but Whitey knew he could not because of the face. No one could know about the face. It would be too upsetting to realize what it was that had been hiding from them all of this time. Whitey understood and kept private the knowledge that the face gave him in his dreams. He too stood from his chair, but stayed right where he was. He heard the sound of a snowmobile in the distance, but it was not moving away. It was coming closer. Stepping through the open front door of the cabin, Whitey saw that Gilbert was leaning over Hedley's body, pulling to lift the carcass that seemed to be frozen into the snow.

"Leave him alone," Whitey shouted. "You hear me?"

Gilbert did not ever look back. He remained bent close to the body and kept pulling and pulling until he was exhausted and fell off to the side, landing on his knees, and cursing quickly.

The sound of the snowmobile grew nearer as Whitey stepped toward the treeline where Hedley's body was sitting rooted in the coldness, staring straight ahead. Gilbert stayed on his knees, until he heard the steps coming closer. Leaping to his feet, he reached down for his leg, and spun around, slicing Whitey across the stomach with one swift lash of his arm. The blood made the snow very red as Whitey fell sideways, having no time to stop everything from slipping out from the center of his body. The steam rose from his belly and from the scalded snow, and the face — suddenly convulsing across the yard — scrambled toward what had always been slowly leaking out of

Whitey, leaking faster now, all in one quick blast.

"Meeeest," shrieked the face, bucking hysterically along the snow, getting stuck and freeing itself as the crust broke beneath its unsteady weight, and finally rolling onto Whitey to cover the mist that wavered from the boy's wound, the hole where the leakage was steaming from. "Meeeest, meeeeeeest! shouted the face up close, staring flush into Whitey's already depthless eyes.

Gilbert's face was washed with a look of still and perfect shock. The spilling of blood had been one thing that was totally believable, but the coming of the face was something completely different. Gilbert wondered what it was, but found no definition in his mind, no fluid stream of character he could claim as having understood, and so he bent closer with a sour expression and set the knife against the face's back, because it was made of something that defied the eyes and should be opened to see if — at least — it would bleed the way it was meant to. Its skin was white, almost whiter than the snow and it made noises that no one could possibly unscramble, frightening noises that rose to Gilbert, telling him that he himself was wrong, always wrong, but Gilbert could not understand the language, knowing nothing of tolerance. He pressed the knife against the face's back, hesitating, because of the frightening sound as it lay there shivering violently. Hearing the pitch of the snowmobile, Gilbert glanced up to see the vehicle gliding closer with Aggie on the seat. She brought the machine to a stop and turned off the key in its silver slot, the engine dying as she hurried toward Gilbert. Gilbert, finding no time to replace the knife in its sheath, hid it in the deep lined pocket of his snowmobile suit, and slowly backed away, then turned to run off into the woods, not pausing to look back to see if Aggie was after him. But Aggie was more concerned with treading closer to the face. Pausing, her lips opened and she blessed herself, mumbling several merciful words. She saw the blood, and the tears came out of her eyes in an instant. She did not bother to wipe away the fluid, letting it dry cool and hard on her cheeks. The sound of the weeping was of interest, and the face twisted as if to move free of itself, turning to stare up at Aggie with its round eyes that crossed and wandered, con-

fusingly independent of one another. It sensed a presence and
slumped off the body, slowly wading across the snow, and into
the cabin.

Aggie watched it bump over the threshold, then she bent to
Whitey, whose dark skin had washed completely white. His
eyes were shut and Aggie was glad for this, not wanting him to
see anything else of the torment that had finally, and completely, delivered itself. She pulled the boy across the crust of
snow toward the cabin, seeing the thick startling trail of blood
that soon turned thinner, so that she quickly understood how
warmth was an impossibility and changed direction, dragging
Whitey back again until he was close to Hedley. She sat the
boy beside his friend, then wiped at her eyes with her snow-
covered mittens, feeling the chill against her skin and on her
wrinkled lips that wanted to speak, but knew no words, only
the absolute weight of sorrow pressing inside her chest.

The face was making loud whooping sounds of distress
from inside the cabin. Hesitantly Aggie walked across the yard,
toward the open door, and stepped into the warm room where
she pulled off her pointy blue woollen cap. Fussing with her
thin, grey hair, she watched the face scurrying in circles on the
floor in front of the wood stove.

Taking off one mitten, then the other, Aggie glanced back at
the two bodies across the yard, facing toward her, as if wondering what she would do next, wanting to give her a hint as to
the truth of what they had already settled close to.

She turned away from them, bending down to offer kind-
ness to the face. Her fingers reached forward as she carefully
tried to touch its wet skin. Inching closer, her fingertips found
their mark, and the face stopped instantly, sensing the heat of
contact. It stared at Aggie, and tried to laugh, but yelped instead, realizing the thinning shade of mist that was the oldness
of its new keeper.

Rising to stand straight on her feet, Aggie shut the cabin
door. The faint sound of Gilbert's snowmobile touched a place
inside her head as the impression raced off across the land, the
dim hum eventually gone completely. The compact silence
seemed complete. Welcoming it, the face scurried closer, circling around Aggie's boots, and speaking to her — without the

slightest warning — in a way she thought impossible. Blinking, she saw the words inside her head, then blinked again, finding it impossible to erase them. They remained and multiplied as the face twisted its mouth and coughed, telling her of the drum and how it should be pounded now, of the slow painstaking rhythm; a bland pronouncement of the mortal scourge that strikes repeatedly at the face's pale heart.

Birthdays

I

No one knows the girl is dying, until she trips away from us and lands on her back with a meat-slamming sound. It takes a few seconds before we see the wet blackness leaking out of her blouse into a puddle by her side. Her eyes are shut but she is smiling up at the deserted buildings. A strange thing after she had been screaming like crazy with her mouth wide, breathing loud, and drawing back her lips in a way that I could see her teeth trying to bite.

I back away and Skag laughs first. We look at him and all of us start laughing together because it is a funny kind of ugly thing; the way she is lying there flat on the garbage without a word to say anymore. And it is we who have done it. Made her change that way. Left those red glossy lips smiling sad and happy forever.

"Easy dreaming," Skag says. "She's still warm." Squinting a view of all of us, he kneels down and fingers the girl's skin between the slashed white jeans and pink blouse. I pull off her shiny red shoes (they make a sloppy-wet sound because her

socks are soaked and sticky) while Skag takes hold of the waist
of her jeans, yanks them down, and slides on top, walking on
his hands until his face rests above hers. I know how Tat can
make use of the shoes. Hers are worn down from skimming
her heels over Slattery West, back and forth along the same
block, waiting to score. They are expensive shoes and they are
red like wet cherries. A nice colour. This dead girl was rich and
she had herself locked away behind a tall gate in a big house,
but curiosity brought her out and we got to her. We showed her
what a mistake it was to think she was so special.

The white car she'd been driving is parked on the street at
the end of the alley, blocking us from sight. She'd stopped to
watch us slapping and shoving at each other, pretending to
fight. After a while of looking and smiling easier and easier,
she rolled down her window to laugh in a bubbly way, and ask
for a light. All good looks and teasing with her lips around the
cigarette. Bad idea. Now she isn't living on the hill anymore.
She has come down among us, down real low. Everything that
was hers wound up meaning nothing. She will be worthless in
a little while; once Skag and the others taste what they have
done to her. No one can use her again. A hunk of flesh and
bones with her greedy soul cut loose to shop in Fucking Hell.
But there will be money for the car. That's the one good thing
she did for us. Dead now, easy and giving of herself. Charity
working between her numb legs. We have the money from her
purse, too. All a big mistake on her part. Being afraid. Living
her life so afraid of us poor children. Staying locked away behind big gates to make sure she never gets what she is really
searching for; the danger that is the only thing of value, the
only thing she does not possess. It frightens her and makes her
come closer. Having everything and needing only this now.
Her silent body finding movement in savagery. It makes me
smile, but the smile is more in the way the eyes go narrow.
That kind of way. Sexy. A funny ugly thing is a bad joke, but
it's better than no joke at all. Skag tells us, "She should have
known better. Look what acting snotty got her." He spits down
and the saliva lands on the dead girl's smiling lips, staying
thick, not warming where it creeps down over her cheek, leaving a trail through her heavy makeup, so that I wonder what is
underneath.

Skag saying, "The rich got no idea of how to mix."

Skag tastes the blood. One finger in the dead girl's side where the knife went in after we were only pricking her with the tips for fun, watching her bounce around, stumbling and shuffling, until she tripped and moved too fast, taking the full length of the blade, even part of the steel handle, and making a surprised sound, drawing in one long breath, which opened her eyes wider like the last of her air was being forced into them.

Skag pulls his finger from the hole and there is that hard-on sucking sound as it comes loose. He tastes his finger like it is icing from a cake, then smiles up with the blood wet and smeared across his teeth.

"It's my birthday," he says and he is right. We all realize that. But he is waiting to tell us again, knowing his birthday, or pretending to, making up the date, because most of us know nothing about the first day we squeezed from the whores who held us inside, letting us grow there for no good reason, then dropping us out like one mean bowling-ball crap, left all alone to roll around and squirm and kick our way to our feet.

We all clap our hands together and shout into the settling dusk, "Happy birthday, happy birthday," while Skag works on the girl's body, stabbing with his hips and squeezing one place, then somewhere else, squeezing and watching the girl's dumb eyes, waiting for something to change, but the smile stays there regardless. Will not be frightened away.

Skag pumps and tears away handfuls of her clothes until he slows down and I think he is getting bored with the idea. The girl is already dead enough and not even Skag can make her any worse.

"I'm fifteen today," he shouts, shaking back his head as if it is raining and the water is washing him clean but there is no rain falling. The sky is black with clouds but they aren't letting anything go. They are holding on. But Skag is doing no such thing. His face tightens up and his eyes jam shut and I know that he is letting loose into her, cursing as his neck twists as if casting off a pain, the veins there stretching like rope pulled tight by something that is trying to leave. Sweat all over his skin. I see it when he stands and rubs the dirt from his hands in his black t-shirt and jeans, then zips himself up. The streetlight at the other end of the alleyway shows the sweat down the right side of his face, one eye glowing. He gives me a close look, thinking about something he wants to share, wondering just how to put it, to make it special.

"Best birth control you could ever want," he says, squinting and smiling with his small flat teeth barely seen behind his lips. Staring down at the dead girl, seeing, watching into her, his face changes to let him whisper, "Momma, no more little bastards coming out of you."

II

The police car is stopped in the road and the back door hangs open. A gang of people are beating and kicking a man, stepping back and swinging forward with their shoes and boots. Two policewomen are trying to break up the commotion, but they look like they are worried about getting hurt and there is too much of a crowd and I hear sirens wailing in the distance; more cops finding their way closer toward us. We stand and watch, listening to the kicks and punches whacking the body, and the popping sounds that the guy on the ground is making, until the round-sounding sirens and the blue flashing lights get really close and the crowd runs off, scattering, leaving the man on the pavement with his arms wrapped around his head and his legs twitching, like the twig-like parts of a crushed bug. The two policewomen stare down while the other cop car pulls up.

"We were taking him to the courthouse," this fat-faced policewoman says to one of the new arrivals. We listen to her clear voice in the silence and I hear a few of us snickering, "and they stopped the car, all in a line across the road, and pulled him out the back door."

The new arrival walks around with his hands on his hips and his long green raglan sweeping around his feet. He keeps walking in circles, licking his lips again and again and glancing over at us on the other side of the street.

"These people?" he asks without much concern in his voice, nodding our way, while the two policewomen help the bruised and bloody prisoner into the back seat of their car.

"No," the fat-faced policewoman calls over her shoulder, "others."

"Other ones?" he asks, shaking his head and giving the policewomen a look like he can hardly believe that only two of them have been driving through this part of town without the company of a big bad man like him in there with them.

"Yeah," she says, not too pleased with the way things are going. She slams the door and looks around for something to wipe her hands in. Finally, she decides just to rub them against each other, then tuck them into the armpits of her jacket like her fingertips are cold.

All of them keep looking at us, knowing we are innocent of this, but maybe planning something quite the same, understanding we are guilty of a hundred other crimes, staring as if they are trying to make up their minds, piecing things together, making decisions, until we know it is time to wander off.

"Go home," the policeman shouts, sighing, maybe with relief because we are finally moving clear of them.

"Where's that?" Skag shouts back. Reaching into his pocket, he pulls out the roll of bills we had stolen from the rich girl; the one we killed the night before. He spreads the bills like a deck of cards and holds them that way, elbowing me, then glancing back at the cops, who are farther behind us now.

"Home," he says, staring at the money. "I heard something funny once, Dogger."

"What's that?" I ask, walking, feeling the heat of the gang around me, the shuffling echo of footsteps and the quick shouts — threats tossed at the condemned buildings on both sides of the street. A bottle kicked here and there. The sound of a howl. Laughter.

Still staring at the money, Skag tells me, "Home is where the heart is. You know this man." He holds up a bill and shows me the face that is printed there, flicking the bill with his finger, "This man's the best Daddy I could ever hope for. He takes me *everywhere*."

III

Tat has a cloth up to her face when I see her at Sparkles' apartment. I trace the dark-blue tattooed bracelets around her wrists and the mess of tattoos up higher on her shoulders. She is wearing the skin-coloured top I like; the one that clings to her chest and is tied up behind her neck. I can almost see through it. And her shorts are so short and tight they cut her up the middle, seeming like they might just split her right in half. She looks ready, and I tell her so, but she does not seem too happy, with all the noise going on around her. I stare off at Sparkles' baby, and hear the mean sounds it is making, and I want to make it still for being so useless. It does not know anything; nothing about why it is even crying or what crying is all about. A baby that is just there, reaching up and grabbing at the air. That's what makes me feel crazy. Just grabbing, already.

"Why don't you kill that noise?" I ask Sparkles, the red shoes hanging from my fingers. Sparkles comes over to me and slaps at my chest with her little hands. Tears start spilling out of her and she wipes at them right away.

"Stop it," she says, dragging her sleeve across her eyes, smearing her blue eyeshadow and knocking her fake eyelashes loose. "Jesus, Dogger," she sniffles, pressing at one eye and blinking, "you know I'm waiting for his father."

I look at Skag and he laughs and squints, shrugging with a funny frown on his tight lips.

"Father?" he says, only moving his mouth, not really speaking.

"What happened to your eye?" I ask, holding the red shoes out to Tat, the back straps hanging from two of my fingers. She takes the cloth away from her eye and I see the bruise there. It makes her look extra-sad, and I feel like touching her to set it better, or to make it hurt worse. All of it leading to the same point; creamy touch or a good smack connecting to the breathing and screaming and the spilling of come.

"You get the money?" I have to ask because we need the cash to keep what we have together.

"What money?" Tat smiles real sly, looking nasty with those few bottom teeth gone, showing me what is really on her mind. She tips her head to one side, then reaches to take hold of the shoes.

"The guy who did this," I say, letting her slip the shoes off my fingers.

She keeps smiling, like she understands I know the answer but she is not going to tell.

"I got it," she says, turning the shoes over in her hands and taking her time to admire them. "Cash always...up front." She sleazes a look up at me and I stare at the holes between her teeth and the long crooked scar over her top lip where she was sliced by a cop who was having much too much fun with her. She pats her jean pocket so I will look there and see the bills tucked away in a safe place.

"Click, click," she says, letting me know that she cut the guy with her switchblade. "After he stuck it in me, I stuck it in him. Got his own little momma hole now."

"Good," I say, smiling over at Skag, who is eating a spoonful of something yellow sitting on the table. "Fair is fair," I tell him and he nods with a serious look on his face, then swallows, laughing and wiping his mouth with his arm before dropping the spoon.

"Thanks for the shoes," Tat says. But I am not interested in hearing what she has to say. I have other things on my mind.

"It was Skag's birthday yesterday," I tell her, hoping she will pick up on what I am thinking, so I do not have to finish.

Skag opens his arms so Tat can get close. Their mouths come together and they kiss hard for a long while until things get a little wild and he has his hand down where I had been looking before and he is shoving hard there so that Tat grinds and pushes back. It takes no time at all before Skag carries her off into Sparkles' bedroom.

They leave the door open, so I go down there and watch, leaning in the doorway and thinking about things, knowing it will be Tat's birthday in another two weeks and wondering what to get for her.

"How old you gonna be, Tat?" I ask, but she is groaning with the breath jerking out of her, and I cannot hear the number because of how Skag's tongue is pushed far down her throat, although I think she tries to say "thirteen." I am not certain. It is just her wet lips blubbering behind the kiss, then laughing at how stupid the sound is.

"I'll be sweet sixteen," Sparkles calls from the living room. Her voice is shaky as if she thinks I am trying to make up with her for saying what was on my mind about the baby. "Why you want to know?"

"Nothing," I yell down the hallway. "Forget it. I wasn't talking to you."

"Okay then," she shouts back. "Forget it, right."

I am only interested in Skag and Tat, how it is like they are wrestling with each other to get free of something, tearing away at their hair and lips and bodies. Tat smacking Skag across the face and then him slapping her until they are laughing at how the slapping is beginning to sting.

Sparkles starts crying again and slamming cupboard doors to let everyone know that it is her apartment; how we are here because of her. And the baby starts crying. I watch Tat and Skag hitting and screwing, Skag's legs pinning down Tat's, then shifting up with his knees around her head, as he sits there, leaning back with a handful of her hair in each of his fists, rocking, and I have to hold onto myself because the force of what they are doing is leading me to think of the baby. I have to tighten up inside to stop from running into the other room, going to the crib and showing the baby some kind of fucking mercy by making sure it never reaches birthday number one.

IV

Sparkle runs out of money and food and what is left of her patience. She is thrown out of her apartment because she cracks, and no one will make it with her anymore, so she has no money for rent. But the cops never know who does it when they find the baby in the dumpster with its bald skull turned to splinters and its bones cracked in too many places to count. Although I know they will get her because Sparkles will talk. She will tell them everything. She will confess. Weak like that. Shaky, and she cannot hold it together. Always crying, even when one of the boys is doing it to her, crying and crying, wanting another baby, not wanting to slap and kick, wanting another baby and that is all, so that she gets one, needs one, has another in her belly when they finally arrest her for crushing up the first one with a leg from the kitchen table.

V

"What're you doing, Dogger?" Tat asks me. My hands are over her eyes and I lead her through a doorway with no door into a building with walls still standing, up the stairway and down a long hall that must have been some kind of office place once. It is stinking in here, but Tat stumbles along without passing comment. She never mentions the sounds of people sleeping or screwing in the rooms, rolling over and grumbling, or whispering nasty things while they do it, struggling to shove right through each other's skin to finally bury what is troubling them.

"It's a surprise," I tell her, taking my time guiding her through the dark building to a room in the back that I claim as mine. A room with a window looking down on the black street. No lights. No kind of movement. A place like how I feel inside.

"No surprises," she says, sounding a bit worried now, knowing about my kind of surprises. "Stop it, Dogger."

I will not take my hands away for a while, even when we stop walking. I leave them over her eyes and I stare at the little flames that are all side by side and surrounding each other. I wait before I show them to her. That is what a surprise is. Waiting, and then seeing what has been put before you, in one big rush. I lift my hands away and she looks down at the cake, icing glowing against the grey concrete floor.

"One year older," I say, looking at her eyes and how they are changing now. "You know when you were born. I got the day right?"

Tat turns to me and smiles in a sad kind of way. "I forgot," she says and kisses me like she means it, nice and easy, with her arms around my neck. I keep watching her eyes and the bruise that is changing colour, from black to deep purple and yellow. Her face kind of darkens for a second because she is looking at me, some kind of meaning trying to find its way out of there.

"When's your birthday, Dogger?" she asks, her eyes gone nervous because she is watching me up close.

"I don't have a birthday."

She stares at me for a while, still holding on, then looks back at the cake as if she has not heard a word. She is liking the sight of the flames and how they give off a soft kind of light to the garbage around our feet. Papers and clumpy chunks of cement. She kicks something that sounds hard and does not go too far.

"Everyone has a birthday," she says real low, like she is in a trance.

I think back, nothing there, except that dark hole swelling. "I don't know," I say.

Looking up, she finishes it for me, "when you were born."

"If," I say.

Her arms slip from around my neck and she stares at my feet. I hear her breathing the smell of wax. Then her eyes rise for me, completely changed, turning sly like she knows how she is going to pay me for remembering. She opens her mouth and curls the tip of her tongue out the way she likes to do, teasing. Taking hold of my hand, she lifts it to her lips, sucks and licks my fingers, but her face scrunches together, and she spits and spits.

"What's that," she says, opening and closing her lips, tasting with a sour look.

"Just dirt," I say, laughing at what is happening with her face because I know what she has tasted.

"Tastes like blood."

"Maybe," I say, pressing my fingertips against my jeans, rubbing them clean, hard and slow, up and down until my skin feels hot.

Tat wipes her lips and paws at her tongue with both sets of fingers. "Jesus, Dogger. What're you doing to me? Wash your hands, for once."

"Make a wish," I say, thinking that this was not such a good idea after all, making it known by the sound of my voice. "And blow the candles."

Tat's actions calm and she seems normal again after a little while. Agreeing, she closes her eyes and holds them shut, smiling nice and warm, but in a second or two, she looks frightened. Wishing not that easy, bringing unwanted things to light. Her eyes open wide, rushing away from whatever is shoving closer in her head.

So I take a dollar bill from my pocket and hold it up to her face. "Did you see this picture of my father?"

"Yeah, right."

"Yes, it's true. He's a pretty big guy. You know what I mean?"

She forgets okay then, laughs once with her look turning back to sly — the way I like it.

"What about *your* father?" I ask, wanting her to pick up th joke.

But it does not go that way. She starts thinking real instead, her eyes hardening on mine, like she wants to hurt me now with what I have made her see.

"My father really knew how to screw me," she says, staring, then turning to look at the little flames. They move around in her eyes and it seems like there are all these short little fires glowing inside her, trying to get bigger, wanting to climb. "My mother, too. I killed them when I was eight."

I stare at her face and make up my mind: It is her three missing teeth that I admire most. Those, and the tattoos. My finger goes for the space where the teeth once grew, and her gums are as soft as anything I have ever touched. I hold my fingertip there for a while, playing with the gap.

"Now why'd you go and do that?" I ask, tilting my head to look into her eyes. "Fuck your stupid past." I can smell the candle wax, burning. There are fifty or sixty candles on top of the cake. I just kept putting them on for all of us, not just for Tat, tearing open the packs and sticking them through the real sweet coating, lighting them for the flashes of fire that warmed my eyes, then going outside to get Tat.

Now I can smell smoke in the room. Something sweet and sickly getting out of hand. The icing melting.

Tat opens her jaws wide, until I think the corners of her mouth will rip apart. She turns to face me and I stare down her throat, see things shivering: her heartbeat jerking in the roof of her mouth, spit rolling into a pool on her tongue.

Her tongue moves and her breath steams against my face: "I killed them with a blade across their filthy fucking throats. Easy as cutting through shit. They were in bed, drunk." She shrugs and does not even bother shaking her head. "Prick and Cunt never even woke up. They couldn't even care that much."

"Then what?" I ask.

She waits and her face turns hard and mean, the gap in her bottom row of teeth deepening, the scar along her top lip flinching in the light. She says, "Nothing."

"That's right," I agree easily, snapping my fingers once. "Just like that. Nothing."

Only a few birthday candles are burning now, so we stand

ing, until they blink out too and everything is dark. hell worse right away. In no time at all, tiny sounds from the corners, across the walls. Bugs scurrying for cky cake, getting stuck there, kicking and twitching drowning in the sweetness. The idea is a smiling kind of and a laugh bubbles up from the black pool trapped inside me, but there is no way I will let it out. It thickly rounds up, en silently settles.

A funny ugly thing is a bad joke, but it's better than no joke at all.